THE BLEEDING WORLDS

BOOK ONE

HARBINGER

Justus R. Stone

Red Bucket Publishing

Published by Red Bucket Publishing, Toronto, Ontario, Canada.
http://redbucketpublishing.com

Front cover artwork by Starbottle.
Twitter: @starbottle
Pixiv: pixiv.me/starbottled

Third Edition

Summary: Our reality is founded on secrets. Beings with god-like powers pass through society unnoticed. Some aim to protect us. Others seek our destruction. Guided by prophecies and twisted beliefs, they all watch for the Harbinger. Many believe it heralds the ultimate end, Ragnarok. A select few see it as a tool to manipulate creation itself.
Gwynn Dormath knows none of this. He's a barely noticed kid going through the motions of his every day.
That comes to a halt when Sophia sits down across from him.
For years, Gwynn has admired her from afar.
When the most shocking words he can imagine come from her mouth, he knows his world is forever changing.
It begins with a simple date. A date which ends in explosive tragedy.
Injured, confused, Gwynn realizes he sees things no one else can. He begins wielding powers no human should. The world is cracking open, its secrets bleeding out.
In those secrets lay the revelation of grave danger. Forbidden agents of darkness gather, intent on killing thousands of worlds. And they believe Gwynn Dormath is the Harbinger.

[1.Mythology-Fiction 2.Supernatural-Fiction 3.Soul-Fiction]
ISBN: (Print) 978-0995969742 (eBook) 978-0987743909

For my Father,
who inspired my love for reading and the fantastic.

And to Tina, Meredith, and Leanne
Because a promise is a promise.
Even ones made at the age of 12.

Contents

The Fine Line Between Dreams and Nightmares

It could've been a battlefield. People dashed about, bartering deals and solidifying alliances. The noise level ebbed and flowed from dull roar to deafening thunder. At random intervals, complete chaos would ensue as projectiles launched to screams of "take cover."

Another Friday in the school cafeteria.

Headphones in place, volume high enough to drown the noise, Gwynn pulled his hoodie tighter over his head, hoping to remain in the eye of the storm.

His seat resided at the center of the cafeteria. His seat. If asked, he'd never call it that, nor would anyone in the school have a clue where such a thing might be. But every lunch hour, here he sat. No one else ever occupied the seat. The Chair always sat vacant awaiting his arrival.

Something poked Gwynn's shoulder. He reached up to brush it, assuming it a stray bit of thrown food. He jumped when he met another hand. Gwynn tried to compose himself. He yanked out his headphones and swept his hood back.

"Hey, Gwynn. Mind if I sit?"

"Sure," he stammered. "What's going on Sophia?"

Sophia Murray occupied his dreams since he'd been old enough to have dreams about girls. In all the time he'd known her, they'd exchanged few words, but something drew him to her. Unlike Gwynn, who lived in a bubble of self-isolation, Sophia traveled in the popular circles. All school society revolved around her. The others in those circles cared little for school. Instead, looks and material wealth were far more important.

But Sophia strove to succeed. Her answers were intelligent and her eyes never filled with the vapidness of her other friends.

Gwynn couldn't concern himself with the games, gossip, or competitions of his classmates. He didn't belong. Though he lacked any evidence, he'd always suspected Sophia was much the same.

Sophia gave her blond hair an absent-minded twirl around her finger. "I wanted to say thanks again for your help with Mr. Baker's assignment. My mark would've been crap without you."

Gwynn's heart pounded in the back of his throat. He regretted the speed he fired down the cafeteria's lukewarm dollar store pizza.

"No worries. You did as much work as I did."

"We made a good team." She stopped playing with her hair and bit her bottom lip. "Maybe we could be partners again sometime."

"Sure. I'd like that." Gwynn flushed. He hoped he didn't have the sweat to match.

"So..." Sophia averted his eyes, her hands fidgeting. "Do you have plans for tomorrow night?"

"Tomorrow?" He gulped on the word.

"Yeah. You do know it's Halloween, right?"

"Right, Halloween." He'd forgotten. No sense keeping track when he didn't receive any invitations. "Um, I don't think so."

Gwynn's stomach knotted. He had recurring dreams where Sophia asked him out. Which became a nightmare ending with him on a table, pants around his ankles, and everyone laughing while pelting him with food. Gwynn suppressed a shudder and swore that even if she begged he would not stand on any tabletops. Quite the opposite, he had a sudden urge to crawl under the table and beat his head with one of the tacky orange cafeteria serving trays.

She smiled at him, and all thoughts of retreat melted away. If she asked with that smile, he wouldn't think twice about getting up on the table, nightmares or not.

"Think maybe you'd wanna hang out with a few of my friends and me?"

"Sure." He tried not to cringe, waiting for the moment his pants would hit the deck and food would start flying. But the world appeared oblivious to the momentous event occurring in his life.

"Sweet. Meet me in front of the 7/11 on Williams at seven, okay?"

"Yeah. Sure. Looking forward to it." He tripped over several words answering.

"Me too," were the words she used, but Gwynn noted something more. Satisfaction? Mission accomplished? "See you tomorrow." She smiled and left without a further word.

The noise and hectic atmosphere of the cafeteria melted away, and a vacuum of silence surrounded Gwynn. The ten-year-old who carried a torch for the past seven years started jumping up and down, then skipped along singing so loud it obliterated any sense of tune. The solitary seventeen year–old Gwynn had grown into remained guarded, but optimistic; unsure whether he should join in the festivities, or stay leaning against the wall on the sidelines. He shook his head trying to suppress the stupid grin threatening his lips.

A heavy hand slapped him on the shoulder, interrupting his dreamy state.

"Hey Gwynn, I hear we're going to be hanging out tomorrow."

Seeing the face, he wanted to shrink under the table. Eric Haze, captain of the school football team. Gwynn had done everything he could to stay clear since Eric beat him up in the seventh grade.

Haze thrived off two types of people; those who glorified him, and those he intimidated. Seeing Gwynn's discomfort made Haze's square, Neanderthal features even more animated.

"Relax man, it's Halloween," he laughed. "I was psyched when Sophia told me you were coming along. We're going to have an, uh, unforgettable time!"

Haze started walking away, but then turned and shot Gwynn a thumbs up with a smile suiting a crazed hyena.

Gwynn couldn't help thinking he would've preferred being in his boxers with food pelting him.

***

Gwynn walked through the halls in a daze.

He'd slipped out of the cafeteria ten minutes before the bell rang, wanting to avoid the crush of bodies dashing for class. Gwynn despised being caught in the surging waves of students. Many times those waves swept him away, and he missed his destination. He hated feeling powerless. More than that, he hated that so many people surrounded him he could barely breathe, yet he still felt alone.

The unsettling events of lunch left Gwynn rattled. Being stuck in the halls would just be too much. Not that arriving at class would lessen his anxiety. He had English class with Mr. Baker. Sophia would be there. So would Eric.

The classroom tables formed a horseshoe shape, allowing the whole class an unobstructed view of Mr. Baker and each other. In what Mr. Baker described as a whole other life ago, he was a Shakespearean actor. Gwynn's decided old dramatic habits die hard, as Mr. Baker performed Shakespeare as though he stood on a stage as opposed to a high school classroom. Other students made fun of Mr. Baker behind his back, but Gwynn found his delivery gripping. While his classmates debated the need or use for Shakespeare, Gwynn wondered more at how people could ignore the power of words. When Mr. Baker launched into a soliloquy, the world shifted. The ebb and flow of the world moved in time with the teacher's voice. He wished he could share that feeling with someone, but anxiety clawed at his chest over what his peers would think. So he kept quiet and hoped his rapture went unnoticed.

He found the classroom silent and empty. Gwynn took his seat at the center of the horseshoe and bored a hole in the floor with his eyes. He took in a slow breath, trying to abate his growing anxiety. The bell rang, and he grabbed the books for class.

Besides his awe-inspiring delivery of Shakespeare, Mr. Baker became Gwynn's favorite teacher for pairing him up with Sophia. He'd assigned them a scene to analyze from the Tempest. While Mr. Baker touted numerous advantages of group work, Gwynn suspected it had more to do with Mr. Baker wanting to grade half the number of papers.

Much to his delight, Sophia didn't seem to mind working with him, despite their different social standings. While in the same classes off and on for the past seven years, he never spent any time with her alone.

"You shouldn't get too worked up," his Aunt Jaimie cautioned.

She'd been his guardian for almost ten years. She treated Gwynn well, though she never wanted the burden of a child, let alone someone else's. Still, this life felt secure. He tried to insulate it from everything else. Meaning he often left his social life at school out of it.

"What would you know?" he grumbled.

"Oh, I remember. You pointed her out to me during your school play on the Greek pantheon. You looked so cute in your Ares outfit." Jaimie gave a conspiratorial laugh. Gwynn had a sinking suspicion photographs existed that would one day find their way into the hands of any girl he brought home. "You were so worked up. 'Aunt Jaimie, did you see the girl playing Athena? That's Sophia Murray! Isn't she amazing?'"

Heat filled his cheeks. He remembered the play. They were all dressed as various Greek gods, and Sophia wore a toga with a laurel wreath in her hair. He still remembered her tears about having to cut her hair short when the laurel tangled in her long blond curls.

"Geez, you must have it pretty bad for her if you're this worked up after all these years."

He stiffened. "She's just my partner for this assignment. It's not that big a deal."

"Sure, sure, Romeo. Just keep that in mind when you're working with her. Otherwise, you'll make an ass of yourself and flunk too."

Gwynn clenched his fists and gritted his teeth. No wonder he didn't share personal details with his Aunt. But, she gave him sound advice. In the end, he did what she said—kept calm and professional. The two of them had fun. He'd even managed to make her laugh. Being near her was comfortable, easy. On top of that, they aced the assignment. Now Sophia had asked him out. How well her advice worked out would no doubt surprise Jamie.

Students started shuffling into the classroom. Gwynn averted his eyes from the door, appearing to focus on his books. Out of the corner of his eye, he saw Sophia come in alone and then Eric followed shortly after with two other members of the football team. The boys guffawed about something, though Gwynn couldn't hear what. They stifled themselves after entering the class. After everyone arrived, Mr. Baker made his entrance. The teacher's gray-streaked hair stuck out at random angles, and his tie was flung over his shoulder—all hinting he met an unexpected wind turbine somewhere in the hall.

He launched into his lesson. They were wrapping up the Tempest today, and Gwynn leaned forward in his seat, eager for his teacher's typical performance.

"Now everyone, I'm going to be reading this soliloquy from The Tempest. We'll be going over it in detail because it might be on your test tomorrow." Mr. Baker gave an exaggerated wink and launched into his performance.

The words reverberated around the room. With each syllable, Gwynn remained entranced. Sophia caught his eye and gave him a small smile. It should've made him happy. Instead, his insides churned. Beyond her, Eric talked in hushed whispers with his cronies who stole occasional glances toward Gwynn and then averted their eyes if they saw him looking their way. A shadow seemed to hang over him since Sophia asked him out. Maybe he should cancel before the dream tumbled into the realm of nightmares.

In some distant place, Mr. Baker called the tempest down. Thunder rumbled. Or had Gwynn imagined it? In the pit of his stomach, something twisted. His body threatened to collapse in on itself.

Bell-like laughter, playful, but verging on mockery, filled the classroom.

Gwynn searched the room for the source. His classmates were listless. Most kept occupied passing notes to each other, or catching a few minutes of sleep.

The laugh again. This time, he followed its sound and found the source. On Mr. Baker's desk, less than five feet from the teacher himself, sat a girl Gwynn's age.

She sat cross-legged, her long legs encased in black stockings disappearing beneath a black dress puffing outward over white frills. Green eyes regarded him with a childlike playfulness, and her smile begged for a game of tag or hide-and-go-seek.

She jumped down from the desk, her movements filled with a dancer's grace. She passed within a foot of Mr. Baker, ducking under his gesticulating arms, who paid her no attention at all.

She leaned both elbows on Gwynn's desk and rested her chin in her hands. Long black hair divided into two long strands fell on either side of her face.

"Hello Hidhaegg"

"What? Who?"

Her eyes filled with hurt. "You don't remember me, do you?"

Gwynn stole a quick glance around the room. No one seemed to notice her. "I'm sure I would remember you" His voice wavered with uncertainty.

"You used to know me." She gave his nose a gentle poke. "Soon there will be a time when you need me. I am Gnosis. You are Logos. I am the Knowledge, and you are the Word that will give the Knowledge shape."

She moved and took hold of Gwynn's right hand. Flames of pain raced up his arm. His head exploded in agonizing white flashes.

"Soon," the girl said, "the Word and Knowledge will become one and deliver the Gospel."

He fell. Everything went dark with stabbing punctuations of painful light. A crushing weight rested on his chest.

"Gwynn, Gwynn, are you all right?"

At first, he didn't understand. It took a moment to register he was on the floor. He nodded, unsure as he got back to his feet.

"Do you need to go see the nurse?" Mr. Baker asked, his eyes questioning far deeper than whether Gwynn needed a nurse.

Snickers came from the direction of Eric Haze. Gwynn didn't think the school nurse would be much help. He took stock of the room. The girl in black had disappeared—if she was ever there to begin with. What the hell? Hallucinations and blackouts? Even if the nurse couldn't help him, he'd rather be there than in the classroom.

"I think maybe I should," he managed.

"Don't worry about your books. Will you be okay getting down there, or should I send someone with you?"

Gwynn wanted to pull his hoodie up and disappear. "I'll be fine. Thanks." He left the class as quick as his wobbly legs would carry him.

***

School had long since ended.

Mr. Baker wandered the deserted hallways toward his office. He liked this life. A mix of theater and a dash of power. Sure, the little bastards made their snide comments behind his back. But seeing their faces fall at their low marks made for sweet revenge.

He kept his office Spartan—nothing but a desk and filing cabinet. Keep things simple—it made maintaining the charade easier.

Mr. Baker fished a key from his pant pocket and unlocked the filing cabinet. From inside, he pulled a plain black flip cell phone. It lacked the streamlining of modern phones, but function concerned his people more than form. He collapsed into his office chair and reclined. He punched a series of numbers and waited.

A gruff male voice with a thick accent Baker couldn't place answered.

"Hello."

Mr. Baker cleared his throat. "I'm calling with a status report."

"Ah, Mr. Baker. How did things proceed?"

"He reacted to the Ambrosia field as predicted."

The man's voice filled with an eager anticipation. "Did he awaken?"

Such an idiotic question. "No." Mr. Baker's patience ran thin. If the boy awakened, there would've been little need to call in an update. It would've made the evening news. "He did have a reaction. I believe things are in place. This weekend should reveal everything."

"Then we will fulfill the final prophecies of Delphi."

"Yes," Mr. Baker said, a grin infecting his voice. "It will be glorious."

Be Warned of Another's Woe

Gwynn opened his eyes. The cold, damp sheets clung to his skin. He lay in bed trying to calm his ragged breathing, his eyes unfocused on the dark surrounding him. His heart drummed a ferocious staccato against his rib cage.

He woke this way almost every night since regaining consciousness in the hospital nearly ten years ago. The nightmare became so familiar, nights without seemed odd and uncomfortable. Gwynn viewed the dream as evidence he still loved and grieved for his parents. He worried that when the dreams ended for good, it would be the night he no longer cared.

Unknown minutes passed. When the dreams first woke Gwynn, he would stare at the clock, counting the minutes until his breathing normalized—it became a game to see how many times his heart pounded a minute. Almost a decade later, he didn't care about those things. The dream became a part of him. It couldn't hurt him—just be a reminder of the fracture staggering amounts of therapy hadn't fixed.

Nervous energy and jumpy legs convinced him sleep wouldn't come again. Gwynn turned over to see the harsh red digits of his clock. It read four thirty in the morning, Saturday, October 31. Halloween. Most importantly, the day of his first date with Sophia Murray.

He stared at the clock, willing it to move faster. Gwynn had little desire to get out of bed, but lying doing nothing seemed even worse.

He avoided telling Jaimie about the incident in Mr. Baker's class. He didn't want to worry her when he had no idea what was happening.

The memory of the girl, her laugh, somewhat familiar, still hovered over him. Was he losing it? Had Sophia's first move snapped his tenuous hold on reality?

"I never thought being a Shakespeare nerd would land you a girl." Jaimie had difficulty containing herself when he told her.

"I think it's more than that." He said the words, but his churning stomach served reminder he doubted it.

"Wow, this may come as a shock, but I was seventeen once. I can almost guarantee you no girl asks a guy out because he's a Shakespeare nerd."

Gwynn started to grumble. But Jaimie's smile and the joy in her eyes stopped him. Jaimie was twenty-four when she took him in. Pressed to describe their relationship, Gwynn would say they were friends more than anything. Without knowing it, Jaimie gave him what he needed. She never tried to replace his mother, but she did keep him in line. She gave Gwynn space, respect, and in turn, he attempted to make her proud.

"So what are the big plans for the night?"

"I, um, don't know. We're meeting at the 7/11 on Williams and then going from there. She said we would be with some of her friends."

Jaimie's eyebrow arched. "Ah, a trial date."

"A what?"

She laughed. "A trial date. You know, when a girl thinks she likes a guy, she invites him to hang out with her and her friends. Because it's not just the two of them, it isn't the same pressure as a formal date, and she can see if the guy fits in with her friends."

"Oh."

"Come on, don't get like that. After all, with that, ah, wit and charm of yours, I'm sure you'll pass the audition successfully."

"Now you're making fun of me."

"No, no. Just remembering what it was like to be a younger girl crushing on a guy. I used to do it all the time. Hell, even if I thought I was in love, I did the trial date. Half the time I did it so my friends would keep me from making a total ass of myself. Anyway, I hope this girl is as special as you think. Cause if she hurts you, she'll have to answer to me."

There were a million things to say, but he kept it to a simple "Thanks."

Now the day had arrived, and his stomach twisted in an increasing tangle of knots. Agonizing hours passed. How many times could he wash or change clothes in a single day? No matter how many showers he took, no matter how many outfits he tried, nothing ever seemed right. Even his skin conspired to be awkward and uncomfortable. He would catch Jaimie out of the corner of his eye watching. Much to his surprise, she said nothing, but he saw the odd devious smile.

It seemed several days had passed when six thirty in the evening arrived. Gwynn dressed in black jeans and a gray sweater.

He checked the brown mess he called hair. Despite his best attempts, it remained defiantly unkempt.

"On your way?" Jaimie came down the hall.

"I think so. No jokes, how do I look?"

"Very handsome. If I was fifteen years younger, and we weren't related, I'd date you."

"Kinda creepy." He smiled. "But, thanks."

"Go on, Romeo. Don't keep the girl waiting. If you're late, that'll be a strike against you right from the start."

"Okay. See you later."

"Sure. Be safe and have fun."

Gwynn bounced out the door. His heart raced, and his stomach lurched back and forth. He gave a giddy laugh. Lord, he needed to get this out of his system before meeting Sophia. Scared, excited, his body couldn't seem to decide.

The 7/11 was around the corner. Before entering the store, Gwynn gave himself a final check—didn't want any zippers to be left down. In doing this, he realized he was missing his cell phone. Jaimie got it for him two years ago. He carried it out of habit. He shrugged. No loss. The only person who ever called him was Jaimie, and he hoped she would have the good sense not to call him tonight, of all nights.

The unseasonably warm air smelled fresh and miraculous. Especially compared to the last week where a chill and dampness seemed to creep into everything. Tonight had to be magic. Children ran in their costumes, filled with excitement they didn't need to hide under heavy coats this year. Gwynn missed many Halloweens. After his parents died, he lacked the heart to go out alone. Not that he'd forgotten the allure.

Free candy and treats, the inherent joy of a night where you could be something, someone...anything else. On Halloween, everyone lived between worlds. Maybe Halloween was the one night he belonged.

A shadow moved in the corner of his eye. He spun around, expecting to see another child, but found nothing. Chills ran up his neck and his head prickled. He couldn't help but take continuous glances over his shoulder.

Despite the 7/11 regularly being a busy hang out, it seemed deserted. Gwynn supposed most people had somewhere better to be. He checked his watch. It read six fifty. Was ten minutes early enough? He didn't see any sign of Sophia, so he decided to kill time inside.

The hard fluorescent lights stung his eyes and washed out the cream–colored walls that had once been white but had discolored with age and grime. A girlie mag occupied the clerk behind the counter—he couldn't even be bothered to grunt some form of hello. Gwynn wandered the aisles, showing enough interest to deflect suspicion, but he didn't intend on buying anything. Anxiety ruined any hope of eating, and the meager offerings on the magazine rack offered little that would entertain Gwynn as much as they did the store employee.

Gwynn took another anxious glance at his watch. The blocky digits caused him further gastric discomfort. Five after seven. He started to worry Sophia asking him out was a cruel joke. In his mind, he had visions of Eric Haze, Sophia, and a half or more of the football team having a good laugh, making bets on how long Gwynn would wander around the 7/11 before giving up. Were they hiding somewhere nearby, so they could confirm the time of his defeat and pay out the winning bet? The back of his throat tightened, something heavy tugged at his core, and his right hand burned with pins–and–needles.

"Go home," a voice whispered.

The cashier remained buried in his magazine and oblivious to the store. Gwynn edged to the end of the aisle and peeked down one, then the other, but there was no sign of anyone else. In one of the security mirrors placed in the corner of the store, he caught sight of dark hair dashing outside of view. Another spin, taking in the store. No matter what he heard, or thought he saw, he seemed alone with the clerk.

Gwynn took a deep breath, counted one, two, three, four, five, and let it out slow.

I am losing my mind.

Before any phantom voices agreed, a roaring engine and thumping bass outside shattered the quiet. The sound even made the cashier bother to lift his head.

Outside, a black car pulled up—some sports car, though Gwynn had no idea what—having never been much interested. The door opened, and some person Gwynn recognized from school hopped out. Gwynn waited for the pointing and laughing, but it didn't happen. Instead, his schoolmate turned and popped the front seat forward so someone could climb out of the back. Gwynn caught sight of blond curls, and for the first time that day, his stomach settled. His heart beat harder than usual with a joyful rhythm.

"Go home now," the phantom voice said in a growled whisper. Gwynn ignored it. It must be his nagging doubts and insecurities trying to hold him back. It sucked being alone. He didn't want to feel separate and detached. He wanted grounding, to have something warm and meaningful to root him to the world. He wanted to be the one to make Sophia smile.

Sophia got out of the car, searching the area. Gwynn raised his hand in a shy wave. When she caught sight of him, she gave a wide grin and bounced into the store.

"Hey!"

"Hi, Sophia."

Her eyes got serious, and her bottom lip pouted. "Sorry, we're late. Eric *had* to get gas. You haven't been waiting long, have you?"

Gwynn deflated at hearing Haze's name, but when she grabbed his hand, a surge of invulnerability struck through.

"Come on," she said with a laugh. She nudged Gwynn out of the store to the waiting car.

The guy who let her out still stood holding the front seat down. He gave Gwynn an obligatory "hey" as he came out of the store. Sophia gave Gwynn a shove into the back and then hopped in next to him.

The "doorman" let the seat go, and it sprung back with a thwomp. He flopped in and pulled the door shut behind him.

From the front, Eric turned around with his hyena grin. Gwynn never liked seeing Haze smile. Not a hyena tonight, more like a shark admiring his dinner.

"Hey Gwynn," he drawled, having to shout over the blasting volume of the music. Gwynn couldn't even make out the song; the pounding bass obliterated all sense of melody. "Hope you're ready. We're going to have an awesome night."

The sound of screeching rubber accompanied the car peeling away. With Eric's driving, the night could be dangerous.

Sophia thrashed in her seat to the beat of the music. She laughed wild and high. "Isn't this great? I *love* this song!"

She seemed out of character. Her happy face seemed forced.

Nerves? Gwynn wondered. No.

Sophia nervous of being with a loser like him? Maybe *that* was the issue. Maybe she regretted asking him out and worried about what her friends thought. Cold doubt strummed his heart with its icy touch. Maybe this had been a mistake.

Gwynn took a deep breath and counted before releasing. Some random therapist in the past taught him about breathing and counting. While he bitterly regarded therapy as useless quackery, he'd found a use for the breathing techniques. It quieted his mind and helped bring things into focus.

The car made an abrupt illegal U-turn and banked to the left, heading west on Williams.

"So where are we going?" Gwynn asked more to Sophia, but loud enough he might get a response from anyone.

Sophia continued to thrash away to the pounding bass.

Eric yelled from the front seat, "Big surprise, Gwynn. We're meeting with some more people at the coffee shop on Kennedy, and then everyone's following us to our, uh, final destination."

Eric raised a hand, which his buddy high-fived with a laugh.

"So am I the only one who has no idea where we're going?" Gwynn started thinking exit strategies.

"Nah. Me and Mike are the only two who know. That's why we're meeting up with everyone else so they can follow. Even Sophia doesn't know what we're up to."

Gwynn found that hard to believe. Sophia never struck him as being the type to relinquish so much control. "Really?"

She smiled and shook her head. "Not a clue. They've been keeping it to themselves for weeks."

"So why didn't I meet you guys at Kennedy with everyone else?"

"I knew the 7/11 was closer to your house. We had to drive this way, so I thought it would be easier," Sophia said.

A hazardous right turn and they were heading north on Kennedy toward some no-name coffee shop managing to survive the chains through the generous support of cheap students who enjoyed paying half the price for coffee and doughnuts. It also helped they had a huge parking lot and never kicked out the dozens of kids hanging out there.

Eric wrenched the car into the lot, causing a half dozen of his classmates to scatter for safety. A who's who of the popular kids from North Field High had congregated. At least two–thirds of the football team, almost as much of the cheerleading squad, and some mix of the basketball team were present. Even their championship volleyball team was there. In all, there had to be thirty or more kids hanging out in the parking lot. This wasn't Gwynn's crowd. In truth, he didn't have a crowd. It made him wonder how many levels of hell he'd see on this date with Sophia.

The car stopped, and Eric turned it off. The sudden silence seemed odd and out of place. Haze jumped out, and his friend Mike stopped long enough to pop the seat forward to allow Gwynn and Sophia to clamber out. Gwynn expected Sophia to dash off and start talking with the other groups of girls. Instead, she turned, her face apologetic.

"I'm sorry I dragged you into this. We should've gone to see a good horror movie instead."

"It's okay." Gwynn inspected the gathering of people with trepidation. Did any of them know him? He knew all of them by reputation. His mind started working, and he couldn't resist the question it kept asking. "Why *did* you ask me to come along?"

If the question surprised her, she didn't show it. She gave the asphalt an absent–minded kick. "Honestly?"

"Yes. Please."

"I hate it when all these people get together. There's never enough room for everyone and their egos. You've always struck me as being kinda cool. You seem like you don't need to get involved in all the games of who's popular, who's got the best car or clothes or make-up."

"Yeah well, I'm sure I could use some make-up, but my skin's too sensitive."

Sophia laughed. Proving an intoxicating melody to Gwynn.

"See what I mean. You're just... You. You don't need to play all the games these people do. I wanted someone...real. Guess it was kinda selfish. Sorry if you're having a lousy time." Her eyes locked on his, filled with a desperate hope he was not as miserable as she suspected.

"It's fine. If we survive tonight, we'll do a movie next time, okay?"

"What do you mean survive tonight?" She sounded panicked.

Gwynn laughed. "Seriously? Haven't you been paying attention to Eric's driving?"

Sophia laughed, though it sounded nervous and relieved, as though she avoided a taboo subject.

Eric approached with Mike. The two of them were slapping each other on the back, their smiles full of conspiracy.

"Okay," Eric said, "We're good to go. Sophia, Gwynn, back in the car. We're on our way to the night's main event."

The assembled masses made for their cars. Gwynn gave Sophia a small shrug and opened the door for her with a slight bow. "After you Milady."

She gave him a smile and dropped into her seat.

When all four were in the car, Eric headed out. This time, he kept to the limit, allowing the vehicles behind to keep pace. They headed north on Kennedy, heading toward the city outskirts. The subdivisions passed, their streets emptying of sugar giddy trick-or-treaters. It was almost eight. By now, Gwynn figured the ones left in the streets would be the kids too old to be seeking candy.

Mayfield Road formed a near magical boundary. On the South side, the suburbs with their houses and convenience stores surged like a wave right to the lakeshore. On the North side, farmland and wooded areas stretched out. If they continued driving north, they would not hit another city for about twenty-five minutes. In time, supposed "progress" would storm the boundaries and tear them down. Green fields and tall ancient trees would fall to bulldozers and their remains buried beneath concrete.

They drove for another five minutes then turned east on a small side road Gwynn didn't catch the name of. There were no streetlights, but the near–full moon washed the open laneway in an ashen white light.

Sophia shifted in her seat. Her eyes darted about, and she gave her nails a nervous chewing. Eric and Mike were talking up front, so Gwynn moved a little closer to Sophia and kept his voice hushed.

"What's wrong?"

Fear filled her eyes. "We're getting close."

"Where?"

Sophia, wide-eyed, shook her head and drew her legs up against herself.

Touching the Maelstrom

From the front seat, Eric bellowed, "'Kay. We're here."

Gwynn peered out the window. They were in front of an old house. Though the windows and doors appeared intact, the oppressive darkness and stark loneliness spoke of abandonment. The old Cameron house. Gwynn had never seen it, but like every kid in town, he'd heard the stories. Urban legends always take on a life of their own. They always happen to a friend of a friend or distant relative. Unlike those far-flung stories, the Cameron house sat right outside of town. A short drive away. A Bogeyman house, haunted by the angriest of spirits. The most recent story said a group of kids went in ten years ago, and one came out. The boy's hair turned white, and he never spoke of what happened up to the day they found him dead of an overdose. The note he left behind said, "I'm sorry. Destroy the house."

The house seemed to swallow every life associated with it. Who even owned it now? Whoever it was, they fixed the windows and doors and started to renovate inside. Something must have scared them off because now the property stood waiting for the day a Wal-Mart or grocery store would consume it. Until then, the house stood as the ultimate dare. As Gwynn understood it, no one dared lasted more than five minutes, but also no one had disappeared or been hurt. It surprised him the windows were intact and the house free of graffiti. But he could see the reverence his classmates had about the place. No one would think of desecrating this building of myth.

Sophia brushed against him. She trembled. Though he had no idea why they were here and little fear of the house, his stomach still tied itself into a nauseous knot. Something tugged at him, drawing him toward the cold stare of the house. He took one step closer and the pull increased. His right arm throbbed like he'd pulled a muscle. His forward step made it worse.

"What the hell?" Gwynn wondered aloud.

"I don't want to think about it," Sophia groaned.

He leaned close to her, his question insistent. "What's wrong?"

"I've had nightmares about this place. Now that I'm here, I'm... Scared."

"Do you want to leave?"

Her eyes made it clear she did, but she shook her head. "No... I need to be here."

"It's not a big deal. We'll ask someone else for a ride. I'm sure some other people wouldn't mind getting out of here."

"But..."

"Look, blame it on me. You're right; I don't care what anyone thinks. Let them call me a coward. I don't care."

She placed her hand gently against his chest—the spot feeling a bit warmer. "You're sweet. But I can't. Whatever happens here, I need to see it through to the end."

Gwynn meant to say more to convince her. Something in the house reached out to him, whispering a louder call every second. But Eric came tromping toward them first.

"Come on. Awesome, right? Where better to come on Halloween?"

He took a deep breath. "Sure Eric, but what are we doing here?"

"We're going to have a séance on the front lawn. Mike's got a Ouija board and a bunch of other shit in the trunk of the car."

Gwynn went to say Sophia had nothing to worry about; they would be staying outside with thirty or so people. Before he got the chance, Eric bellowed to the group.

"'Kay, before we get started with the main event, nobody comes to Cameron house without being issued The Challenge. So! Who's got the balls to go inside?"

Eric turned his gaze on Gwynn, and he understood why Eric dragged them out here and why so many people were present. The "big surprise" would be public humiliation. The back of his throat burned and he clenched his fists. He expected this from Eric, but Sophia as an accomplice blindsided him.

He would answer Eric's challenge, even if death waited for him inside.

Before he could, Sophia stepped in front of him and said in a shaky, yet firm, voice, "I'll do it."

Shock and unbridled anger filled Eric's eyes.

Gwynn reached out and put his hand on Sophia's shoulder. "You don't have to do this."

"Shut up." Her voice sounded ragged and full of tears. "I told you I had to see this through to the end."

She stormed up the lawn toward the house. She made a show of almost barreling Eric over as she went. When she reached the front door, her hand hesitated. Gwynn started moving after her. A dull ache began to accompany the throbbing in his arm, and the tugging at his insides proved impossible to ignore. If he moved forward too fast, no question he would throw up. Sophia's hand shook as she made a hesitant reach for the doorknob. Gwynn wanted to call out to her, but his throat went dry and stole his voice. He bit hard on his cheeks and tongue, trying to get any moisture possible. No one else made a move. No one else spoke. They all gawked. Gwynn made silent pleas for them to call her back, for someone to tell Eric to end this stupid prank. Instead, nothing. They were thankful someone else stepped forward. Some seemed confused. A few glanced to Gwynn and then up at Sophia, who still stood at the door. They came to see him humiliated. The easy target. He belonged to no groups—no one would stand beside him. There would be no reprisals. Everyone could tell the tale and have a good laugh at his expense without worrying about consequences. He knew he didn't fit in, but he didn't realize it made him so disposable.

But he wasn't at the door. Sophia was. If she began as willing to help in his humiliation, something changed. Gwynn fought against his body. He tried to move faster, push her aside if he had to. But his chest collapsed in on itself. The illness in his stomach seeped out to his legs.

The pulsing sensation in his arm quickened, and the ache remained consistent, even getting sharper. His heart crawled up into the back of his throat, pounding, strangling. Pressure, like two arms, wrapped around him, crushing his torso.

Sophia pushed the door open. To Gwynn, it appeared the house opened a dark, horrible mouth, to devour her. He couldn't make out anything beyond the threshold.

God, Jesus, anybody, stop her! His mind screamed. The words still wouldn't come. His stomach tightened and his legs cramped.

Move. Move. Move! He howled at his body.

If she went in the house.

If the door shut behind her.

Gwynn shuddered.

The house hungered. If this didn't stop, they would lose someone.

Sophia crossed the entrance. With every step, the darkness ate at her, swallowing her before Gwynn's eyes. The moonlight played across the threshold, battling with the darkness beyond. In the dim light, he still could see her blond sea of curls. The house had her now—far enough the dark obscured her like a blackened veil. Sophia didn't move any further. A wind picked up, kicking dust and years of trash into the air. It stung his eyes, but Gwynn wouldn't turn away. Out of the corners of his eyes, his classmates turned and shielded their own eyes, yet none protested or said a word, shock and a creeping horror having stolen their voices. When most were no longer looking, the door of the house swung shut. As it closed, Sophia spun, and for the briefest moment, Gwynn caught her terror-filled eyes. The sound of the door slamming shut echoed across the fields surrounding them and the wind dropped. Everyone stood staring at the house. Time crawled for Gwynn. He fought against the invisible restraints binding him. He prayed Sophia would come strolling out of the house, giggling, unscathed.

A scream shattered the silence.

The sound sent a lightning bolt through Gwynn. Despite the ill feeling in his stomach, the pressure on his chest, the strangling feeling in his throat, he surged forward. He reached the door and yanked on the knob. It refused to turn. He used both hands. He yelled at it, kicked it, and swore—the swearing giving way to a strangled sob.

"Somebody help me," he cried. His classmates gawked in mute silence. "At least use your cell phones to call for help." Someone might have made a move for a phone. Meanwhile, his head worked on getting into the house.

"Sophia!" He kept calling her name, waiting between to listen for any reply. Nothing came.

Gwynn stalked the perimeter of the house. A door at the back refused his attempts at entry as much as the front. He found a large rock and moved to the front of the house. He hurled it with all his might at the front window, rewarded with a resounding crash. Gwynn pulled off his coat and found the night had lost all its warmth. He wrapped it around his arm and punched away at the remaining shards of the window. When he widened the gap enough, he crawled into the house.

Though his stupefied classmates were a wall away, they might as well have been in another world. The house creaked and groaned—a beast awakening from slumber. After ten years of silence, the Cameron House hungered again. Gwynn crouched on the floor, allowing his eyes to adjust to the gloom. He found himself in the front sitting room. The paint on the walls was the color of old blood. A thick blanket of dust covered the cracked leather furniture. The dark wood floors showed recent movement in the trails of dust.

Gwynn's insides were a town–destroying twister. A sharp pain stabbed up the length of his right arm. An invisible line hooked into his core and dragged him upstairs.

Sophia will be there, some alien instinct told him.

He moved cautiously. Deserted for years, the Cameron house could be a death trap of rotted boards. The last thing Gwynn needed now was to go through a floor and break something.

Gwynn shifted toward the door that led to the main entrance hall where Sophia entered. Beyond the door sounded a sporadic, heavy, Thump, Thump. He edged the door open and peered into the hall. A chill ran up his spine, and the taste of bile filled the back of his throat.

A body hung in the hall, swinging back and forth, hitting the stair railing. Gwynn looked for any other sign of movement but noticed nothing. He eased out and moved toward the body. A rope extended from the second-floor banister and wrapped around the body's neck.

"Not Sophia. Please, please not Sophia."

He got closer. Not only was the body not Sophia, it wasn't even a person. Someone created a life–sized doll out of clothes stuffed with newspaper. Being closer to the door, he noticed a bucket suspended above it. He didn't want to know what the bucket contained. The full extent of the plan became apparent. Eric intended for Gwynn to come in the house all along. He'd been counting on it. Someone, maybe the two or three members of the football team who were missing from the coffee shop gathering, came ahead and prepared to scare Gwynn. But Sophia entered first. Did one of the football team's pranks scare her? Maybe they were keeping her quiet, hoping to get a shot at their intended target.

Above him, something sighed, and a floorboard creaked. At the second floor landing, a dark mass darted to the left—fluid and fast. Gwynn blinked several times, trying to focus on what he'd seen. From the direction where it fled floorboards groaned. He tried to convince himself it was one of the football team.

He started up the stairs. They gave a loud moan with each step. The third gave way, his leg crashing through the wood. Gwynn eased it free. Bloody scrapes covered his leg, and his pants were garbage. The dim light made it difficult to see any embedded slivers in his leg. It stung like hell. He gritted his teeth and moved up the remaining steps—a slow and tedious endeavor as he tested each step before putting his weight on it. Above, the sound of something heavy dragging across the floor joined the noises of complaining floorboards.

Gasping, Gwynn reached the top of the stairs. His feet slipped. A dark liquid covered the ground. He bent down and dipped a finger into it. It was tacky and smelled metallic. His stomach lurched, and acid burned his throat. His right arm screamed. Gwynn crept left where the shadow disappeared. In one of the rooms, a set of steps led upward into the attic. The dark liquid he tried to convince himself wasn't blood, trailed upward.

From the bottom of the steps, the attic lay in complete darkness. Gwynn couldn't see any movement, and the noises ceased.

If he turned around now, he could wait outside with the others for the police. They would be able to help Sophia. The police would punish the football team for the prank. It made sense. If the football team didn't have Sophia, wouldn't it be dangerous? Why should he throw away his life? Would anyone have risked themselves for him? If no one cared or respected him, why should he do it for them? What about Jaimie? She had no one else.

Sophia might not even be alive.

Gwynn shook his head. No, that couldn't be true. Not because he still nursed a nine-year-old crush, but because she protected him. No matter how this started, she stepped in to take his place. Even if this was foolish, even dangerous, he had to see it through. He refused to live every day seeing a coward in the mirror.

And as much as he tried, he couldn't deny something up there wanted him.

Taking a hesitant step at a time, Gwynn ascended the steps and let his head breach the attic. The musty gloom made it almost impossible to see. He inched the rest of the way until he put his feet on the floor. He reached up, testing the height of the ceiling. To his left, the thing tugging him called. One hesitant footstep after another took him deeper. The smell of rot assaulted him. His nose recoiled, and he swallowed down a ball of sick. But he couldn't stop. The presence in the far corner of the room beckoned.

Approaching the source, he noticed a faint glow. He faced a tall, floor length mirror. The glass showed not his reflection, but instead a swirling maelstrom thrashing beneath the surface of the glass. Gwynn reached out to touch it.

Something smashed into his midsection, sending him sprawling 20 feet in the opposite direction. Gwynn hit the ground hard and gasped as something snapped in his chest. Every inhalation stabbed his chest, and the ragged breaths filled with sloppy wet. Something stood in front of the mirror, obscuring the hazy glow.

The thing reached the height of a man and had a similar build. Its eyes revealed the creature's inhuman nature; yellow eyes, glowing, feline and starved. The thing growled low and then stuttered in what seemed a laugh.

"More...fresh...good," the voice rasped; like bones being ground together.

Death stood before him. He stretched out his right arm, reaching for anything he might grab hold of to defend himself. He couldn't tear his eyes from the monster that seemed to enjoy letting its prey panic. His hand pressed up against something. In the dim light, he couldn't make out the details, but a deeper instinct sensed a familiarity in it. He pushed harder. It tore.

Like an electrocution, a jolt of fiery white rushed through his veins and flooded his senses. Something old and primal rose within him and took control. No longer hesitant, he twisted his arm, so it tore and then pushed into whatever he held.

Gwynn howled in sudden agony with the sensation of a thousand knives carving the flesh of his arm. Even as pain consumed him, a surge of strength poured from his heart to his extremities. His muscles flexed and expanded, his vision adjusted to the darkness, making the attic bright as a midday afternoon.

Now the details of the thing across the room were clear. While it had a body shaped like a man, its face was disfigured. Its elongated jaw accommodated a mouth full of long razor teeth. Gray, rotting flesh hung limply from its bones. Gwynn understood he should feel terrified. Here was all the monsters he had been told didn't exist come to life. Instead, adrenaline pumped a joyful high through his system. He laughed. He wanted to fight. He wanted to sink a blade deep into this monster's heart. He just had to wrest his arm free of whatever still pinned it.

The creature's face contorted with intense anger, and maybe an element of fear. When the beast spoke, it said one word. "Anunnaki."

The beast charged.

Gwynn pulled at his arm, demanded it free. Whatever held it tried to draw him deeper, like fighting the pull of quicksand. The creature was on him, swinging its arm to take off his head. With a final heave, Gwynn freed his arm and rolled under the monster's swing.

Too slow. The beast's foot landed on his back. Something popped inside Gwynn and stole his breath. The swirling mass in the mirror lay within his reach. It called to him. Tugged at him. Taunted him. Anger rose from his guts like black sick. He opened his mouth and screamed, slamming his right fist into the mirror.

The mirror exploded outward. Shards of glass bit into Gwynn's skin. A gale wind ripped through the attic. Some of the older wood gave way and smashed outward into the night. A white–hot light popped like a flash bulb. Gwynn lifted into the air and flew at an opposing wall. He slammed into it and fell to the floor in a messy heap.

The night air rushed in through the gashes in the attic roof. The breeze felt comforting, sobering, against his flushed skin. He took a painful look at the remains of the attic. He couldn't see the creature. In the corner across from him, he saw a form crumpled on the floor. Sophia.

He tried to crawl toward her. Pain hit him like a fist in his stomach.

"Sophia," he croaked. She didn't move. His vision blurred and dimmed. Gwynn collapsed to the floor. Bright flashes of red and blue from outside shone through the holes in the roof. "Help's here Sophia. Everything...going to be—"

The darkness claimed him.

Tales From the Past

Gwynn drifted.

His body became weightless—up and down ceased to exist. Freedom with no limitations. His body was fluid, twisting and turning like a champion swimmer. His movements met with no resistance. The feeling of something drawing him forward existed as the sole bearing on direction or movement. The sensation intensified. The featureless void shattered with light. Bright, beautiful. Gwynn's feet touched down on a firm surface.

The light narrowed and thinned, transforming into a set of headlights cutting across his vision. Blinded, disoriented, he couldn't move. The silence filled with the sound of wheels locking against pavement, a vehicle twisting in a manner never intended. As the lights veered away, his vision returned, and he found himself staring into his own confused, eight-year-old, eyes.

The car flew off the road, disappearing into the woods. The bell-like sound of shattering glass and the tortured screams of ripping metal tore a gaping wound into the night.

Gwynn's eyes opened.

A foreign ceiling greeted him. Harsh florescent light stung at his eyes.

Gwynn tried moving his head. The room spun, and he fell back against the pillow with pain stabbing at his temples. Feeble attempts at movement revealed his right arm immobilized with restraints.

"Hello?" His voice sounded dry and hoarse. "Anybody?"

"I was starting to think you wouldn't wake up," a male voice, one Gwynn didn't recognize, said.

Trying to respond felt like walking through neck–high mud. The stranger's words spun around in his mind. Why *wouldn't* he wake up?

"How long have I been sleeping?" Gwynn had a hard time forming the words. They creaked and groaned—their bones old and settled into place.

The man stepped into sight. He wore the long white coat of a doctor. He studied a clipboard

"According to this, you've been in a coma for four days."

"Four days?" Gwynn's shock sent him straight up, which resulted in yelps of pain and him retreating to lying down.

"Easy, don't overdo it. From what the chart says, you've had a hell of a time," the man said, his voice warm and full—baritone with hearty low notes. A slight lilt accompanied his words, some accent long abandoned but not forgotten.

"What happened?" It hurt even to talk. Gwynn wished he had slept longer.

The stranger pulled a penlight from his pocket and clicked it on. He leaned over and shone the light in Gwynn's eyes.

"Do me a favor. I'm going to hold the light in front of you. Follow it with your eyes."

The light moved side to side. It stung worse than the fluorescents.

"Do you remember your name?" the man asked.

"Gwynn. Gwynn Dormath."

The light clicked off, and the stranger gave Gwynn a long, probing look. "My name's Pridament Alcandre. I'm a doctor here at the hospital, though I'm not assigned your case. When I heard your name, I had to check. I knew your parents years ago. I went to university with your dad. I've checked in on you the past couple days, but I haven't seen them."

"They...died. In a car accident." It didn't matter how much time passed, admitting his parents were gone still hurt like hell. His physical pain paled in comparison.

The man, Pridament, swept his hand through his bushy brown hair and let out a remorseful sigh. He gave his short-cropped beard a long, thoughtful stroke. "I'm sorry to hear that. They were the best kind of people. So who are you living with now?"

"My mom's sister, Jaimie."

"Really?" Pridament's voice rose in surprise. "I didn't know her, but from what your parents used to say, she didn't strike me as being very...maternal."

Gwynn couldn't help chuckling. Waves of pain and nausea ripped through him. "Oww. I mean, yeah, she's not exactly. Still, she's great. I'm lucky to have her."

"I hope you tell her," Pridament said with a parental air.

Gwynn shifted painfully in the bed, his mind returning to its purpose. "You didn't answer my question," Gwynn huffed. "What happened?"

Concern filled Pridament's gaze. "You don't remember any of it?"

"It's hazy." Gwynn tried to search his mind, but his jumbled memories read like a book written backward. Recognizable enough to decipher, but foreign enough it wouldn't give up its story without effort.

"All I know are the sketchy news reports," Pridament said. He rubbed his temples. "An explosion happened at an abandoned house outside of town. Two teenagers sustained injuries and were taken to the hospital. A third person, a homeless man, died. What *actually* happened there, that's up to you."

Wheels clicked into motion in Gwynn's brain. Images splashed across his mind's eye in a rapid and painful succession. Pridament's words gave him the most important cue. "Sophia."

"I'm sorry?"

The memory of pain kept Gwynn still, but he wanted to leap from the bed and tear through the hospital searching for her. "Sophia Murray. She must've been the other person brought in with me. Is she okay? Can I see her?"

Pridament held up his hands. "Whoa, slow down. First, I guess she is fine. Everything I heard said you were the worse of the two. Second, and this is another reason I think she's okay, no you can't see her because she was discharged yesterday."

Gwynn drew a deep breath. He tried to quell the anxiety making his legs jumpy. "You're sure?"

Pridament shook his head. "I wish I could tell you I was. Like I said, I overheard things. Once I knew it was you, I let a few docs know. They've kept me in the loop. All I know for certain is her injuries weren't that severe, and she left the hospital yesterday."

"Good." Fatigue wrapped its soft fingers around him. "That's good."

Pridament gently clasped Gwynn's bandaged hand. A stranger whose touch should've been foreign and unwelcome. Instead, a feeling of calm emanated from it. The stirring in his soul eased.

"I need to do something," Pridament said, his voice soft, comforting, but tinged with a current of earnest concern. "It's vital I remove the bandages from your right arm and inspect it."

His arm. Despite Pridament's voice and the calming touch of his hand, the mere mention of Gwynn's arm flared his anxiety. Clouded memories hovered out of reach, dark storm clouds threatening unknown terrors.

"But...you said you weren't my doctor. Why would you do that?"

Pridament locked eyes with Gwynn. His touch and voice were calming, but his eyes showed fear. "I need to check your arm. If I'm right, if I see what I think is there, then I'm the only person who can help you. I won't do it without your say–so." Pridament's grip on Gwynn's hand tightened. "If I'm right, and you wait until your doctor takes those bandages off, you'll need someone here who can explain what you're seeing."

Gwynn's stomach knotted. Every muscle tensed, sending waves of ache and stabbing pain. Anxiety didn't describe it. No, fear penetrated deep into his soul. Doubt and a sense whatever lay beneath the bandages would change everything, fed his fear. But why should he feel that way? And this man, who claimed to know his parents. What proof did he have? Should he trust him?

"You said you knew my parents?" What could he ask Pridament? What would a real friend of his parents know? "How did they meet?"

Pridament gave a gentle laugh. "How did they meet, or how did they discover they were in love?"

That answer kept Gwynn's fear at bay. The confidence in Pridament's tone, the knowledge there *was* a difference between the two things. Yes, he did know the story. But Gwynn wanted to hear it. "How they met."

Pridament shook his head, his smile widening. "Now I have to wonder, what version have you heard? I can't imagine you were told the whole story."

A pained laugh escaped from Gwynn. "Jaimie gave me the uncensored version a few years ago."

"Fair enough. So your dad, he was at York University at the time. That's where he and I met. Both of us drifting through a general BA 'cause we had no idea what to do with our lives. We were at the Absinthe Pub in the Winters residence. The place was dark wood, dingy, a hangout for arty types. We were only there the one time. I think maybe because everywhere else was too busy. Anyway, your dad, he's had more than his fair share of beer. This girl walks into the bar—"

"Mom."

"Hey, kid, who's telling the story? But, yes, your mom walks into the bar. She is wearing this little black dress that has, uh, well—let's say she looked *good*. So your dad, catching sight of her, jumps up on a table and starts reciting some of the worst poetry I've ever heard. I mean, I don't know if he wrote it, or read it in some bargain basement book, but wow, it was cheesy. Now, he's not just saying it—he's performing. He's got his hand over his heart; he's reaching to the Gods screaming thanks they have brought this beautiful creature to earth. Anyway, your mom isn't impressed. If anything, she's pissed." Pridament laughed full on, tears streaming down his face. He had to stop and take the odd breath between words. "So, your dad gets a little too energetic in his performance, and the table falls over, sending him falling on his ass. But he's so drunk—he doesn't notice. He gets up on his feet, saunters over to your mom, and plants a big kiss right on her lips."

"And she...?" Gwynn loved the punch line.

"Kicked him so hard in the nuts he puked all over her."

Gwynn's body convulsed with his laughter. "I can't believe they ended up together after that."

"Well, it took some time, and your dad *could* be quite the charmer. When he was sober."

They laughed for a while.

Pridament quieted, sadness creeping into his eyes. "I should've done more. I shouldn't have let that relationship go. I transferred to another school to pursue medicine. Your dad stayed for law. We talked a little, traded the odd email over the years, but we never were as close as we could've been. I'm sorry for your loss."

"Thanks." His parents. When would remembering them get less painful? "Go ahead."

"Go ahead?"

Gwynn gave a little shrug. "My arm. Look at it. If there's something wrong, I'd rather be here with someone who knew my parents. Besides Jaimie, that's as close to family as I get."

"Jaimie's been here every day. I'm sure something came up."

"I'm sure she has. Probably work. Seems they can never go a full week without her going in."

Pridament drew a breath. "Okay, here we go."

The bandages went right up to Gwynn's fingers. Pridament maneuvered around, searching for the best place to start. He ended up cutting from the elbow down. Pridament eased the wrapping up a little to move his scissors along. The tender skin howled and burned with the new irritation. Gwynn panted, trying to ignore the arm.

"I'm almost there. Hang on another second."

As Pridament promised, the tugging and pulling soon ended.

Gwynn couldn't—wouldn't—look. His fear heightened when Pridament let out an involuntary "damn."

"What is it?" He kept his eyes averted.

The visitor's chair groaned as Pridament flopped back. The man sighed. "It means we need to have a long talk."

He didn't want to see. But the unknown suffocated him more than any truth he could imagine. He turned his head to inspect his arm.

It took everything in him not to scream.

Something, or someone, carved his arm up. It remained intact but covered in odd symbols from his elbow to his fingers. They were like nothing he'd seen. Combinations of shapes and foreign looking letters. It reminded him of the heady math equations geniuses solved in movies.

"Why..." His voice a wreck of fear, anger, and tears. "Why would anyone do something like that?"

Pridament took his hand again. The same sense of calm, no, security, emanated from it. "No one did this to you, Gwynn. This is your body reacting to something inside of you."

"Inside of me?" Gwynn was incredulous. "What could be inside of me that would do this shit to my arm?"

With his free hand, Pridament rubbed at his temples. "I'm going to tell you, but you won't believe me at first. No one ever does. If you trust me, if you give me time to show you, I will prove everything I say is true."

The fight drained from Gwynn's body in a rush. Sorrow took hold. An impetuous decision, chasing after something he had no right to claim, had left him scarred again. At the age of seven, he trespassed on the old Wilson farm and sliced his abdomen on the barbed fence. Being impulsive, crossing over into worlds you had no right to be in, led to pain and scars. But how did scarring like this happen? If Pridament had the answers, would it clarify the cloudy nightmare Halloween night had become?

"Tell me what you know," Gwynn's words were slow and labored, "I'll give you a chance."

Pridament paused. He seemed to be searching for the right words. "Thousands of years ago, a group of people were born with special abilities. Normal humans elevated them to godhood. The masses praised and worshiped them. In their own way, those gifted people tried to be fair and benevolent gods. They called themselves the Anunnaki. Over time, others were born with similar powers. In some cases, people raised them up as gods through adoration. Others assumed the role through force. Many others chose to hide their abilities. All over the world, patches of these people appeared. Our modern world remembers them as the Olympians, the Aesir, and the gods of Egypt."

"So what does that have to do with me?"

"Those people," Pridament said, nodding toward Gwynn's arm, "were marked the same way you are."

"So you're saying I'm one of these people?" His mind reeled. When Pridament said he wouldn't believe, he had no idea how outrageous the story would be. Him? Gwynn Dormath, a god? What a ridiculous joke. He would've said so to Pridament, would've told him to save the fairy tales for toddlers, but nothing but conviction resided in the older man's voice and eyes. Yes, he understood what he said sounded foolish and impossible. But he believed every word of it.

"I know. It was a lot easier to have faith in a world not dominated by science. But the truth is, science plays a role in this. You see—"

"What the HELL is going on here?" a male voice—old leather worn through years of smoke and alcohol.

Pridament made a startled jump to his feet. "Please, let me explain."

"I think you damned well better." This man's gray and thinning hair made him look much older than Pridament. He wore thick glasses which fell halfway down his hawkish nose. His attire marked him as a doctor.

Pridament extended his hand, which the other doctor showed no interest in taking. After an awkward minute, Pridament withdrew his hand. "I'm Doctor Alcandre, Pridament. I was friends with Gwynn's parents."

The older doctor looked to Gwynn, who nodded his agreement.

"It's true. He knew them."

"Well, I'm Doctor Saduj. I've been overseeing Gwynn's care since he arrived. While I don't mind you visiting my patient, doctor, I'm wondering how you justify removing the dressings on his arm."

"When he came out of the coma, he started tearing at it. He seemed in distress. When I got him calmed down, he said it felt like it was on fire. I removed the bandages so I could see what was happening."

Had Pridament practiced that very speech just in case? Even knowing it as a lie, Gwynn thought it sounded flawless and convincing.

"What did you find?"

Gwynn couldn't shake the odd feeling being around Pridament made this Doctor Saduj uncomfortable.

"As you see. Scarred, but no obvious issue. Once Gwynn got over the shock of seeing the scars, the sensation ceased. It might have been merely psychosomatic."

Doctor Saduj scratched the top of his nose and pushed his glasses further up. "Well, nonetheless, let's not make butting into other doctor's cases a habit, shall we Doctor?"

"Yes."

Pridament came closer to Gwynn and gave his hand a gentle squeeze. "I should let Doctor Saduj do his job now. As soon as I can, I'll come back and finish our conversation. Deal?"

"Yes." He said the word but felt conflicted. Did he want the conversation to continue? It meant either he was a freak, or an old friend of his parents was insane. Neither option seemed appealing.

"Again, I'm sorry Doctor Saduj," Pridament said. He left the room, hesitating long enough to give Gwynn a final wave.

"Well," Doctor Saduj sounded flustered, "I'm glad to see you're awake Mr. Dormath. Let's do a few tests and see how you truly are."

***

Several hours later, Doctor Saduj paced his office.

This assignment made him very uncomfortable. He had grown accustomed to inactive duty. Now, powerful eyes focused on him.

He went to check his watch and, much to his dismay, found his hand trembling. How long since he called? They told him the man who called himself Pridament might visit the boy. Now it had happened, Doctor Saduj had to admit he never believed it would. They didn't tell him much, his role minor in the grand scheme. But the tones used to discuss Pridament were akin to the reverence saved for the Bogeyman.

A knock at the door.

Saduj opened it a cautious crack. The familiar face on the other side wore a mask of contempt, as usual. The unpleasant man ran his hand through a shaggy silver mane of hair.

"You called?"

"Yes," Doctor Saduj stammered. "Please. Please come in."

Saduj's visitor pushed passed him into the office. Doctor Saduj leaned out and checked the hall to ensure no one was paying attention. Once satisfied, he closed and locked the door. Saduj went to address his visitor when it occurred to him he didn't even know the man's name. In his mind, he always referred to him as 'The Tie' due to the habit the man had of having his tie flung over his shoulder.

"So what do you have to report?" The Tie asked.

Doctor Saduj's brow dampened. "You were correct sir. He came to see the boy, as you suspected he would."

Despite the apparent importance, no, danger, of Pridament, The Tie's interest seemed casual. "He used the usual alias?"

"Pridament. Yes, sir."

"Did the boy give a description?"

"I saw him myself."

Doctor Saduj related a description of Pridament.

"And were you able to find out what they discussed?"

"The boy claimed it was stories about his parents. It seemed like there might've been more, but he refused to say. I confess I think I interrupted them."

The Tie waved it off, a minor offense not worth addressing.

"And what of the boy? Is he well?" The Tie asked.

"Given he's been comatose for four days, I'd say he's doing splendidly. There are no cognitive deficits I can find. Most of his injuries seem to be mending at, well, honestly, an abnormally fast rate."

"What of his arm? What does his right arm look like?"

Doctor Saduj gave his nose an absent-minded scratch. "It's been horribly scarred. It looks like someone intentionally carved symbols into his flesh."

An excited anticipation filled The Tie's eyes. "How extensive is the scarring?"

"I'm sorry?"

"The scarring, Doctor Saduj. Is it a small patch of symbols, or does it cover the majority of his arm?"

"Oh." Saduj gave another scratch to the bridge of his nose, pushing his glasses back to their proper position. "It covers from his elbow right onto his hands. I can't imagine what sort of madness would drive a person to do such a thing."

"Yes, yes. Decent work. I appreciate your prompt action in this matter, Doctor. If you hear anything further concerning Pridament or there's any radical change in the boy's health, be sure to contact me."

Saduj attempted to snap to attention. He'd never been in the military, and he didn't know if the organization even did such things. "I will. I'm here to serve, sir."

"Glad to hear it." The Tie seemed amused by Saduj's feeble attempts at military order. "Take good care of young Gwynn, Doctor Saduj. Return him to health and get him out of this hospital. *We* will see to him after that."

"I will, sir." In a conspiratorial whisper, he added, "To heal the world."

"Yes, doctor," a hunger filled The Tie's eyes, "to heal the world indeed."

Instrument of the Shadows

Gwynn sat on his bed, inspecting the scarred mess covering his right arm. It burned and itched. The markings played across his flesh from the elbow and onto his hand. They held some meaning, but it eluded him like the whispers of a dream. When he stared at them long enough, the answer seemed so close, something he could reach out and take. But it always danced away before comprehension solidified.

"We're not too sure how," the doctor at the hospital said, "but you are completely healed."

"So? Why's that a problem?" Jaimie asked.

"Ms. Roberts, please try to understand," Doctor Saduj huffed. He pushed his heavy glasses further up his nose and scratched at the wrinkled skin of his forehead. "When Gwynn arrived in hospital, he had several broken ribs, a punctured lung, and head trauma. He remained comatose for four days, and we had every reason to believe the possibility of extensive brain damage. Now, after a total of seven days, he is completely healed."

"Again, what's wrong with that?"

"There's nothing wrong with it" Doctor Saduj failed to hide how flustered he'd become. "Except it's impossible. Not only has he healed at an accelerated rate, but there's no indication the injuries ever existed. Even when bones heal, they leave evidence of the previous break. None of that exists. It's as if the injuries never happened."

Fire filled his aunt's eyes. She hadn't birthed him, she might not have been ready to be his mother, but neither of those facts kept her from a fierce defense. "That's not our problem. Is it safe for him to go home?"

"Well, yes," Doctor Saduj spluttered. "We would like to do some more tests to try and understand how—"

"No. There will be *no more tests.*" Jaimie turned to Gwynn, her small form full of power and determination towering over all others in the room. "Gwynn, get dressed. We're leaving. Thank you, Doctor, I'm sure Gwynn's speedy recovery is due to your outstanding care."

Doctor Saduj shrugged. The doctor didn't think for a moment his care cured Gwynn, but the droop of his shoulders and the distant look in his eyes spoke of defeat at Jaimie's hands.

Seven days after admission with life-threatening injuries, Gwynn left the hospital. He should've been ecstatic, felt blessed. But doubt, cold and gnawing at his innards, kept a simple question ever-present in his mind; why am I alive?

When his parents died, he felt angry. Why had they died? Why did his dad have to switch jobs anyway? If they just stayed where they were...

To ask why he survived never occurred to him. At the age of eight, you expected to live, death seemed odd. Being older, he understood people died for far less. How many people sidestepped the reaper twice? If this was luck, how long would it hold?

Life changed. His room, exactly as he'd been comfortable in for years, today seemed cold and foreign. The white walls, barren of posters and color, loomed high and seemed too close.

Gwynn pulled a long-sleeved shirt over his head. It did nothing to cover the scars on his hand. He couldn't recall a time when the opinions of others meant much to him. But the scars were private. The thought of someone else seeing them filled him with uncertainty, like a dirty secret. Gwynn searched the room for something to cover his hand. Nothing on his floor or the small desk with his computer proved of any use. His eyes fell on his dresser and inspiration took hold. The top drawer contained socks and underwear, the second, sweaters. The third, and bottom-most, drawer had clothes he classed as other. He rooted around the drawer, digging to the bottom. A search rewarded him with a pair of biking gloves. The black gloves had leather sewn to the palm, and the fingers cut off. Aunt Jaimie purchased them. But Gwynn preferred to feel the rubber of his bike handles, so the gloves were retired. Gwynn slipped on the right-hand glove. He flexed his hand a couple of times and left the bedroom behind.

The smell of breakfast cooking awaited him.

"Aren't you supposed to be at work?" He asked Jaimie as she stacked pancakes on a plate.

"I took the day off. I thought, maybe I should be available. You know, in case..."

"I go postal at school?"

She gave him a strained smile. "I thought if you decided it was too soon to be back at school, you might appreciate a friendly face at home."

Gwynn threw his arms around her. Her body stiffened with surprise, but then relaxed and she returned his embrace.

"Thanks, Jaimie."

She sniffled. "Come on, are you telling me you don't like having pancakes ready for breakfast?"

"Freshly cooked instead of nuked? Yeah, I'm not going to complain."

Complaining around the warm, syrupy morsels stuffed in his mouth would've been impossible anyway. Jaimie gave him a warm smile. Her eyes fell on Gwynn's gloved hand, and her face hardened.

"Aren't you going to get a hard time about that?"

"Better than people staring at the scars."

"You don't have to go in you know. Take a few more days off."

Gwynn shook his head while he chewed. He swallowed loudly. "I'm going to have to go back eventually. Besides, I've got a few days of work to catch up on already. I don't need to fall any further behind."

"You're hoping to see Sophia?" Jaimie wore a sly smile.

Gwynn caught her eyes for a moment, and then mumbled around a mouthful of pancake, "Maybe."

With breakfast finished, Gwynn thanked Jaimie and grabbed his backpack.

"You want a ride?" she asked.

The offer tempted Gwynn—November arrived wet and cold. But something in him wanted to feel the wind biting his skin. He wanted to smell the oncoming snow. Mostly, he didn't want to arrive at school looking like an invalid.

"I'm good. Thanks."

Despite the doubt crossing her face, she didn't press him.

"Anything you want for dinner?"

"Homemade breakfast and dinner on the same day? I should get blown up more often."

Her face told him he shouldn't joke, but he couldn't help it. He faced his mortality, and if he couldn't laugh, if he couldn't force it down into the dark places where the loss of his parents lived, he'd lose his mind.

"Sorry. I'm good with anything. I'll trust you."

She shook her head. Jaimie hated it when he was noncommittal.

"Have a good day Gwynn. If you want to come home—"

"I'll call. Promise."

Out in the morning air, the cold wrapped around Gwynn and prickled at the exposed flesh of his face. The gray sky cast odd shadows and washed out the finer details of the world. Dark clouds filled the sky. They filled him with a dread he couldn't explain.

Gwynn arrived on the school grounds. Small pockets of students clung together in clumps, seeking shelter in each other's company. Were they seeking shelter from the current chill or the threat of something worse?

No one gave Gwynn a second glimpse. There were no whisperings, no fingers pointed. He moved through the halls, through his classes, like the phantom he had always been.

Lunchtime.

Nothing obvious about the cafeteria had changed, but it felt like a sinister energy undulated beneath the surface. Gwynn found his way to his seat. It still stood empty. Had it been sitting here waiting for him all this time? Would it still stand empty when he'd left this place behind?

He scanned the cafeteria for Sophia. He'd spent all morning watching for her. Laughter drew his attention to the far corner where Eric Haze held court with his cronies. Gwynn's arm throbbed—partially due to how hard he clenched his fist. Gwynn was halfway to their table before being aware he'd even stood up.

He reached the table. Why was he here? Did he hope for some form of apology? Would Eric be remorseful? Would he tell Gwynn where to find Sophia?

All hopes shattered with the grin on Haze's face. Still the hyena.

"Gwynn! Hey, how's it going?"

Haze stood up and put his arm around Gwynn's shoulders. Gwynn's fist gripped so hard—only the glove prevented him drawing blood.

"You all remember our man Gwynn, right? The AH–MAAAAAH–zing exploding boy?"

The others didn't know how to act. But when their lord and master belly laughed, they all soon joined in. Haze turned his malevolent eyes on Gwynn.

"Hey buddy, didn't I tell you Halloween would be a blast?"

Eric flew to the ground, his nose a fountain of blood. In horror, Gwynn realized he had drawn back his fist to deliver another blow. Confusion, maybe even fear, had Eric's cronies paralyzed. A tangible silence gripped the cafeteria. No one stirred. Their faces were a mixture of confusion and shock. Had the quiet loner revealed his true nature?

One face he didn't recognize. It wore an expression different from the others. Her long, straight brown hair framed a pale, heart–shaped face. Unlike the others, she showed no confusion. Her dark almond shaped eyes held determination and a readiness to act. His insides churned in ice. A huge shadow enveloped him. He tried to block the image from his mind, instead focusing on the dumbfounded Eric.

Something went wrong with his vision; Eric appeared blurry. At one moment, he was solid, the next, a phantom duplicate image appeared. The two images moved out of sync with each other. While the solid Eric sat on the ground avoiding eye contact with Gwynn, the ghostly image locked its eyes on him. But the ghost had catlike eyes, and as it opened its mouth, a series of long teeth descended. The ghost tensed, and then it leaped at him. He threw his arms in front of his face to protect himself. When nothing happened, he lowered his arms to see Eric still sitting on the ground.

The eyes of the cafeteria weighed on him. The silence gave way to hushed murmurings. The girl he didn't know, the one tensing for a fight, appeared as confused as everyone else. Gwynn's right arm throbbed, a sharp hammer and nail pain pounded on his temples. Phantom Echoes of everyone in the cafeteria appeared. The solid versions remained seated. Some of their ghostly counterparts laughed, while others growled and prepared to pounce and devour. Only the girl remained free of an echo. No ghost image of her moved or acted in ways opposite of Gwynn's world.

His stomach lurched, and he ran from the cafeteria, slamming hard into the doors, throwing them aside and fell into the closest washroom where his stomach gave a violent heave.

He fumbled in his pocket for his cell phone. He stared at the keypad for a while. "Should I? Shouldn't I?" He didn't want Jaimie to worry, didn't want her to hear what he had done. He didn't want to admit she'd been right. He should've stayed home. He slid the phone back into his pocket and moved to the sink. The acrid taste of sick burned the back of his throat.

Cold water cleansed and soothed his mouth. Clean, simple, and pure. He splashed some on his face, hoping it would wash away whatever illness caused his head to sting and his arm to throb. Soon, he admitted defeat. No amount of cold water could soothe the burning of his flesh or quell the deep aches.

A shadow moved.

He caught a brief glimpse from the corner of his eye. A hulking mass shifted from the wall and passed behind him. He took a hesitant glance in the mirror, but nothing was there except for his own, mad-looking, face. He made a slow three–sixty, and again, the shadow moved. It never remained in his direct vision where he could get a clear look. A bead of cold sweat burned down his neck. He threw himself against the wall so he could view the whole washroom. He saw nothing else.

Gwynn shut his eyes tight. He counted, opened his eyes, and returned to the sink. He tried to muster a sane and steady look in his eyes as he confronted the haggard young man in the mirror. "It's a dream or stress. Some leftover thing from when I got hurt." He ran his hands down over his face. "Maybe I need my eyes checked." No one offered a different opinion.

Gwynn groaned and shuffled out the door, colliding with an innocent passerby in the process.

"I'm sorry. I, I'm really sorry," Gwynn said.

Intense dark almond shaped eyes probed him. Gwynn took several awkward steps back. The girl said nothing, just continued walking down the hall, hesitating a moment to give Gwynn the same glare he saw in the cafeteria. A chill ran down his back.

He started down the hall, moving away from the chaos of the cafeteria. He had two choices, leave school, go home and hope the whole thing blew over. Or go to the office and face the consequences. He played the options in his mind for a few minutes. What would Jaimie have him do? There was only one choice. Gwynn made his way to the office.

6

Luck Only Lasts So Long

Gwynn felt restless. Did they buy uncomfortable chairs in the office intentionally—a sadistic torture to further the uneasy experience of being there?

Gwynn's left knee bounced in time to a marching rhythm beating at the edge of his consciousness. He'd never been in the office. Almost finished high school and he managed to keep his head down and never attract much attention. Now he'd smashed the nose of the reigning school football hero. No doubt, he was a dead man.

After a seeming eternity, the principal's door opened. Gwynn's guts twisted as he caught a glimpse of the now familiar heart-shaped face. Thankfully, the murderous intent in her dark eyes seemed to have vanished.

"Thank you very much Fuyuko, I appreciate it," Mr. Davis, the school principal, said.

Fuyuko gave a slight bow and left the office.

Mr. Davis turned to Gwynn and sighed. "C'mon in Mr. Dormath."

The words, *Dead man walking*, echoed in Gwynn's head as he trudged into the office.

Mr. Davis shut the door and assumed his seat behind a large desk, barren except for a computer.

"Let's get right to it, shall we." Mr. Davis steepled his fingers. "You're here because of what happened in the cafeteria?"

"Yes."

"Well, I'll give you some points for coming here yourself. At least it shows you're willing to accept the consequences of your actions. That said, striking another student is unacceptable."

"I know sir. I'm sorry." Gwynn searched for an excuse. Something to explain what happened. In the end, he had to admit the truth. "I don't know what came over me."

Mr. Davis' smile held some sympathy. "Fuyuko tells me Mr. Haze goaded you into it. Given what happened to you and Miss Murray, I can understand why you reacted the way you did."

Gwynn tried to process what Mr. Davis said. "Fuyuko? You mean the girl who was just in here?"

"Yes, a new transfer student from out of province who started last Monday. She saw what happened and felt she should tell me. I guess she figured I would believe her because she's impartial."

Gwynn started to feel the noose loosen around his neck. "Did you?"

"Gwynn, Eric Haze has a certain reputation in this school I am well aware of. Yes, I do believe what Fuyuko told me, but that doesn't change the fact it's a serious infraction, and you need to receive some form of punishment."

"Yes, sir." Gwynn shrank in his chair.

"I think you should go home for the rest of the day, and take the next two days off as well. Officially, it's a suspension. But I think you and I can both agree you need some more time off to...relax."

Gwynn tasted rising sick. Jaimie would be pissed.

"Yes sir," he gulped out the words.

"Is there anything you need to get from your locker?"

"Just my coat."

"Good. Your Aunt is coming to get you. I'll accompany you so you can get your coat."

For nine years, Gwynn had an obligation to be a model young man for Jaimie. She'd taken him in. He had no one else. She'd abandoned so much for him. He appreciated it. He valued her. The feeling of letting her down was a punch to his stomach.

"Mr. Davis?" he hesitated. Maybe he should keep quiet.

"Yes, Gwynn?"

Desperation took hold. Gwynn needed answers.

"I was hoping to see Sophia, to talk to her about what happened. But I haven't seen her all day."

Mr. Davis cleared his throat. "As far as I'm aware, Miss Murray has been away from school since the incident. I don't think she was severely hurt, but she hasn't been well enough to come back to school."

"Okay. Um, thanks." That had him worried. Pridament said Sophia left the hospital before Gwynn woke up. Had he lied? Were Sophia's injuries worse?

Mr. Davis escorted Gwynn to his locker. Thankfully, the hallways were empty as it was still the lunch hour. When they returned to the office, Jaimie arrived. Mr. Davis explained Gwynn's punishment and the events leading to it. Gwynn couldn't read Jaimie's eyes. He wished she would yell at him; hit him, anything other than be the calm, understanding Jaimie. His insides twisted so bad they managed to overpower the continuous throbbing in his arm and head. Gwynn trudged behind her to the car and crashed into the passenger's seat.

"I'm sorry," Gwynn said when Jaimie finished putting on her seat belt.

Jaimie closed her eyes for a moment and took a deep breath. "I'm not mad you hit Eric. Hell, it's about time someone took that kid down a peg. It's lousy timing. You fought me so hard about staying home a bit longer."

"You were right. I should have listened."

Jaimie opened her eyes and smiled. "You're a good kid. This shouldn't have happened. First that damn house, now a suspension on your record. You don't deserve this. It seems unfair. I think that's what upsets me most."

"Thanks, Jaimie."

They drove home in silence. Once there, Gwynn went up to his room. At first, he flopped down on his bed. But his legs bounced, and the throbbing in his arm and head wouldn't let him relax. Instead, he ended up pacing his floor. Halloween. He replayed the night in his mind. Maybe Pridament would be able to clear up some of it. The man seemed to want to talk more. Gwynn caught sight of him several times while at the hospital. More than anything else, Gwynn wanted to know what role Sophia played. Only she could answer that for him.

After a few minutes, he went downstairs. Jaimie shuffled about the kitchen. She seemed lost.

Gwynn cleared his throat.

Jaimie turned, her face red and flustered. "I was going to start dinner, but then I couldn't remember what I was going to make." She sank into a chair.

"You know it's only two o'clock, right?" Gwynn asked.

"I know. I was hoping to make something...happy."

Tears stung at Gwynn's eyes.

"I'm sorry I let you down."

Jaimie's face fell. "No, no, it's not you Gwynn. If anything, I'm the one who's doing something wrong. I mean, in a little over a week you're almost killed and then suspended from school. God, my sister would disown me."

Gwynn searched for words. The mention of his mother had him flustered. Bad enough to feel he failed Jaimie, but failing to live up to what his parents' would have wanted for him? He'd become a failure.

Jaimie sniffled and wiped her sleeve across her eyes. "Crap, I'm a mess. Did you want something?"

Gwynn hesitated. It was the wrong time to ask. At the same time, something felt wrong. Something gnawed at his insides, and only one person he could think of had answers.

"Jaimie, I know I shouldn't be asking, but, I hoped you would let me go see Sophia."

Jaimie exploded. "You're goddamn right you shouldn't be asking me. You think 'cause you're off school you should be able to go make out with your girlfriend?"

Gwynn didn't let her continue. "Make out with her? Girlfriend? I think she set me up so Eric Haze could get me into that house. But then something changed, she took the bullet for me. Why? I'm not interested in making out with her; I want to know what the hell really happened."

Jaimie's eyes were stern, but she weighed his words. He considered pressing his argument, but that risked going too far.

"If she wasn't at school, do you think she's in any condition to see you?"

The building tightness in his chest started to unravel—Jaimie seemed to be considering it. "She wasn't badly hurt; they discharged her from the hospital before me. I think she's laying low. I think she kind of ruined Eric's plans by going in the house first. Maybe she's avoiding that crowd until everything blows over."

Jaimie shook her head.

"Fine. On the condition you call me from your cell if you're staying and call me again when you're on your way home."

"I will." It dawned on Gwynn how much faith his aunt put in him. "Thanks, Jaimie. I promise. I'll call you soon."

"You better, or I'm not going to be Ms. Nice–and–Understanding–Aunt any longer. Got it?"

Gwynn gave a salute.

"Got it."

Gwynn bolted out the door before she could change her mind.

***

He had walked the route to Sophia's a number of times, though he'd always made it seem he had another destination in mind. He would often hope Sophia might be outside her house alone and call him over, or maybe join him in his walk. It had never happened, and as he had gotten older, he realized his actions were kind of creepy and that he needed to dial back.

He passed the 7/11. A shudder ran along his spine.

He was so preoccupied with memories—he slammed into someone at the stoplights. He stumbled back, catching himself before falling.

"I'm so sorry. I wasn't looking where I was going," his voice stammered.

"That seems to be a habit of yours."

Gwynn stared at the girl Mr. Davis had named Fuyuko. Genuine anger filled her eyes. Not wise to make this girl an enemy.

"I know. It's been a rough day for me. I'm sorry I keep running you over."

Fuyuko shrugged. "I've had worse things happen."

She took a step closer to Gwynn, moving beyond his barrier of personal space. It wasn't unpleasant, just awkward. She seemed to be inspecting him.

"I heard a rumor you were in an explosion."

Gwynn tried to laugh it off. It sounded unnatural and even uncomfortable. "That's what they tell me. The whole thing's a little blurry."

"When I came into the school last Monday, the other students said you were going to die."

"Doctors got it wrong. I'm fine."

Fuyuko's gaze fell to his hand. "Trying to start some new fashion trend?"

"Hmm? What?" Gwynn looked down. Oh, she meant the glove. His face reddened. "No, no. There's, uhh, some scars. I didn't want people staring at them."

"I see. Well, goodbye."

Fuyuko turned to cross the road.

"Wait," Gwynn called.

She turned back. "What is it?"

Thankfully, she didn't sound annoyed.

"I wanted to say thanks. For speaking to Mr. Davis. It saved me. No one else would've bothered to help me out."

She smiled, small and brief, but Gwynn had seen it.

"I thought Mr. Davis should know the whole story. The way others were talking, I knew none of them would," she said, her voice smooth and silky—no accent he could detect, just an air of intelligence and sophistication.

"Well, I guess I don't have many friends. Thanks, I appreciate it."

"You are very welcome. Good day."

With that, she turned and crossed the road.

Gwynn waited for the light to change and continued to Sophia's.

Crossing Dixie, he made his way through a walkway and turned right when it came out to a residential street. He kept walking until he came to another walkway. Through this, left at the street, and down three houses. While most of the homes in the subdivision were an average family home, the ones on this street were all custom builds. Sophia's home would fit at least two of his house.

Gwynn took a deep breath and started walking toward the front door. His forehead dampened and his stomach knotted. The constant throbbing in his arm and head didn't help. Several times, he considered turning back. So many times the walkway to the Murrays' door seemed miles in length.

When he reached the door, Gwynn gulped another breath and rung the doorbell.

Several moments passed. Gwynn figured he should give up when the door echoed with the sound of locks clicking open. The door opened to reveal a grim, middle–aged man whose eyes fell disapprovingly on Gwynn.

"I'm sorry to disturb you, sir," Gwynn stammered. "I wondered if Sophia was home."

Thinly veiled anger filled the man's eyes. "She's not seeing anyone right now."

"Oh." A pit gnawed at Gwynn's stomach. "Can you please let her know Gwynn came by to see her?"

The man hesitated. "Did you say you were Gwynn?"

"Yes, sir."

The man, Mr. Murray, Gwynn assumed, inspected him.

"The same Gwynn that went into the Cameron House after Sophia?"

"I am."

Mr. Murray's eyes softened. "I heard you were gravely injured. I figured you'd still be in the hospital."

"I'm not sure what happened. I guess I wasn't as bad as the doctors thought. I got out two days ago."

"Gwynn, Sophia's not here," Mr. Murray shuddered. "But I think it's important you see her. She keeps asking for you."

Despite his dark suspicions, Gwynn's heart raced. "I'd be glad to come back when she gets home."

Sophia's father's face fell. "I don't know when that'll be, Gwynn." Her father's eyes misted. "It's not very good. Sophia's back in the hospital."

7

The Girl He Used to Know

Jaimie made a dash for the ringing phone.

"Hello?" She puffed.

"Hi, Jaimie."

The sound of his voice helped ease her nerves. "Hi, Gwynn. How are things with Sophia?"

A long pause. Maternal fury burned her insides. If Sophia hurt Gwynn further, if she *had* betrayed him, Jaimie would make the girl wish she were back in an exploding house.

"Sophia's not here." He sounded hurt. "Her dad says she's in the hospital."

Jaimie scolded herself silently for jumping to conclusions. "I'm sorry Gwynn. Were her injuries worse than they thought?"

"No, nothing like that. Her dad says she's in the psychiatric ward."

"Oh my god. Gwynn, that's awful."

"Her dad says she keeps asking for me. He wondered if I could go see her tomorrow."

"Maybe you should, but I can't tomorrow Gwynn. I think I stretched my boss' goodwill to its limit taking today off on short notice."

"Sophia's dad says I can go with him. Her mom's spending her whole time at the hospital. I'd like to see her Jaimie. But I understand if you don't want me to..."

Jaimie sighed and rolled her eyes toward the white ceiling of the kitchen. How did she deny him? Until his suspension today, he never once gave her a reason to be mad at him. And didn't Eric Haze deserve a smashed nose after his prank nearly got Gwynn and Sophia killed?

"Okay Gwynn, you can go. But I don't want you being a burden. I'll give you some cab fare, so the Murrays don't have to worry about driving you home. And I expect you to keep me informed throughout the day, deal?"

"Deal. Thanks, Jaimie. I'll tell her Dad, and then I'll be on my way home. Bye."

Jaimie hung up the phone and focused on some distant point. What was happening? Until a week ago, their lives were so consistent. No excitement, no change, just a dependable existence. She and Gwynn found a good balance of friendship and parenthood in their relationship. Gwynn started to have more nights without nightmares than with. The kid had good grades. She had a steady job with decent benefits. They had a comfort zone. Now, security was slipping away. Her sister, her parents, they had all gone without warning. That taught her life does change in a matter of moments. She couldn't shake the dread one of those moments had come again.

***

Gwynn hadn't slept.

Down the hall, Jaimie's alarm clock sounded with an angry squawk. He threw on some pants and an old T-shirt and headed downstairs for something to eat.

From the kitchen table, Gwynn could trace Jaimie's progress in getting ready for work. A few stumbling thumps after the alarm were her getting up. The pipes creaking with a sudden burst of water from the washroom. Then a constant hissing meant a shower. More thumps, their pace hurried from before, were her moving to the closet. He waited for the sound of her bare feet slapping against the wooden stairs. He smiled to himself. She moved with the grace of a peg-legged pirate.

"There's a bowl of cereal here for you and some toast with jam," Gwynn said.

"Thanks." Jaimie stuffed the toast in her mouth and went to the powder room where she would fuss with her hair for a few more minutes.

She returned to the table and sat down, finishing the toast and working on the cereal.

"Are you sure you're okay going with the Murrays?" she asked.

"I'll be fine."

Her eyes said she doubted him. "I left some money on the front hall table for you. It should be enough to buy some food and get a cab home. Don't make the Murrays feel like they need to worry about you. They've got enough on their hands."

Gwynn groaned. "I know Jaimie."

Jaimie smiled. "Sorry, sorry. I didn't sleep too well." After a brief appraisal of him, she said, "Doesn't look like you did either. I hope you don't fall asleep on the poor girl."

The statement lacked Jaimie's usual joking tone. It sounded humorless and biting.

"I won't," Gwynn snipped

Jaimie held her hands up in surrender. "I know, I know, that came out too harsh. I seem to be channeling my inner overbearing mother today."

"And after I made you breakfast."

Jaimie leaned back in her chair and rubbed at her temples.

"You're right. I should relax. Things have been so...strained. I'm afraid everything's falling apart."

"Jaimie, I punched some asshole who deserved it. If it hadn't been in the school, no one would care."

"Maybe. But that's the thing. Since when do you punch assholes, whether they deserve it or not?"

"Well, it's not like I've been blown up before."

Even Gwynn winced at the growing annoyance in his voice. What was happening to him? When did his fuse get so short? Jaimie's face showed she got the message.

"Okay, I'll leave it alone. Just keep me in the loop. You've got my work number?"

"Yeah."

She got up from the table and kissed him on the forehead. "Love you, Gwynn. Sorry, I'm getting all overprotective. Don't want my favorite guy to get hurt, that's all."

Gwynn checked himself before answering. She loved him. That would be a lousy reason to attack her.

"I know. But geez Jaimie, sometimes I think you forget I'm almost eighteen."

"Maybe I do. Almost a man. You're right. I need to remember that. Have a good day Gwynn. I hope everything goes well."

"Me too. Have a good day at work."

"I will. Oh, and Gwynn?"

"What?"

Jaimie winked at him. "Thanks for breakfast."

Gwynn couldn't help it, he laughed. "You're welcome."

With Jaimie gone, Gwynn dashed up the stairs for a shower and proper clothes.

He had come back downstairs when the doorbell rang.

"Good morning Mr. Murray," Gwynn said. Mr. Murray seemed dressed for a business meeting.

"Good morning Gwynn. Are you ready to go?"

"Yes, sir."

They drove to the hospital in silence. It struck Gwynn Sophia's father was not one to talk much. What kind of relationship did this man have with his daughter? Mr. Murray's discomfort level seemed to rise with every step bringing them closer to the locked doors of the psychiatric unit.

Mr. Murray punched a code into a numeric pad beside the door. An orderly had them sign in and escorted them down the hall to a waiting area where an older woman sat staring out the barred window. The blond curls identified her as Sophia's mother.

"It's nice to meet you," Mrs. Murray said. She smiled, but her eyes were tired.

"Thanks. Pleasure to meet you too."

"The orderlies are making Sophia...presentable. We should be able to see her soon."

Mr. Murray cleared his throat. "Could I speak to you a second, Sweetheart? Privately?"

They went out into the hall and left Gwynn alone in the waiting room. The hospital painted the room a pale green with soft fabric chairs bolted to the floor. There were no other pieces of furniture and nothing hanging on the walls. It felt cold and sterile. A disheveled stack of magazines, the newest of which being over a year old, seemed the single thing giving the appearance of life. How could anyone's mental health benefit from such stark surroundings? Minutes Gwynn didn't keep track of passed. The door opened, and Mrs. Murray returned.

"They say we can go see Sophia now."

Gwynn looked behind her. "Umm, where's Mr. Murray?"

The question made her look flustered, maybe even angry. She recovered and attempted a weak smile. "He had a mandatory meeting today. He appreciates you coming, Gwynn. He needs to keep working. I think it's his way of coping."

"Okay. Well, let's go see Sophia." Gwynn said it with enthusiasm, but it filled him with dread.

The orderly escorted them down the hall. They stopped, and the orderly opened the door. Gwynn worked hard to compose himself. The walls had numerous drawings taped to them. There were terrifying images of creatures Gwynn had never seen, circular lines spinning inward until becoming a mass of darkness. Gwynn found himself more disturbed by those circles than most of the monsters. In the center of the room, a small girl who had once been Sophia Murray rocked back and forth. Her radiant blond curls now hung limp and dull. None of the life and vitality he knew Sophia to have lived within this shell. Gwynn understood why her father ran away to work. Seeing such vibrancy diminished was devastating.

"Sophia?" Mrs. Murray gently touched her daughter's shoulder. "Sweetheart, you have a visitor. Gwynn is here to see you."

Sophia's eyes locked on Gwynn's—too many swirling emotions made them unreadable.

"Alone," Sophia muttered.

Mrs. Murray probed Gwynn, concern in her eyes. He shrugged his shoulders and put his hands up.

"Sweetheart, since it's his first visit, maybe I should stay."

"Alone!" Sophia shrieked.

Mrs. Murray relented. She backed out of the room. "If you need me, Gwynn, just knock on the door."

"Uh... Okay."

The door shut behind him and Gwynn stood alone with Sophia. He tried to speak to her, but he stumbled over his words.

"Sit," Sophia said. She rocked back and forth, her hands in constant motion, but her eyes fixed on Gwynn. He sat.

Seconds took minutes, minutes hours, time played tricks with Gwynn. He started to believe the few intelligible words she said were a fluke. The girl in front of him seemed broken beyond any hope of repair.

She lunged at Gwynn.

Before he could react, she grasped his face between her hands. He struggled in vain. She wouldn't let go. He thought to cry out for help, but something in her eyes held him a silent prisoner.

"The shadow is moving," she said. Gwynn's eyes darted from side to side.

His mouth went dry, his voice a hoarse whisper. "I don't see anything."

"Behind you."

Gwynn tried to turn his head, but Sophia held him in place.

"Doesn't like *me*. Angry with *me*. Traitor." Sophia hissed.

She released him and sat back.

The Sophia in front of Gwynn was feral, her words coming in growling spurts. But the room held another voice. A voice belonging to the Sophia he knew. Beyond the madness in front of him, there stood a phantom image of Sophia. The phantom had the long shining blond curls, the sparkling blue eyes, and the smile which led Gwynn to Hell.

"I'm so sorry, Gwynn," the phantom Sophia said. "To have to put you through this."

This vision of the Sophia he'd lost broke him. Tears burned his eyes. "I'm the one who's sorry. If I'd stopped you. If I'd been stronger..." He covered his eyes, no longer able to bear seeing her.

Arms wrapped around him. Not the fierce grip she had on his face, gentle and comforting instead.

The mad Sophia, solid and very real whispered. "Phantoms. Other worlds bleeding through. Wounds you need to heal."

"I don't understand," Gwynn said.

"The beast long banished stirs. Blood taken through betrayal will release it. Only blood given can send it back."

"Sophia, I don't understand."

The phantom remained, her eyes full of sorrow and pity.

The near-insane Sophia still held him in an embrace. When she spoke, the warmth of her breath tickled his ear. "Dragons for good, dragons for evil. Messenger, prophets, harbingers. Fall, fall, fall. The shadow rises. Don't let it drown you."

Sophia let him go. The phantom Sophia disappeared. Gwynn tried to process what she said. None of it made sense. Then why did it feel so important? She sat away from him, rocking back and forth. Sophia's eyes—which held such power and focus—were now empty, focusing on some distant point which only she could discern the importance.

Gwynn stumbled to his feet and knocked on the door. Sophia's mother had hope in her eyes when the door opened, but her face fell when she saw Sophia.

"Did she speak to you?"

Gwynn's head buzzed. The world swayed beneath his feet. "Yes." His voice sounded thin. "It didn't make any sense to me, though. I'm sorry."

Mrs. Murray managed a weak smile. "It's fine, Gwynn. We hoped, well, maybe..."

"I'll let you be with her now, Mrs. Murray. Thank you for letting me see her."

The orderly escorted Gwynn down the hall and let him out the secure doors. Gwynn's head seemed to be hurting more, and his right arm throbbed so bad his fingers were numb. Shadows danced in the corner of his eye—something following him, something wanting him. He increased his pace, the hospital hallways becoming a blur of formless white. Gwynn trusted the deeper recesses of his mind to guide him out.

"Gwynn Dormath," someone called, sounding like it echoed from an impossible distance.

Gwynn stopped.

Someone jogged down the hall toward him.

The man came up to him, his breath huffing. "Gwynn, I'm glad I caught you. I thought for sure you'd still be in the hospital."

Who was this person? He seemed somewhat familiar.

The stranger must have recognized Gwynn's confusion. "It's me, Gwynn, Pridament. We met when you first came out of your coma. I've been trying to see you, to finish our conversation, but there's always been someone there."

"Oh. Sorry. So much has been going on. And I had no way of getting hold of you."

The man laughed. "I'm surprised to find you up and walking around so soon. The injuries your chart listed were extensive."

"Apparently I'm a medical mystery."

Pridament studied Gwynn.

"Are you just being released?"

"No, I've been out for a few days." The reason for Gwynn's visit, Sophia's terrible condition, hit him hard. He said in a cracked whisper, "I was here visiting a friend."

"Sophia Murray?"

Gwynn nodded.

"I heard about it." Pridament's eyes filled with sympathy. "I'm sorry. You look shaken. Did she say something to you?"

Sophia's frantic words played through Gwynn's mind. No matter how he turned them around, they made no sense.

"It was just gibberish."

"Tell me something Gwynn," Pridament's eyes and voice were intense, "have there been some, um, odd things going on with you the past couple of days? You seem a bit disoriented."

"It's been a bit much. I think I need some more rest."

Pridament didn't seem convinced. "Do me a favor, take my card. I'd like the chance to finish our talk. Sooner than later, okay?"

Gwynn took the card and slipped it into his pocket. "Sure. Right. I'll call soon. Seeya."

Gwynn plunged through the hospital doors into the biting November air. The wind stabbed his exposed flesh leaving it feeling raw. On an average day that would have been annoying. Today he imagined the cold eating away the darkness clinging to his skin.

Forget a cab. Gwynn didn't need the risk of someone being chatty. He opted for the quiet anonymity of the bus.

The bus arrived with a few passengers congregating near the front. Gwynn went for the solitude of the back seat. The swaying rhythm of the bus moving through traffic soothed his battered soul. He closed his eyes, drifting in the between places of waking and sleep.

A growl.

At first, Gwynn dismissed it as traffic noise. The next time it came, it sounded nearer, urgent. Gwynn snapped his eyes open. The passengers at the front of the bus were looking at him with hungry, feline eyes.

The Script of Creation

Gwynn rushed from the hospital. Whatever transpired between him and Sophia left the boy rattled. Pridament inspected Sophia's chart after his first meeting with Gwynn. There was little significance in her injuries, and nothing noted about her mental state. That changed two days ago when she returned because of an emotional breakdown. But how did he miss news of Gwynn's release? Could someone be keeping things out of official channels?

Pridament made his way to the elevator. He reached into his pocket, reassuring himself he still had his forged identification. The world operated on simple rules—if you looked the part, acted the part, and carried the right pieces of laminated paper and plastic, you could access anywhere.

The elevator doors shuddered as they opened. The hallway, white and oppressive in its facelessness, lead to a double door where a pin pad waited to allow access. Pridament punched in the code and waited. The doors swung open with a low electric hum. On the other side, an orderly sat at a desk. Pridament approached the man and flashed his credentials.

"I'm here to see Sophia Murray."

The orderly raised a skeptical eyebrow. "You're not a doctor assigned to this ward."

Pridament had played harder roles. One rule served him in all of them; never appear flustered.

"Yes, you're right. See, the girl came in a few days ago to the emergency." Pridament leaned in closer, his voice hushed and conspiratorial. "When I found out she was readmitted, I wanted to check on her."

The orderly wore a sly smile. "Making sure you didn't miss anything doc?"

If only his credentials were real, so he could report this useless excuse for an employee. Breathe, he told himself. Remember the rules. Pridament gave the man a wink, "I'm in the clear, but the other doc on with me, well, you know how it is."

The orderly nodded knowingly. It's not me. It's my friend. Power lay in using cliché excuses. For whatever reason, it always made people more understanding. Maybe because they used it themselves, or because it made them feel a small part of the deception. People, no matter the world, liked being a part of conspiracies, especially if they could do so from a safe distance.

The orderly led Pridament down the hall. To his right, a small waiting room where a woman, a visitor, dozed in one of the chairs. He caught sight of her for a brief moment, but he recognized the agony in her posture. A parent, thinking her child lost forever. Yes, he knew the signs of that pain all too well.

"Popular girl today," the orderly said. "You're in luck. We made her presentable for her last visitor. She doesn't seem to care much about her looks nowadays."

Pridament mustered a weak smile.

The door shut behind Pridament, the orderly promising to return in ten minutes. If the girl noticed him, she made no sign. He took in the display of art on the walls. He shuddered as he recognized some, and felt thankful he had never run into others. The bulk of the art shared a dark swirling pattern. Pridament knew it well. He pitied the girl. Lovecraft was right, "When you look into the abyss, the abyss looks back into you."

Still, it made little sense. If Gwynn's account of events was accurate, the girl was within proximity of the tear for a few minutes. How could it have fried her mind in such a short time?

Pridament knelt in front of her. He almost fell back when the girl's eyes locked onto his with a fierce intensity. Her gaze held him in place, pulling deep at the essence in his core.

"Know Thyself," she said.

"What did you say?" Pridament trembled.

"He will go with them, and you need to let it happen."

"Who? Who's going and with whom?"

"You cannot finish his journey with him, but he will lead you to the end of yours."

Pridament couldn't speak. Then the connection severed, and the girl's gaze fell onto some distant place Pridament couldn't see.

"Sophia?"

She was gone, lost to whatever inner demons tormented her.

Pridament stood up and moved behind her. "Sophia, I don't know if you can hear me, but I need to check something. I'm not going to hurt you."

Pridament pulled the girl's hair up to inspect the back of her neck. Hidden just above her hairline, he found the birthmark. His stomach lurched.

"What the hell have they done?"

He let her hair drop at the sound of someone approaching the door.

"Everything okay doc?" the orderly asked as he entered.

Breathe. How could something so vital and natural be so easy to neglect?

"Yes, fine. Seems my friend has nothing to worry about." Did the orderly notice how he forced his smile?

The man smirked and escorted Pridament out of the ward. The doors groaned as they closed behind him. The arteries in his neck throbbed with the racing of his pulse. This was bad. No, beyond bad. He sensed that first day with Gwynn someone was orchestrating events. But to this extent? He had some answers, but those were leading to more questions, which all led somewhere dark and frightening.

He pondered his next move when his phone started buzzing. He picked up and listened to the frantic voice on the other end.

"Gwynn?"

***

Gwynn leaped to his feet and pulled hard on the emergency signal. The bus came screeching to a halt, throwing the passengers who started to creep toward him back. Gwynn dashed for the closest door and fell out of it.

He smashed to the ground and scrambled to twist and face any potential attackers. Only average, confused, human faces greeted him.

Gwynn drew his breath in ragged gasps. It seemed an eternity before the doors shut and the bus continued on its way. He fumbled in his pockets until he found Pridament's card. The phone number listed was unlike anything he had seen—a series of digits forming no familiar pattern. He pulled out his cell and dialed.

When the line connected, Gwynn didn't even allow the person on the other side to speak. Words fell out of his mouth—mad rantings about monsters and shadows. After he'd spewed out several sentences, he managed to grab hold of himself and take a desperate breath.

"Gwynn?"

Hearing the warm, baritone voice on the other side of the phone loosened the tightness in his chest.

"Pridament," Gwynn tried to control the anxiety in his voice, "I lied. I need help. Can I meet with you?"

A moment of silence on the other end. Despite Pridament's affection for Gwynn's parents, he had to be weighing the pros and cons of getting further involved with their insane son.

"Where are you now?" Pridament asked.

Gwynn did a frantic search for street signs.

"Queen and Highway 10."

"There should be a strip mall on the corner. I'll meet you at the coffee shop there in ten minutes. OK?"

"Sure. Yeah. Thanks."

Gwynn snapped his phone shut and crossed the road to the strip mall. It took him a while to find the coffee shop. It wasn't even big enough to qualify as a hole in the wall, the kind of place that stayed open through sheer force of will. Inside did little to inspire him to sample their pitiful display of pastries and doughnuts. Someone pasted mirrors on one wall in a sad attempt at making the space appear larger. Perhaps it would work if someone cleaned off the grime. The painted parts of the walls bore numerous chips and scratches. Gwynn shuddered at the thought of using the washroom.

Gwynn ordered a large coffee. Not that his nerves needed any caffeine. But being the only customer, he didn't feel comfortable sitting without having something.

The lone employee seemed far more interested in a phone conversation than her workplace.

Within five minutes, Pridament arrived. He ordered something and joined Gwynn at a back table.

"I remember this place being a lot nicer," Pridament said.

"Maybe twenty years ago."

The older man laughed. "You might be right. Still..." He sipped his coffee. "The coffee tastes just as good." Pridament adopted a serious air. "How can I help?"

"When I met you the first time," Gwynn's voice wavered with anxiety, "you started telling me a story. I need you to finish it. I've seen things... I... I've been feeling out of control. I need to know what's going on."

Pridament leaned forward and rested his head on his steepled fingers. He remained silent, his eyes probing Gwynn, who squirmed in his seat. After a few minutes, he leaned back and shrugged off his jacket.

"Perhaps the first thing you should know," Pridament pushed up his sleeve. Symbols similar to those on Gwynn's arm formed a circle around Pridament's forearm. "You aren't alone. What I'm telling you I've learned because I've lived it as well."

Gwynn inspected the symbols on Pridament's arm.

"Why do mine cover my entire arm? At least yours looks like some crazy tattoo."

Pridament gave a dry chuckle.

"Among our people, you're considered the lucky one. Mine is incomplete. I'm a Fragment. Yours is the full deal—a Script."

Gwynn tore at his already tangled hair.

"Let's get something straight. I'm losing my mind, okay? I'm not interested in riddles or names. I want to understand what is happening and how I stop it."

"You don't stop it." Pridament's eyes held compassion, but his voice left no room for negotiation. "This is who you are. Before, I started telling you about the history of our people, but I'll cut straight to the chase. The symbols on your arm are the story of creation."

Gwynn sighed and let his arms flop on the table. His coffee shuddered as the table wobbled on the uneven floor. Why couldn't this be like going to the doctor and handed your diagnosis? 'Gee, Gwynn, you have freakitis. You'll grow three heads and die alone in a cave.' Done. Simple. Straight forward.

"You can't make this simple, can you?"

Pridament shook his head. "Nope."

"Fine," Gwynn waved his hand. "Keep going."

Pridament cleared his throat. "What do you know about the soul?"

Gwynn blinked. "What?"

"The soul. The energy within you."

"Wait," Gwynn's voice elevated. "First you tell me some nutso story about being a god, and now you want to talk about my soul? What kind of crazy religious shit are you trying to sell?"

"The kind of crazy that'll save your ass. So answer my damned question."

Gwynn froze in stunned silence. Pridament's voice hovered above a whisper, yet every word carried an intensity that battered Gwynn like physical blows.

Pridament's eyes drilled him with expectation. Gwynn's mind played with options. He almost persuaded himself to walk out, but the man's presence, his force of will, kept Gwynn rooted. Despite his growing apprehension, he had to admit only Pridament seemed capable of helping explain this mess. He drew a long breath and let it out slowly, ticking off the seconds until his lungs were empty. He reached ten. Another breath.

"The soul is some kind of energy. It's supposed to be what makes us who we are."

Pridament nodded. "Good. But you don't believe any of it, right?"

"Not really," Gwynn shrugged. "Probably because I don't follow any religion."

"The concept of the soul, or life energy, is widespread. There's Chi, Atmas, Jeeva, Hun and Po, just to name a few. You'll find myths, legends, and even some religious ideas like a soul, have some basis in reality. Regarding the soul specifically, I can say it is true. Our physical forms contain the threads of an energy far greater than our frail bodies can hold. The bulk of that energy lives within the Veil."

"The what?"

Pridament shook his head. "So much to explain." He rubbed his temples. "In this world, the Nazis lost World War Two. Can you imagine a world where they won?"

"I don't think I'd want to."

"Well, you don't need to imagine it, because a version of Earth exists where the Nazis did win. There's a version of Earth where the dinosaurs still rule the world. There are countless versions of Earth. Maybe as many as every choice any person ever made. The Veil is what keeps those different realities separate. The Veil is a realm of pure energy we can't see. The Veil is the seat of the soul, the source of creation, and those symbols on your arm connect you to it like a plug in a socket."

Gwynn fell back in his chair. He ran his hands through the mess of brown he called hair. He let his fingers twist and pull at the strands. Could you feel pain in dreams? Would he have to tear his hair from its roots to wake up from the madness his life had become? Hell with this dream, nightmare, reality, it didn't matter. He wouldn't sit and listen to babble when he had real problems to deal with.

Pridament didn't move. One minute, the man sat in his seat, the next he gripped Gwynn's arm with such force no amount of strength Gwynn possessed would break it.

"You asked me for this," Pridament hissed. "You *will* stay and hear me out."

Gwynn fell back into his chair. Blood and adrenaline pounded through his veins making his limbs tremble. His right arm throbbed. Tingling pinpricks crawled across his skin.

Pridament nodded. "You're reaching for it. The thing you don't believe in, the crazy thing I'm talking about. Your head tells you I'm insane even as your body searches for that impossible power to break free. Tell me what happened in that old house on Halloween night. Explain to me what kind of explosion destroyed the roof without burning you or Sophia to cinders."

Gwynn's mouth went dry. "How am I supposed to know?"

Pridament's grip tightened.

"If you're going to lie to me kid, you'll have to do a lot better."

The grip loosened, enough Gwynn breathed normally again.

"Let's try this a different way—tell me what happened on Halloween?"

"I went with Sophia and a bunch of people from school to the Old Cameron house." A tremor of anger snaked down his spine. "Eric challenged someone to go in the house. He meant the challenge for me, to make me look bad, like a coward. But Sophia went in instead."

"She must care about you."

"I don't know how she feels about me. The only reason I was there was because of her."

What were the emotions in Pridament's eyes? Shock? Concern? Gwynn couldn't figure it out.

"Sophia asked you to go?"

Gwynn nodded. "I've thought she was in on the whole thing, setting me up. Maybe she started to feel guilty about it, and that's why she went in instead. Only..."

"What?"

"I'm not sure." He recalled her face. So determined, her voice telling him she had to see it through to the end. "I can't shake the feeling she knew all along she would go in. It's like she planned it from the start. I wanted to ask her and get some answers. I don't know if I'll ever get them now."

Pridament released his grip on Gwynn and sighed.

"After I saw you at the hospital, I went to see Sophia myself. She said some things that made sense to me. The problem is there's no way she could've known those things. I think you're right—Sophia had a plan for that night. I have no idea what it was, or if it succeeded. So what happened after Sophia went into the house?"

"I went in after her. I heard something upstairs, so I went up. Then I ended up in the attic." Flashes of something human shaped, pain, and monstrous eyes. "Something attacked me. Probably the homeless man they said died."

Pridament tapped his finger on the table. "You weren't attacked by any ordinary homeless man, were you?"

"I..." He resisted the words. If they left his lips, if he spoke the truth of his memories, it meant he'd gone insane. Because his memories said one thing—he saw a monster. But what if that *was* the truth? He had to know. "No. I thought that at first. But the way he spoke and how he threw me across the attic like I weighed nothing, he couldn't have been just a man. Then I saw his eyes, and I knew. He was a monster. I tried to find something to fight him. I thought I found something, but..."

"You pressed your hand against something. Instinct told you to push harder. But when you did, something changed. *You* changed."

Gwynn stared wide-eyed at Pridament.

"How did you know?"

Pridament tapped his right forearm. "Told you, I've been there. While Anunnaki can draw on their soul for strength, our greatest power comes in tearing the Veil. It's like giving yourself an energy boost. The first time you do it, it marks you. Hurts like hell too. But it's dangerous. Stay connected to it too long, draw too much energy, you can lose yourself. Is that when the explosion happened?"

"No. There was a... mirror. I felt pulled toward it. When I got close enough, I saw a whirlpool, or like, a black hole, inside. After I... tore the Veil, I touched the mirror, and that's when everything exploded."

"There must have been a natural tear already there. That explains the Taint." Pridament took a sip of the coffee and made a face saying he lied about the coffee being good. "A Taint is a person exposed to the raw energies of the Veil too long. Poor bastard was probably squatting in that house and never knew. Anunnaki can draw power from the Veil, but even for us, it can become toxic after a while. Normal humans have no resistance. It twists them, turns them into monsters. Almost every nasty thing of legend is from some poor soul turning to a Taint. But something more is happening. You said you'd seen things and during your call, it sounded like something was attacking you."

"I thought so." Had that happened? He gave his head a shake. "I thought I was going to be. Ever since I woke up, I've seen things. Eric, who set me up on Halloween. I smashed his nose in the middle of the school cafeteria before I even knew what I was doing. I keep seeing people change into... Taints, but they're not. After a minute, they're normal again. I don't know whether I'm seeing the future, hallucinating, or going crazy."

"Did you close the tear?"

"What?" Anguish, or perhaps madness, choked the word.

"When you tear the Veil, you must seal it. Like I said, tearing the Veil is like putting a plug in a socket. It keeps drawing power until you pull the plug." Pridament went pale. "Odin's eye, you're still connected to it, aren't you?"

"I don't know."

"No, it makes perfect sense. It's why you healed so quickly and why you see things. You're not going crazy or seeing the future. You're seeing an alternate world. You're seeing *through* the Veil."

Pridament stood and put on his jacket.

"You and I need to get back to the Cameron house, and you need to close that tear."

"What? Right now?"

Pridament leaned close, his voice filled with an intensity demanding obedience to any order it issued.

"Haven't you been listening? If you don't close that tear, you'll cease to be human."

Closets Never Stay Closed

Jaimie was pissed. Or maybe worried. She couldn't decide, so settled to be both.

Despite his assurances, Gwynn failed to contact her. Jaimie tried his cell several times. On the fifth try, she left work. No matter how much she tried to tell herself he had no reception in the hospital, she couldn't believe he was still there five hours later. Jaimie leaned against the doorframe of the kitchen and tried his cell again. From her vantage point, she saw down the hall to the front door. Maybe his battery died. She counted the rings; one, two, three, four and then the click as a computerized voice told her she could leave a message. Jaimie tried to calm her voice.

"Gwynn, it's me. I'm at home. Please call me when you get this message, thanks."

She replaced the wireless in its cradle on the wall and sat at the table. A mug of cold tea sat there. She made it, thinking to calm her nerves. Instead, her hand shook so bad she splashed the hot tea on herself. After swearing and rinsing cold water over her hand, the tea was in danger of going down the drain. But it still sat on the table, a remaining question— would she drink it, or dump it? Would it stay, or go? Its surface clouded over with the dash of milk she added. It brought back the time nine years ago when a similar decision felt so cloudy.

The doorbell sounded. Deep in memories and thoughts better left buried, the bell sounded foreign, something odd she initially didn't understand. It took a second sound of the bell to register what she should do in response.

The front door's decorative glass obscured the person on the other side. When Jaimie opened the door, her heart fell.

"Hello, Jaimie."

She hadn't seen him in five years. At the time, she hoped she would never see him again.

"You don't look happy to see me."

Her stomach churned. "Sorry. I wasn't expecting you."

"Are you ever?" he asked, his bushy brown eyebrow raised, his mouth curved in a cruel half-smile.

"What do you want?"

"Now, now Jaimie. Why the hostility? After all, haven't we delivered on everything we promised?"

She hated to admit the answer—yes, they had. Guilt clung to her soul like filth. Here stood the devil with whom she struck her bargain. Every time he visited, she wondered if he came to collect.

The man cleared his throat. "In any case, I'm here to ask a small favor. Nothing too much, I promise."

"What is it?"

"Gwynn is going through some...changes. I need you to understand. I need you to allow the boy some space. He'll want to go out more, meet up with people you don't know. You need to trust him and let him do as he asks."

Jaimie anger welled up, filling her chest to bursting. "Who the hell do you think you are? You think you can just show up and tell me how to parent Gwynn?"

The man held his hands up in defense. "No one is telling you how to parent Gwynn. No one is questioning the job you've done so far. After all, you brought a boy, shattered by tragedy, and turned him into a successful young man. But I don't think Gwynn is going to know how to talk to you about what he's experiencing. I want him to be able to do what he needs without damaging the relationship the two of you have."

"So what? Now you're Doctor-Fucking-Phil, here to save our relationship?"

"I'm saying the boy might act more secretive. He might not be his usual self, and I don't want you to worry he's doing drugs or anything illicit."

"Then what is happening?" She was pleading, even though she hated appearing weak in front of this man.

"When the time is right, he'll tell you."

She opened her mouth to say more, to press for answers, but the man held up his hand.

"He is the one who should tell you, Jaimie, leave it at that."

Jaimie bit into her lip, afraid to ask the next question—knowing she must. "And when will you show up to collect on what's due?"

The man smiled. "There will be no need for us to do anything. In the end, Gwynn will come to us."

The Man on the Other Side of the World

Gwynn barely noticed the world passing by out the car window. The last time he traveled to the Cameron House, Sophia sat beside him. Now, not even two weeks later, she'd gone insane, and he'd become a freak. The man in the seat next to him remained quiet. He should be asking more questions. Hadn't he wanted to know more? Hadn't that been why he called Pridament?

No. Gwynn called out of fear. Having seen Sophia, alone and mad, he worried he would go the same way. Maybe Pridament could validate his experience. Maybe he wasn't insane, and there was a logical explanation.

But Pridament opened more doors than he closed. His clarifications led to more confusion. In trying to convince Gwynn of the noble and powerful origins of his experiences, he overloaded him. Now he just couldn't make himself feel interested.

When his parents died, it taught him things just happen. Although Pridament seemed to think some act of fate existed, Gwynn couldn't see it. Life consisted of a series of accidents. Patterns appeared because people searched for them—a vain hope it all served some purpose. What happened to him was just the universe having another brain fart. Just another random complication to shove in a dark place and forget.

Pridament shattered the silence. "What does the sky look like to you?"

Gwynn peered out the window. "Gray, overcast."

His head pounded. Staring up at the sky made it worse.

"Mhmm" Pridament responded.

They were reaching the outskirts of town, crossing Gwynn's imaginary line between the concrete realm and that of nature. In the concrete world, things made sense. Humans forced their will on the world and broke it into order. Out here, beyond the control of steel and cement, things were wilder. Had he seen beauty in it once? Just several days ago, as they passed into it, had he not considered it a bad thing the cement should push further? Yes, but the Cameron House taught him, just as a dark country road nine years earlier, nature should not be trusted—could humans and their unfeeling manufactured stone? No, but people were far more predictable.

They turned down the country road. Nearing the house, Gwynn's headache and throbbing in his arm intensified.

"Shiiiit."

"Getting worse?" Pridament asked.

"Yes." Gwynn grit his teeth and drew breath in short gasps.

"It's because you're getting closer to the source. All Anunnakis feel some discomfort when we're near a tear in the Veil, but because this one has been leaching onto you for an extended period, you're far more susceptible."

"Whatever. Let's just get this done."

The car stopped, and Gwynn lurched out. His stomach convulsed and the meager contents of his stomach met the ground with a splash. Pridament patted him on the back.

"Thanks for waiting until you got out of the car, kid."

"Piss off."

Pridament laughed and walked toward the house. Yellow police tape now decorated the perimeter of the property. Despite the place's infamous reputation enticing thrill seekers, the tape appeared undisturbed. Ironic after all these years, something finally happened to validate the house's reputation, and now people stayed away.

Pridament pointed toward the boarded-up front window. "That how you went in the first time?"

Gwynn nodded.

"The door wouldn't open?"

"That's right."

Pridament walked up to the front of the house and threw open the front door with a flourish. "Appears we get to do things the easy way today."

Gwynn stumbled up the walk. "Show off."

The two stepped over the threshold.

The world lurched to Gwynn's right and then left. His stomach knotted but refused to let go of anything. He fell. Pridament grabbed him by the arm. "Gwynn, are you all right?"

Gwynn did his best to nod.

"Take your time, kid. Something happened when we entered the house. I felt it too."

Gwynn took a moment to survey the house. "This isn't right."

The house had changed. In areas where the walls previously showed years of decay and neglect, the walls now stood with fresh paint. The stairs gleamed in a dark cherry hardwood. A sound from upstairs grabbed Gwynn's attention. He braced himself for a Taint. Instead, a man who walked across the upper landing. Tall, well dressed and groomed, he lacked certain solidity. Gwynn opened his mouth to speak, but Pridament clamped his hand over it. The ghostly figure descended the stairs and walked into one of the adjoining rooms.

Pridament held a finger to his mouth. He released it and spoke— his voice barely a whisper. "This is serious. Another world is bleeding through."

"That's what I've seen the past few days."

Pridament shook his head. "That's because you're still wired into the Veil. I shouldn't see anything out of the ordinary. If I see it, it means the worlds are starting to bleed together."

"What?"

"I'll explain it later. We need to get that tear sealed, quick. But be quiet."

"Why?"

Pridament sighed. "Right now, the bleed is still early. The man in the other world is ignoring us. If we draw his attention, he'll come through the tear into this world. Remember how energy from the Veil changes people?"

Gwynn nodded.

"Imagine what happens to someone who gets dragged through it. That person becomes a Full Incursive, a Curse. Taints are contaminated, but they retain *some* humanity. A Curse, they're nothing but horror."

Even in a hushed whisper, the fear and pity were evident in Pridament's voice. Gwynn thought of the feline eyes and deformed fangs of the squatter he faced in the attic. That man had just been in the same house. What sort of changes would happen to a person dragged through the Veil's energies? He didn't want to find out.

"Right," Gwynn said. "We need to go upstairs."

Gwynn led the way. He inched up the stairs. His head felt light and his body slow to respond. Halfway up, he took a step and misjudged. His toe slid back from the slick, polished surface sending his knee hammering down with the sound of a gunshot on the step. Shockwaves of pain radiated up through his hips and into his already jarred stomach.

Heavy footsteps approached from below.

"Damn." Pridament didn't bother to whisper.

The phantom male appeared from the door he passed through earlier. What could they tell him? That they weren't there and he should just ignore them? To think of it like a bad radio station where multiple channels bled into each other.

The phantom locked angry eyes on them. Words would be useless.

The man began to solidify, but as he did so, his body distorted. His limbs elongated in a series of sickening snaps and gushes. The eyes staring at Gwynn and Pridament went yellow and feline. His jaw gnashed and extended downward, revealing rows of razor sharp teeth.

Gwynn couldn't move. Something stirred in the darkest corner of his mind. A memory of some past horror started to shuffle forward. He tried to block it out, focusing on the real horror taking shape in front of him.

"No. No. No. God, no," Gwynn's voice shrieked.

Pridament gripped Gwynn's shoulder. "You need to go and close that tear."

A chill seeped through Gwynn's limbs, freezing him to the spot.

"Gwynn!" Pridament yelled and shook him. "Gwynn!"

Gwynn stirred. "What?"

"You need to close that tear."

"How?"

"Just touch it with your right arm. Imagine a door closing in your head when you do. Just trust yourself, you can do it."

The creature below them howled a high pitch that tore at Gwynn's ears and nerves.

"Go!" Pridament yelled.

Gwynn stumbled, but turned and clawed his way up the remaining stairs. The slapping sound of flesh against wood signaled the monster's ascent.

The hair on Gwynn's neck stood on end like he had built up a static charge. He spared a moment to glance back. Pridament, armed with a staff, stood ready to meet the monster's advance.

Gwynn launched himself onto the landing and slammed hard into the wall. He fell to his knees as the air went out from him. The hall became a fun–house parody of the place Gwynn recalled—it twisted and curved under his feet. Gwynn fell from the wall to the banister as he made his way to the door he hoped would still lead him to the attic. From behind, the sounds of battle drew his attention—Pridament sparring with the creature.

Gwynn inched toward the door at the end of the hall and saw the attic ladder still lowered. He seized hold and started to climb.

Breaching the attic felt like surfacing from beneath water. It seemed unaffected by the madness in the rest of the house. A cool breeze blew through the hole the explosion tore through the roof. For a moment, Gwynn could forget the insanity his life had become. The air smelled pure. Sounds of the battle raging below his feet broke the moment, and Gwynn poured his eyes over the attic. After the third pass with his eyes, he started to panic.

I don't see anything!

What if he couldn't close it? Would he lose his mind? Would phantom monsters keep bleeding into his world? He pushed himself forward in a frantic search. As fear threatened to crush him, he brushed a cold spot. The chill ran up his arm into his spine. Seeing it now, he understood why he missed it. From one angle, nothing. From another, a slight ripple similar to the horizon on the road during a hot day. Gwynn reached a tentative hand toward the tear. The first time hurt so much, and he couldn't ignore the destruction in evidence all around him. His life, Sophia's life, all torn apart in a single moment. Should he take the plunge again?

His fingers stroked the top of the tear and tingled, like touching a balloon rubbed vigorously through someone's hair.

Something hit him hard and sent him flying away. He struck what remained of the roof and tasted blood in his mouth.

Above the ringing in his ears, a voice said, "Time to die, Suture brat."

***

She never questioned orders. Even as she made her way to his office, Fuyuko's stomach churned. She paused outside the door with her hand raised, ready to knock. Maybe she should forget it. Perhaps she should appreciate the easiness of this assignment. After all, schoolwork was the hardest part so far, and it was pedestrian compared to her regular studies.

"Are you going to stand out there all day, or come in?" a loud, deep, voice boomed from the other side of the door.

Fuyuko entered the office, taking note of the Spartan conditions. How did others interpret it? A lack of interest? The desire to separate personal and professional life? From her years in Suture, she understood; leave fast, leave little impression. A ridiculous proposition for ones such as themselves. The last assignment she had they left more than an impression, they left a crater.

The office's only occupant sat at the desk. The last time she saw him, he was over six feet tall, with longish brown hair. The man sitting at the desk appeared much older, shorter, and pudgier. What had he said to her all those years ago? "It's all about mass."

He smirked. "Is the appearance disturbing you? I could change back if you want."

Fuyuko shook her head. "No, no, that's not necessary. Though it's quite the change. I never would've recognized you."

"Well, that's the point, is it not?" He laughed. "So what's troubling you Fuyuko?"

"Troubling me?" She chastised herself for allowing a nervous tremor to enter her voice. "What would make you think I'm troubled?"

The man, she knew him as Justinian, steepled his fingers and drilled into Fuyuko with his eyes.

"You did send in a request to speak to a senior active member, did you not? I mean, I've been undercover here for several years. I'm certain you wouldn't have known who I was unless the home office informed you."

"Yes, of course, you're right." Fuyuko hesitated. Even if orders weren't clear, they were still orders, right? Still, she needed to know. Too many things were happening which failed to add up. She took a deep breath and voiced what bothered her since her arrival in this faceless city. "It's, well, I'm wondering why I'm here."

"Aren't we all?"

Frustration, insecurity, and Justinian's smug tone opened the floodgates—she unleashed with reckless abandon.

"Don't get smart with me Justinian. As you said, you've been under cover for several years. Why? What is so damn important about this town? Why aren't we cleaning up the tears like we always do and calling it a day? Why am I here alone? I mean, what good am I alone if a tear needs closing? I'm not a Script."

She huffed and her cheeks flooded with heat. It took two long breaths for the horror of her actions to sink in.

Justinian's demeanor remained cool. If he'd taken offense, he didn't show it. He gestured to the seat in front of his desk.

"Have a seat, Fuyuko."

She sat, not sure what to say next. She'd learned, more from her parents than Suture, often silence said more than a stammering apology.

"You shouldn't belittle yourself. If I recall, you're the most formidable Fragment in the program. I hear you managed to pull a rabbit out of the hat."

"How would you have heard that?"

He smiled. "Information is my business. Now, don't worry about what you just said, you can speak freely with me. I've known your family a long time. I was one of Katsuro's first teachers."

She flinched. Despite her best efforts, that wound remained fresh.

"I'm sorry," Justinian said. "I didn't think. A good man, your brother. I'm sorry I couldn't be there for your family."

"It's fine. That's how Suture works. We don't choose where we'll be. My brother embraced his abilities as fate. He'd be proud of how he died. He knew the risks. We all do."

"Yes, yes I guess that's true. But you came here for a reason, not to dwell on the past."

Fuyuko sighed. "It's just things are usually so straight ahead. Go in, find the tear, and close it. This time, I know there's a tear, I can feel it in every part of my body, yet my orders are to do nothing but watch some boy who's only been to school one day out of the past two–and–a–half weeks I've spent here."

"I understand your frustration Fuyuko. When I first arrived, I had no idea what to do. I received virtually no instructions. Over time, instructions did come. Because of small things I did, larger events were set into motion. After a while, I started to see there were larger plans at work. Perhaps plans so large I considered myself lucky I didn't know all the details. Instead, I continued my day–to–day routines and waited for further instructions. I suggest maybe you should do the same. Consider it a break from the routines of Suture."

"Maybe. But what have you been doing here Justinian? Maybe I could figure out what to do if I heard about your experiences."

He smiled and shook his head. "You know it doesn't work that way Fuyuko. I'm a senior active. I'm here to be a sounding board, a mentor, and if the worst should happen, to save your ass. Outside of that, the rules of 'right to know' still apply. And I'm sorry to say—you lack the clearance."

Fuyuko's chair became far more uncomfortable. Talk of clearances, rights to know. It sounded too much like the conversations at home. Too much like the answers she received about Katsuro.

"So what should I do?"

"Well, you said you were sent to keep an eye on him. Do that. Try befriending him. I can tell you from what I've seen; the boy could use some friends. Other than that, relax, keep your eyes open. One day, a letter will be in your mailbox, or an email, or you'll get a phone call. Perhaps none of those things will come. Instead, you'll be in the right place at the right time and do the right thing. All I can say is do what you think is right. If you're wrong, I'm sure you'll hear about it."

Fuyuko didn't like the cryptic nature Justinian's instructions were taking. She headed to the door.

"Thanks for your time Justinian."

"Anytime Fuyuko."

She turned on her way out.

"One last question. Why didn't you say anything to me when I first arrived? Why wait until home office instructed you to talk to me?"

Justinian's smile cooled. "It's been six years since we last met, Fuyuko. A lot can happen. I wouldn't break my cover for anyone unless instructed. If I can give you any advice, it would be to keep who you are close and to yourself. Only break your silence when you have to. That tip might save your life someday."

He steepled his fingers and leaned back in his chair. His posture stated Fuyuko's questions would get no further answers.

As she rose to leave, he seemed to recall something, sat forward, and fixed a penetrating gaze on her.

"Before you go, let me ask you a question."

"Sure."

"What did you think of Gwynn?"

She pictured the clumsy, apologetic boy, and cross-referenced it with the boy with the raised fist in the cafeteria.

"A typical teenager. Angry, conflicted, and hormonal. Perhaps I would add impulsive and distracted. Why?"

Justinian gave an icy laugh. "When I first saw him, I saw a killer."

Grasping at an Offered Hand

Since the car accident, life continued on stolen time. Now someone in the guise of a woman with silver hair and hands engulfed in blue flame had come to collect.

She grabbed Gwynn by his collar and hoisted him into the air above her.

"Aren't you even going to try to fight back?" She hissed.

Her free fist caught him hard in the abdomen. The impact reverberated up his spine followed by cold, biting, and clawing his flesh. Gwynn couldn't make out details of the world anymore. He tried to focus, but his vision alternated with flashes of light or shrouds of darkness. Another hit to his midsection and then she threw him. He crumpled on the floor, the sensation of a thousand knives stabbing him. He coughed and choked on fluid flooding his lungs.

The woman said something, but Gwynn couldn't focus on it. Why hadn't he lost consciousness yet? Why wasn't he dead? Pain pressed inward through his head, his skull collapsing in on itself. He tried to ignore the agony, tried to see, speak, or do anything.

She left him on the ground, pausing her attack.

Gwynn's vision began to clear. The pain made everything brighter, blowing details out of focus. Gwynn could discern the blurry outline of the woman, who knelt down near his head. Did he see pity in her eyes? Or was the pain playing with his head?

"In another life," she said, "this would've been unnecessary. We shouldn't be fighting; we should unite in guiding the world to a greater vision. Please understand, I bear you no ill, but I can't let you stop this. In the end, you should hate Suture, sending children to do the work of adults. Maybe when you join with the Veil, you'll understand. When that happens, I hope you'll forgive me."

She raised her hand, and the fire widened and roared.

I'm going to die. A laugh played in Gwynn's mind. *It's not as scary as I imagined it would be.*

Before she delivered the killing blow, a blurry form Gwynn couldn't focus on, slammed into her. The shape and woman sprawled out of Gwynn's line of sight. He tried to move, to see, but even small movements sent explosions of pain raging through his body. When he caught sight of them again, he recognized the shape as Pridament. The two stood facing off against one another.

The woman lunged at Pridament, who turned her away with a stinging shot of his staff. It meant nothing to her. She pressed her attack, stepping toward the staff, just to feint one direction, stepping and twisting to the other. Pridament seemed in control, though Elaios' blows were coming close to hitting his head. He swept at her feet with his staff, and she catapulted backward, landing outside his range. She charged forward, connecting a blow to Pridament's shoulder. He spun and struck her in the back as her momentum carried her forward. The woman hit the ground but rolled to her feet unfazed.

Gwynn waited for the woman's next onslaught. Instead, she straightened and brushed the dust from herself. Pridament didn't release his defensive stance. Pridament's chest heaved with each breath, but his staff remained steady.

"Pridament," the woman said. "It's been too long since we danced with each other."

"Not long enough, Elaios."

"So," an audible sneer in her voice, "you've thrown your lot in with Suture?"

"You should know better."

She gestured toward Gwynn. "The boy?"

"Just that, a boy who tore the Veil and is trying to understand what's happening to him. You remember how that felt Elaios? To tear through the Veil for the first time—the pain, the energies you couldn't control? He's here because when it happened to him, he didn't close off the Veil. He's been attached to it since."

"How long?"

Pridament hesitated. Gwynn couldn't see the man's eyes.

"Almost two weeks."

The woman, Elaios, looked at Gwynn with dismay. "Impossible. He's still intact."

"Even after what you've done to him."

"Then he's..."

"Yes. A Script."

Elaios shook her head. "You know I can't let him go. If Suture finds him, they'll use him to stop us. That can't happen."

"What you're doing is wrong Elaios. Have you lost your vision? Can't you see the calamity that is coming?"

Gwynn couldn't follow their conversation anymore. An elephant's worth of weight sat on his chest, collapsing ribs into lungs. Any moment, the fighting would begin again. How long until Pridament lost, or the woman got close enough to Gwynn to finish him off?

"I think, once upon a time, they were lovers," a soft, high-pitched female said.

Gwynn rolled over to try to see the source. The crushing in his chest increased. He gasped for air.

A face came into view over the top of him. Pale porcelain skin contrasted with midnight black hair and clothes. Her green eyes shone like flawless gems held up to the sun.

"Do you remember me, Gwynn?"

He remembered her—the girl from Mr. Baker's classroom. Now, something else played at the fringes of his mind. Through the delirium of dying, or maybe being free of the distraction of his classmates, he truly saw her. Staring into her eyes caused a memory to lurch into place. A name filed away and forgotten began to surface.

"Adra...stia?"

She caressed his cheek with a frigid hand. "Sweet boy, you do remember."

Gwynn wanted to protest. It couldn't be Adrastia. She was an imaginary friend, a secret confidant.

"Let me help, Gwynn. Let me take the pain away. Grab hold of my hand, and I promise everything will be better."

Gwynn hesitated. If she was Adrastia, something in his universe changed. Like all childhood imaginings, he'd left her behind.

"Take my hand."

Gwynn wanted to close his eyes and forget life and its cruel jokes. Every time things settled, every time happiness seemed possible, life found a way to fall apart. He wanted things to be better. He wanted the pain to go away. He reached toward Adrastia's outstretched hand.

A sound came to Gwynn. It sounded distant—echoing like it raced toward him through a long tunnel. Maybe a voice? He didn't care anymore. He'd lost Sophia, his mom and dad were gone, and it seemed to follow he should go too. Maybe Jaimie could find the life raising him had denied her. Maybe he should let go.

"Take my hand Gwynn," Adrastia urged again. "Before you give up, before you slip into nothingness, grab my hand. The pain will go away. It's time you take your rightful place in the story of your life."

Gwynn took hold.

The world exploded into a million shards of glass.

Everything fell away into darkness.

As a single drop of water, Gwynn hurtled toward a vast ocean. He struck it, and his consciousness rippled to the furthest reaches.

He was nothing, yet he was everything.

The ripples rushed back toward him—an overwhelming wave of power. He drowned in darkness. He sputtered and choked. Something tugged at him from below the surface. The tendrils of the ages curled around him—a thing defying names, definitions and time itself.

Falling, falling.

Becoming the shadow.

***

Pridament choked on the pounding of his heart. He gripped his staff harder, trying to keep it steady and from slipping through his sweat-slicked fingers. The cold air blowing through the remains of the roof bit at his face, even as his body pulsed with heat.

Four feet behind him, Gwynn made the sounds of a mortally wounded man on the battlefield.

"Step aside Pridament," Elaios commanded. "The boy is dying, and you can't stop it. At least let me make it mercifully swift for him."

"You forgot what mercy was when you threw your lot in with the Fallen, Elaios."

From behind, Gwynn said something. The word made Pridament's blood chill. Despite the threat from Elaios, he broke his eyes from her and chanced a glance over his shoulder at Gwynn.

Then he started shouting.

"No, Gwynn. No, don't."

The boy started convulsing. He'd waited too long.

"Gwynn..." Elaios said from behind him. "My God, Pridament. You kept going. Even after I told you not to, you still went ahead. Do you understand what you've done?"

"What I had to."

The floor creaked under the shifting of her weight. Pridament closed his eyes, drew a slow breath, waited for a fraction of a second more, and then spun, throwing his weight behind the arc of his staff. The resistance as it struck Elaios' midsection gave him great satisfaction.

Pridament opened his eyes to see Elaios crumpled on the ground. She drew herself up to a crouch, holding her side.

"You're a fool. Don't you remember what I told you?"

"You said if I kept searching, it would be your undoing."

She laughed—a sick, humorless rattle. "Men. Your memories are so selective."

Gwynn began to scream.

"Do the right thing," Elaios said. "Kill him while you still have the chance."

She began to fold space. Pridament moved toward her. If he didn't grab hold of her, keep hold of her, he would have no way of knowing where she'd gone. His fingers wrapped themselves in the cloth of her cloak.

"You'll have to choose," she screeched. "What's more important to you? Me or the boy?"

Behind him, Gwynn's situation was dire. The transformation began. His fingers slipped away from Elaios' cloak, the world snapping back into place as she fled.

Gwynn's eyes were bloodshot. His bones creaked and cracked as his hands elongated into claws. Black splotches mottled his skin, spreading and expanding like a virus. He sat bolt upward and fell to his hands and knees. His right arm tore at the air in front of him. A slight loosening of Pridament's abdominal muscles gave him a familiar signal; Gwynn sealed the tear in the Veil.

"Thanks, Gwynn," Pridament whispered, "but this is going to hurt."

Pridament waited. Gwynn rose up on his knees, revealing Pridament's target. Pridament jammed his staff into Gwynn's midsection. Maybe he would interrupt the flow of the energy coursing through Gwynn's body. Or he would finish the job Elaios started.

Gwynn howled and fell backward. He thrashed for the longest five minutes Pridament ever experienced and then fell silent. Pridament willed himself to breathe. The black splotches on Gwynn's skin began to recede. The boy's bones slid back into their original shape.

When Gwynn's outward appearance returned to normal, Pridament risked a quick assessment of the boy's condition. He moved his hands along Gwynn's extremities and risked putting some pressure against his chest. Everything appeared to be in place and whole. Gwynn's breathing became steady and free of any crackles. The bruising and lacerations on his flesh vanished. All evidence of Elaios' beating disappeared.

"Adrastia" Gwynn said in the hoarse, hushed voice of the dreamer.

"No Gwynn. Don't go with her. Come back. Let go of her hand." Pridament caressed Gwynn's face. He placed his hand on the boy's chest, willing Gwynn back to the waking world. He felt something beneath Gwynn's shirt. Pridament reached down and pulled the chain around the boy's neck. Attached to it was a Saint Christopher medallion.

"I hope he does a better job of watching over you, kid," Pridament said.

Gwynn began to stir. Pridament tucked the medallion back inside Gwynn's shirt.

Gwynn groaned. "Am I dead?"

"Not yet kid. How do you feel?"

Gwynn drew open his eyelids and took a hesitant look around his surroundings. "Not as bad as I should. Where'd the psycho bitch go?"

"Would you believe me if I said you scared her off?"

Gwynn's eyes said *Bullshit*. "Am I that scary when I'm unconscious?"

"No. Can you get up?"

Gwynn inched his way to a sitting position.

"Hurt?"

"No." Gwynn seemed perplexed. "A little stiff, though."

"What about your headache, or the throbbing in your arm?"

Gwynn blinked. "Gone. Wait, no, still a little, but nothing like it was. What did you do?"

"Nothing. You closed your tear in the Veil. What about the sky? How does it look to you?"

Gwynn turned to the gap torn out of the roof. "Overcast."

Pridament gave the boy a once over. "Are you sure? Overcast?"

Gwynn shrugged. "Yeah. Why?"

"Because it's been sunny for the past couple of days. Quite unusual for November."

"That's not what I see."

"I know." Pridament's expression darkened. "I thought it was your connection with the Veil playing with your senses."

Gwynn got to his feet and walked over to the hole in the roof, his gaze moving up to the sky.

"My God."

"What do you see?" Pridament asked. His stomach twisted.

"It... it looks like a whirlpool in the sky." He turned back to Pridament, his eyes panicked. "What is it?"

Pridament sighed, a weight heaving itself on his shoulders. How many worlds? How many would be enough?

"I've heard of it before." He shook his head. "A madman once described it to me. He said, "'The Veil will open its maw and devour the world.'"

Refusing Destiny

The key slid in the door, sounding hollow and alone. Fuyuko opened the front door of the small bungalow she called home for the past three weeks. The silence blanketed her. She had a cot in one of the back bedrooms as her sole furnishing.

Fuyuko dropped her backpack on the counter and opened the fridge. Another night of noodles. She gave a weary sigh and tried to convince herself this served some purpose. Hadn't she contacted Justinian for that reason—to find some hidden purpose? She pounded her fist on the counter. The feel of the impact reverberated up her arm into her shoulder. The sensation gave her comfort. Something solid pushing back. Her world. No matter what ideas or philosophies Suture taught, *this* world, the one she could touch, was all she knew or cared about. The last time she dared mention this, Caelum suggested she felt that way due to being a Fragment. He made the gentle suggestion maybe if she were a Script, she would understand. She rewarded him with a case of frostbite.

Caelum remained at Suture. She couldn't recall a mission they worked apart. Never had any of them worked alone. But here she was. Strong Fuyuko. Dependable Fuyuko.

Lonely, confused and frustrated Fuyuko.

She pulled the cell phone from her pocket. It felt so weighty and cold sitting in her hand. Like the house she lived in, its design was pure function. No company logos, nothing fancy, just pure function.

She flipped it open. If she pressed and held the five key, she would reach Suture. She did that last night—the first time she used the phone in her three weeks. She let out a long breath. The silence suffocated her. She needed to call someone.

Jason. What she would give to speak to him. She sighed. Even if you could reach individual members of Suture, she didn't know how. She ran through the names of her friends. All of them probably in the barracks or out on some mission. One option remained. Her last option.

"Hello?"

Fuyuko winced at the sound of the voice. She steadied herself before responding. "Hi, dad."

"Hello, Fuyuko." His tone sounded stilted, formal. "How are your studies going?"

"I'm on the secure line dad."

In her mind, she saw him shift. Initially, he would've been reclining in a chair, or leaning against the wall. The mention of "secure line" would have him hunched over the phone, forming a defensive shield with his body. His tone became less conversational—hushed and conspiratorial.

"Good. How is your mission proceeding?"

"I'd be able to tell you if I knew what my mission is."

"Is it a matter of not knowing or that you've failed to put in the proper amount of research?"

Her father had a talent for using words like swords—each one sharpened and stabbed at the right place to inflict the most damage.

"They dropped me off at this house, told me to go to school and keep my eye out for some kid who goes there. How am I supposed to prepare for a mission like this? No technical data, no specifics on the desired outcome. They didn't even give me a map of the city or a floor plan of the school."

"These sound more like complaints of one who fears work. Or perhaps you have doubts in Suture?"

"I have never once turned away from difficulty."

Breathe. Breathe and don't give into him, Fuyuko told herself.

"I am saying this is unlike any mission I've ever done."

"Is that why you called to speak with a senior member in the field?" her father asked.

It sounded more like an accusation than a question.

"You know about that?"

"You must understand my position within Suture by now, Fuyuko. Not much happens I don't know about."

She clenched her fists and gave a silent curse. Her father held an important position with Suture. If pressed on it, she had to admit she didn't even know what he did. But he always knew. If she failed a training exercise or been less than stellar in the field, she could never hide it from him.

"Yes, I understand."

"Did he provide you with enough assistance?"

Had he? Fuyuko almost laughed. He'd done nothing but add to her questions. Having mulled her meeting over in her mind as she walked home, she'd come to the painful conclusion Justinian told her in a polite way to shut up and wait for further instructions.

"I haven't decided yet."

"Then I suggest you spend some time contemplating what he said. In the meantime, your mother is eager to speak with you."

If she was so eager to speak with me, why couldn't she have answered instead of you? Fuyuko tried to calm the raging of her heart. She had no desire to take it out on her mom.

"Hello, sweetheart."

"Hi, mom."

"I understand from your father you've been having some difficulty with this mission?"

"Is that what he said? Difficulty? It's not that, mom. This thing isn't even a mission. Dad would've never allowed Katsuro to get stuck in something like this."

Bringing up his name struck her with regret. Silence dragged on for a minute on the other end of the phone.

"Ah, I see. Well, you know what I used to do as a girl when I needed to figure things out?" Her mother continued past the mention of Katsuro, but the sound of hurt clung to her words. "Go for a ride on a swing."

"You know I'm seventeen, right mom?"

"You are never too old to ride a swing, dear. Besides, it's quite crisp outside. I would think you'd enjoy the chilled air."

"Maybe," Fuyuko grumbled.

"Never mind your father's harsh tone, Fuyuko. He loves you and is very proud of you. It's just hard for him to say."

No, it isn't. He just has no desire to.

"I know mom. Good night."

***

Gwynn's body shook. It had nothing to do with the cold.

"You're telling me you can't see it?"

Pridament hung his head. "No. Like I said, my information is second-hand."

"It looks like a twister is about to rip the town apart! How the hell can you not see it?"

"Because I'm not a Script."

Pridament's weak smile infuriated Gwynn.

"You understand I have no idea what that means, right?" Gwynn's fingers ached from balling into tight fists. "For god's sake, tell me what is going on."

Pridament moved beside Gwynn. "You need to realize not all Anunnaki are created equal. You remember how I said my glyphs were incomplete?"

Had he said that? Maybe. In the coffee shop. That seemed so far away.

Gwynn nodded.

"Because of that, I can't see the vortex in the sky. I can't see, or close, a tear in the Veil unless I made it. It takes six Fragments to seal a natural tear in the Veil. Someone like you, a Script, you can do all those things alone. The symbols on our arms are like a story. When you have the complete story, you can see all the aspects and themes of it. You can understand its rules and characters. You can't when you only have a fragment of it. You can't see the complete picture."

"So what are you saying?" Gwynn inspected his right arm and the symbols extending to his fingers. "I'm some freak? Some super god?"

Pridament's eyes softened. "No, no, not a freak at all. Just, rarer, than the average. At best estimates, about ten percent of Anunnaki are Scripts. If anything, I'm the freak. Fragments are broken, unable to use the full extent of our powers unless as a group. There's some who think we're less pure, less worthy of the title of Anunnaki."

Too much. They were both freaks, one bigger than the other. Gwynn gripped his hair and sunk to his knees.

"So what is that thing? Why is it here?"

Pridament continued to stand, searching the skies, seeming to try to do what he said was impossible.

"When multiple tears in the veil occur near each other, they weaken the boundary between worlds. Think of it this way, you have two glasses filled with water, and they sit open end to open end. A piece of plastic is placed between them, so the water doesn't flow from one into the other."

"I'm following."

"So what happens if you remove the plastic?" Pridament asked. His eyes darkened and appeared even scared.

"The water from one glass goes into the other. Probably spills all over the place." Then it dawned on Gwynn. "Holy shit. You're saying the veil is the plastic?"

Pridament gave a slow and sorrowful nod.

"That woman, the one who attacked me, is she doing this?"

"I believe so," Pridament said. "Her name is Elaios. She belongs to a terrorist group called The Fallen. They believe they must destroy the various versions of Earth throughout the multiverse."

"Why?"

Pridament sighed and sat down next to Gwynn on the floor.

"The Norse saw the universe as a giant tree, Yggdrasil. The Fallen think the trunk of Yggdrasil represents the original universe. From that, the multiple branches are splintered alternate realities. Like you prune a tree to keep it healthy, they believe saving existence means eliminating dead weight."

"By destroying entire worlds?"

Pridament shook his head. "By destroying entire universes. They commit murder in the billions, but they justify it by the belief all those lives continue in a truer, purer, reality. Some are religious fanatics. They believe when they return to the trunk, the roots can be discovered, and then God. I think others do it because it makes them feel powerful."

"Doesn't anyone try to stop them?"

"There is a group..." Pridament trailed off. His jaw clenched, and his eyes were angry.

Gwynn remembered the word. Elaios said it as she beat him. "Suture."

Pridament couldn't contain his surprise. "How do you know that?"

"Elaios. She called me a 'Suture Brat.' It didn't make any sense to me at the time. So what is Suture exactly?"

"About fifty years ago, someone revealed the existence of Anunnaki to world governments." A tremor of anger went through Pridament's voice as he said, "To this day, I'm still not sure of that person's identity." He cleared his throat and took a deep breath. "In any case, the government became aware of the threat of tears in the Veil and that Anunnaki could combat them. Several years of power struggle ensued. Some leaders wanted military applications. Others thought the Anunnakis should guard against invasions from other worlds. Eventually, the threat from outside our world, or a veil collapse, persuaded the world governments to create the entity known as Suture. With the decision made, the varying factions of Anunnakis made a pact. They divided the world into sectors and took ownership of protecting their assigned area."

"So who's supposed to be protecting us?" Through gritted teeth, Gwynn added, "And where the hell are they now?"

Pridament got to his feet and dusted himself off.

"That's the question, isn't it? If this is Suture's job, where are they now?"

"You don't seem like a fan."

"It's good in theory, I suppose." Pridament shook his head. "But how long can you tie egos that large together without a power struggle? These men and women have known the adoration and worship of being gods. They won't take orders forever." He turned his head toward the skies over the city again. His voice softened, maybe doubtful. "We might have to do this ourselves."

"Say that to me again?" Gwynn's voice shook.

"You're a Script. You could stop it."

Gwynn put up his hands and backed away. "Whoa. I'm not sure if you were keeping score, but I got my ass handed to me. How am I supposed to stop something like that?"

"If you look at the vortex, you should see tendrils extending down to the ground. Those are coming from the open tears. This place held one, but you've already closed it. With a bit of training, I'm sure you could close the rest."

"Do you have time to train me?"

"Hopefully."

Gwynn shook his head. "No. I'm not buying that. I think you need to get on your phone and start getting the professionals in here."

"You can do it, Gwynn. You're a Script. A little training on how to use your abilities to fight and you'll be set. Besides, I'd be there to back you up."

"You mean like you were while Elaios used me for a punching bag?" Gwynn's fists clenched. His body seemed healed, but the sting of Elaios' fire clung to his memory.

"You know I was fighting the Curse."

"Sure, and what will keep you busy the next time?"

"There won't be a next time. I didn't know, Gwynn. I thought the Curse was here because of the tear you left open. I wouldn't let you go alone again."

Pridament tried to be kind with his tone, but Gwynn couldn't care. If Suture existed, this was their mess to handle. He wanted his life back.

"Forget it, okay? Are we done here? Did I close the tear I made?"

"Yes."

"Then I think I'd like to go home."

The two descended through the house in silence. It returned to the derelict Gwynn remembered from Halloween. They walked out the front door and got in the car. As Pridament pulled out, a pale girl in a black dress waved to Gwynn from the window. She mouthed some words and Gwynn knew what they were, as sure as if she whispered in his ear. "Be seeing you soon."

Reaching for the Moon

Jaimie paced in the kitchen. The last dying rays of sunlight were retreating beyond the horizon. What had her visitor's words meant? Should she allow Gwynn some more space? Like hell. When the boy got home, he would go to his room and only leave it for food and school. In another few months, he would go to college. When that happened, she would give him space. While he lived under her roof no damn way would he use a school suspension for hanging out.

She never gave herself a chance to ask who he would be hanging out with. In all the years they had lived together, he had never brought home a friend. No, if *that man* told her to let Gwynn do as he pleased, then it was not a good thing.

Her feet and back were protesting. Too much stress, too much time moving back and forth on hard floors without a rest. She embraced the discomfort and used it as further fuel for her anger. Nine years of perfect, predictable behavior. Now, this. Suspension. Disappearance. Some rational part of her mind said she should be worried, not angry. Some part of her understood she felt more frustration and anger toward herself than Gwynn, but those parts were waging a losing battle.

Lights cut across the ceiling in the hall. A car had pulled into the drive.

Jaimie sprinted down the hall and threw the door open. The car lights, still on, blinded her. The whir of an engine fan kicked on as the car idled. A few moments later, a rattling noise accompanied the engine shutting off, and the lights died, leaving her blinking away spots.

Two figures approached from the car. The first one she focused on turned out to be Gwynn. The boy's clothes were in tatters.

The second figure stood taller, a man. He appeared in his mid-forties. Tall, brown hair, nothing outstanding. His eyes though, they were dark and grim. His discomfort of being here wafted off him like stink.

Jaimie allowed them inside the house and shut the door before she started to yell.

"Where the hell have you been? What happened to you?"

Gwynn looked back at the man and then hung his head.

"Well, I'm waiting for some sort of explanation." Jaimie wheeled on the stranger. "And who are you?"

The man cleared his throat. "My name is Pridament. I met your nephew at the hospital."

"What happened to you?" Jaimie asked, turning her attention back to Gwynn.

Again, he seemed to search for guidance from the man who called himself Pridament. "I'm going to go get some different clothes on."

"Excuse me?"

She didn't like this. First, the hated man shows up, now Gwynn looked to some stranger to explain his actions. She wouldn't lose him. "I think you're going to stay here and explain to me why you look like you were in a bar fight and are being driven home by a virtual stranger."

"I don't want to intrude, but perhaps if the boy were more comfortable he might tell you what's happening," Pridament said.

"You shouldn't intrude, and I don't give a damn about him being more comfortable. This is my house, and I want an explanation."

Gwynn was almost up the stairs, but he stormed back down. "*Your* house? What happened to us being in this life together? What happened to us being all the family we had so we had to stick together?"

"Exactly. So don't you think if you've gotten involved in something you should tell me?"

Gwynn shook. "What? Do you think I'm involved in drugs or something? Would you like to come upstairs with me and search my room?"

"That sounds like a challenge." She prepared to storm up to his room and tear it to shreds.

Pridament held up his hands. "Whoa there. This is getting out of control. Maybe both of you should calm down and take a breather."

"Maybe you should get the hell out of my house," Jaimie bellowed.

Gwynn turned a shade of red approaching purple. "I see what this is all about. Nine years I've been the quiet mouse. I never raised my voice. I never questioned instructions. Now, suddenly life is happening to me and you can't handle it."

"That's not it at all."

"Yes, it is. Jesus, I didn't even ask for this. Do you think I want to be some freak? Do you think I need this shit on my shoulders?"

Gwynn shoved by Jaimie and threw open the door. On his way out the door, he grabbed a ratty, too short, jacket. Why had she even kept that coat?

"Gwynn..."

"Let him go, Jaimes." Pridament touched her gently on her shoulder. Even though rage blinded her, she couldn't ignore the feelings ignited in her hearing that name. Her eyes burned as unbidden tears surged forward.

"What did you call me?" she turned to him.

Pridament's eyes were gentle, understanding, familiar. "You've done a fantastic job with him, Jaimie. Give him some time to cool down. He's had a lot dumped on him."

Jaimie's voice came dry and cracked. "Who are you?"

"You won't like the answer."

"Please. I'm sick of all the riddles and games." Pleading filled her voice. She hated it. She didn't know this man, and she hated being weak in front of him. Still, the name. Only one person ever called her that. "I need to know."

"All right," he said. But it seemed the last thing he wanted. "This might be...unsettling.

The air seemed dryer. Jaimie's hair tingled, as though she brushed against a drape and picked up a charge. Pridament's face started to shift. His nose reforming, the position of his eyes moving. Each movement brought the face toward something she recognized. When she had no doubt what final form the man's face would take, Jaimie fainted.

***

Fuyuko still had doubts about the swings.

Mom was right about one thing—the cold night air is comforting.

She learned over the years her mother held a certain amount of wisdom. Doubts or not, if her mom said to ride a swing, then she would ride a swing. A simple search on Google Earth provided her with the location of a nearby park.

It always looks so easy on the map, she thought, correcting another wrong turn. It did seem easier in the two-dimensional space of a monitor. Things got convoluted the more dimensions you added. She laughed. It sounded like a lesson at Suture.

This night provided lots to be thankful for. The moon shone a bright three–quarters in a sky clear and full of stars, and the clean, crisp air tickled her lungs. To top off the perfection of it all, the boots she wore were so comfortable. Every mission before required combat boots. She reveled in the luxury of having well made, civilian, footwear.

At the end of the street, a walkway led to green space. Fuyuko picked up her pace, sensing her destination within reach. Despite her misgivings, her body tingled with anticipation.

Fuyuko stopped at the end of the walkway and let her eyes adjust. A hundred feet from the light of the residential street, the park seemed covered in a shroud that blocked out the artificial light. Thanking the moon for its brightness, she followed the paved walkway, moving through the parkland's series of slopes and valleys. She heard the grinding of cold metal before the playground came into view. Odd, someone else wanted to ride swings late on a cold November night?

She came around a small hill, and the playground came into full view. A large climbing structure with three slides of differing height and shape dominated the space. Another structure for climbing shaped like a dome stood to her left. To the right, the swings, where a lone figure kicked his feet toward the sky.

It's like he's trying to escape the pull of gravity.

Fuyuko inspected the boy on the swings. "Ho–lee shit," she muttered. Fate always proved to be a strange and crafty bitch. "Gwynn?" she called.

He turned his head to inspect her. He stopped kicking himself higher and let gravity reclaim him. Fuyuko moved closer.

"Why is it whenever I'm having a rough time, I run into you?" he asked.

"Lucky?" Inside she cringed. She had little experience in the banter between virtual strangers. She'd known most of the people in her life since childhood.

He laughed. "Maybe."

Fuyuko motioned toward an unoccupied swing next to Gwynn. "Is it okay if I have a seat?"

"Go ahead."

Her stomach fluttered. Something about the boy undermined her confidence. *A reminder this mission is stupid? Why the hell am I even here?*

"So what are you doing here?" she asked him.

"This is my thinking spot."

"Really?"

He looked away from her toward the sky. "When I'm swinging, it feels like I'm leaving the world behind."

When Gwynn's eyes turned back to her, he wore a weak smile. What had Justinian said about Gwynn? 'He looked like a killer.' Fuyuko didn't see that at all. No, just a lonely boy, with life experiences too old for his maturity to handle. She pitied him. She sympathized.

"So what brings you to the swings?" he asked.

Fuyuko laughed. "I'm trying to figure some things out. My mom said I should try it. Apparently, it always worked for her."

"So I'm not the only one who does his thinking on swings? Good to know."

He kicked himself higher into the air, focusing his attention on the sky and the moon above.

Fuyuko shrugged and walked back a few steps. She then lifted her feet from the ground and started pulling herself up to the heavens. Back and forth, kick up, kick back, a physical rhythm. The wind wrapped around her and whistled in her ears. As she went higher, the moon seemed a bit closer. She would then fall back, and the world rushed into view. Rocketing forward, the world disappeared again, replaced with the starlit sky. Motion became everything, the sensation of flight and falling mingled into a sense of freedom. How could anyone think when all these sensations begged to be lost in? Why did this feel so new? She was once a child. Hadn't she been on swings before? Probably. But she'd forgotten those days and replaced them with holes in the world filled with monsters. A simple thing, riding a swing, and yet the joy it brought her seemed beyond reason. Her companion remained speechless. The two of them swung in tandem, the sound of the metal a two–part melody soaring and dipping with the movements of their two bodies.

Fuyuko had no idea how much time passed. It surprised her to find she didn't care.

"So have you figured it out yet?" Gwynn asked.

His words shattered the minimalist symphony. It took Fuyuko a moment to process what he asked her. She laughed, embarrassed because she'd stopped worrying for a moment.

"No. I've been enjoying swinging."

"Like I said, the world goes away."

"How about you?" she asked. "Have you figured out whatever brought you here?"

He sighed—a weary, heavy sound. "I'm not sure if I'll ever sort it out."

"Do you want to talk about it?"

Silence. *Guess not.*

"It's just," the suddenness of his speaking startled Fuyuko, "have you ever thought your life felt stable? I mean, you knew what would happen every morning, you knew where life was heading, you could count on things."

"I don't think I've ever felt that way." Her life could never be that way. She felt faint tingles of jealousy toward him.

"You're lucky. Because when you do feel that way, that's when everything falls apart. I'm just pissed. I should've known better."

"I think that's the way life is."

"It's bullshit."

Fuyuko stopped herself from arguing any further. How could she hope to make him understand? When you became an active member of Suture, you didn't know where you would sleep, wake up, or whether you'd survive. Chaos wasn't something you understood, you called it family.

Without warning, Gwynn launched from his swing. He stood statue still, craning his head forward. He turned back to Fuyuko.

"Did you hear something?"

She hadn't, but he looked alarmed.

Fuyuko landed two feet behind Gwynn. She stepped to his side. "What did you hear?"

He shushed her. Her ears detected nothing but the dying movements of the swings behind her.

Each passing moment clicked in her like the motion of a clock hand. As time and silence continued, her confidence in Gwynn diminished. Justinian saw a killer? No, nothing but a lost little boy, who was increasingly getting on her nerves. She readied to snap. Then the sounds of panting and pawing at the ground on the other side of the hill reached her.

It could be anything, she told herself. But increasing knots in her stomach said differently. Not a tear, but something reeking of its energy.

"Oh God, no" Gwynn said.

Fuyuko followed his gaze to the top of the hill. Hungry eyes and sharp teeth met her eyes.

The Sword of Sorrow

Having company on the swings seemed wrong. His spot to escape and think seemed too private a thing to share. Especially with the day's events crushing down on him.

After his parents had died, he and his aunt moved to this town to start over. She'd found a new job and a house big enough for them each to have space. It took two weeks after they moved for Gwynn to venture out. Finding this park had been a small blessing. Almost ten years had passed, and the swings were still the first place he fled when things became overwhelming. He'd always been alone before, finding solace in the dark where no one saw your tears. Then *she* arrived.

Besides the day he lost his parents, this day ranked as the worst. And here she was like she kept showing up yesterday.

Who are you? he wondered. *I've run into you so often. Can it be more than a coincidence?*

The rhythm of her swing matched his. Two objects, often out of sync, aligning for a moment. Despite his questions and doubts, having her here made it seem, what, safer? Or maybe his experience with Sophia left him feeling so alone, he needed someone else to speak with.

A stab of guilt. Sophia. She'd told him to stop the world from bleeding—to heal its wound. Did she know about the vortex? No, how could she? But what if...? If he *could* close the vortex, would Sophia be normal again? Could they be together? If he could go back, he would do anything to keep her from going into that house. Even if she hated him for it.

His reaction to Jaimie's over protectiveness was childish. She wasn't punishing him, she was afraid for him. Not *over* protectiveness, just love. He should've tried to breathe and keep it together. He had to go home and set things right.

The words 'I'm going home' were about to leave his mouth. Then the wind sighed—a soft humming which grew and swelled until a variety of pitches reached him. Someone sang in the darkness.

Gwynn leaped from the swing. He landed on the ground craning his neck in the sound's direction. Maybe he had heard things—one more symptom of his exposure to the tear.

The singing came closer.

Despite being unable to place the melody, it held a familiarity. A single voice, female, chanting. It wasn't English. Latin? Was it even an actual language?

Gwynn turned to Fuyuko. "Did you hear something?"

She shook her head, no. She jumped from the swing and took a step to stand beside Gwynn.

"What is it?" She asked.

"Shhh." Gwynn tried to still everything in his body. The distracting thump in his chest the hardest to ignore. If Fuyuko couldn't hear it, he could still be hallucinating. Had Pridament been wrong? Could his connection to the tear remain?

Gwynn's body reacted to the singing. His muscles tensed, adrenaline pumped a euphoric high through his system. He felt stronger, ready. But for what?

Then he saw them.

"Oh God, no."

Over the hill padded two creatures. Each had four muscular legs carrying their bull-sized bodies with ease and grace. Red, angry, eyes set in a dog-like head locked on to Fuyuko and Gwynn.

"Gwynn," Fuyuko's voice lacked any trace of fear, "get behind me."

His mouth slackened. If he had super powers like Pridament said, why was *he* the one immobilized by fear? "But..."

"I'll take care of this."

The singing resonated all around him. Gwynn wanted to slam his hands over his ears, but the song crept inside him. A door began to open, a revelation of his secret history. Despite the threat of the monsters, the darkness inside frightened him far more. He willed the door to shut—he had no time for the skeletons there.

His skin prickled. Fuyuko took a defiant stance between Gwynn and the creatures. A faint glow emanated from Fuyuko's right arm. The air around it condensed into a swirling mist, which then thinned out, stretched, thickened. Where once there was nothing, Fuyuko now held a spear. The shaft appeared to be ice; a long, thin, razor–like blade ran along the top. She let out a long, slow breath.

Then she moved.

In the movies, as warriors plunged into potential doom, they always made some sort of cheer, or declaration of their impending victory. Not Fuyuko. She moved like the mist; quick, low and quiet. She almost came within striking distance before the creatures noticed.

But notice, they did.

In a blur of motion, one of the beasts smashed Fuyuko in the side, sending her sprawling to the side of the hill. She made it to her feet before it could reach her.

The monster turned its head to snap at her midsection. Fuyuko slapped one hand down on the side of the creature and propelled herself up and over it. She landed on the other side, slicing a section the beast's tail off.

The creature howled and spun in a wild snapping of jaws. Fuyuko moved beyond its grasp, rolling down the hill.

"Get up to the highest level of the climbers," she yelled to Gwynn.

Fog clouded his thoughts. Everything moved too fast. Fuyuko slapped him, hard, as she passed. He snapped to and followed her.

Fuyuko never touched steps. She jumped from the ground, propelling herself to the next level.

The beasts were in pursuit—the heat of their breath on his neck as he stumbled up the climbers. The spear sliced the air beside his ear, earning a howl in return. Fuyuko continued leaping to the highest level of the climbers. Gwynn didn't chance a look behind him until he stood beside her.

The creatures were both wounded now and stalking around the climber.

"Wait until you see an opening, then run," Fuyuko said.

"What are you going to do?"

Her eyes gleamed with violence. "Give you a chance."

Fuyuko let out a slow stream of air that misted in the cold. She waved her hand through it, then spun and slapped at the mist. A multitude of icicles fired at the creatures, scraping their skin, gouging one in the eye, sending them thrashing as they sought cover. In the confusion, Fuyuko jumped from the climbers, her spear spinning in the air above her head. She fell from the sky, crashing the spear deep into the hide of one of the beasts. The creature bucked and tossed its head, trying to reach back and snap at Fuyuko. Instead, it got a fist encased in ice smashed into its face. Despite the monster's wild movements, Fuyuko held firm to her spear, which remained embedded in the creature's side.

Gwynn searched the playground for the second beast. Had the icicle attack scared it off? No, he caught sight of it stalking toward Fuyuko and the other monster. He panicked and choked on his heart as it pounded into his throat. Did he yell a warning? If that broke her concentration, the creature she already fought with might get her. But without warning, the second would...

Humming. The melody. The world hung suspended, the tableaux of death held frozen in front of him.

"Adrastia," Gwynn said as he turned to toward the girl.

"Hello Hidhaegg"

"What? Why do you call me that?"

The girl's eyes had a catlike glow. "I call you that which you have been and will again become."

Gwynn sighed. "Why does everyone speak to me in riddles?"

Adrastia ignored him and appraised the scene in front of them. Fuyuko dangled from her spear in the hide of the one monster. The other creature crept toward her and stood within a heartbeat of pouncing to finish her.

"Will you let her die?"

Gwynn sputtered. "No. I mean, I don't want to."

I don't know what to do.

"You're afraid," she said.

I'm powerless. Like with Sophia.

His fists clenched so tight his fingers threatened to snap.

He didn't see her move. One moment she stood away from him, the next, behind him, wrapping him in her arms. She smelled like spring. Her embrace made him feel taller, stronger.

Adrastia whispered in his ear. "The last time I tried to help, you weren't ready. For that, I'm sorry. Trust me when I tell you this isn't the same. What you need is already in your hand, already a part of who you are. You just need to Tear the Veil and seize it."

"I can't."

"You can. You mustn't run away." Adrastia ran her right hand down his side and gripped his wrist. She raised his arm and pulled the sleeve back, enough to reveal the symbols on his flesh. "She needs you. Will you fail her?"

No. I can't. Not again. Not her too.

"Then let the song guide you."

Adrastia sang. The strange mashing of vowels and consonants reached down into him, opening a floodgate in his chest sending energy surging through his veins.

Gwynn closed his eyes and drew in a slow breath—the movement of the air traveling down his spine and pooling in the center of his being. The trembling in his body ceased. Yes, Adrastia was right; he did know what to do.

Gwynn's eyes snapped open. The wind gathered around him and propelled him up and away from the climbers.

He tore the Veil. The park didn't seem dark anymore—the darkness resided within him. He brushed against his soul. Not happy memories of days lost, or days yet to come. Instead, he found his misery and pain. Loss and grief spilled out between his fingertips, taking form. Just as an icy mist brought forth Fuyuko's spear, darkness and sorrow summoned what he needed.

Time started again. Fuyuko continued to wrestle the one beast while the other prepared for a killing strike.

Gwynn slammed into the creature before it could attack. The two of them sprawled away. A weight in his hand, a surge of knowing spreading through him. He'd never held a weapon before, but everything he needed to know about it seemed to spread from the hilt he now held through his arm and into every fiber of his being.

A sword with a blade of midnight pulsing with life. Gwynn rolled on the grass away from the monster. He sprung to his feet and without hesitating charged back toward the creature.

First, he vanquished his fear. Now, he would slay the beast.

He wanted it.

He needed it.

Before the beast could regain its footing, the sword severed its head.

The other Taint continued to buck, trying to dislodge Fuyuko.

Gwynn flowed like a crashing wave. From the stroke of taking one beast's head, he flowed toward the other, charging its opposite side. He dragged his sword along the beast's flank, from tail to mouth, finishing by twisting to face the monster and making a smooth pass through its neck with the sword.

The creature's body crashed to the ground.

Fuyuko cursed. She turned to where Gwynn stood and stopped—eyes wide, her mouth agape.

Gwynn felt her fear.

He liked it.

***

When Fuyuko first arrived, she couldn't help but feel uncomfortable. Having been an active member of Suture for three years, the youngest person ever promoted, she'd worked as part of a team and taken part in monster hunts. Dangerous missions, but simple, straight ahead—find it and destroy it.

From the start, this mission was different. First, no one gave her an objective. Her orders were simple; watch Gwynn Dormath. No one discussed his importance, or what she should do while observing him. Second, they sent her alone. No one her age performed a distant mission alone. At least none she recalled. Older specialists like Justinian completed solo fieldwork. The third thing, the most annoying thing, the kid wasn't even there. It took a day or two of listening to gossip to establish some idea of what happened. Her subject was the aim of a Halloween joke. In the end, it turned deadly. Gwynn and another student were involved in some sort of explosion which killed a homeless squatter.

Fuyuko went to investigate the site. The space still crackled with traces of the tear. While that explained Suture's interest in the town, she still didn't know what to do about the boy.

When Gwynn returned to school, he seemed sullen, withdrawn. No one appeared happy to see him. In truth, everyone kept their distance. He didn't seem like anything worth the notice of Suture. Fuyuko had doubts about her mission.

Then he hit the boy, Eric, who taunted him. Emotional stress. She had seen it before.

Within five minutes of Gwynn fleeing the cafeteria, her phone rang.

It took her a moment to recognize the sound. Her phone never rang. "Hello?"

"Fuyuko."

The voice belonged to the man who'd been training her for years.

"Yes, sir?"

"You need to go see the Principal, explain to him how the other boy provoked Gwynn."

"I'm sorry?" She searched the cafeteria for cameras but saw none. "How did you..."

"Do as you're told Fuyuko. Consider this part of your mission."

So she went to meet Mr. Davis. She couldn't understand what she was doing, or why, but it felt comforting to have an explicit component of this mission. Gwynn waited outside Mr. Davis' office as she left. He literally ran into her again at the crosswalk as she headed home. She couldn't escape the feeling of dancing at the end of someone's puppet strings.

Her doubts led to her meeting with Justinian. Now she stood in the dark, cold park, facing a very different Gwynn. She thought Justinian a fool before, but now she understood.

I saw a killer.

"Gwynn?"

The boy inspected the sword in his hand. His expression told her everything. He was an Anunnaki, and for the first time, manifested a weapon from the Veil. If she believed the philosophy Suture taught, Gwynn held a weapon forged of his soul and the energies of creation—a weapon whose appearance stirred memory and dread in Fuyuko.

Giving a portion of the soul substance, often the darkest and most violent part, carried baggage. The energy and emotions it evoked could be foreign and corruptive. Without proper focus and training, it could become mental cancer, carving out the Gwynn of old and turning him into something else. He slaughtered two monsters with little effort or remorse. She had to get him to let go of the sword.

"Listen to my voice, Gwynn." She'd never trained to talk someone down from this. She tried using a gentle voice. "You are the sword's master. You do not have to let it change who you are."

His eyes were hungry. Fuyuko tightened her grip on her spear.

At Suture, they taught them visualization techniques. By imagining the manipulation of energy as physical objects made it easier for the mind to handle and maintain control. Her mind was a filing system full of Suture's lessons. She searched it for the series of images that helped her most when she learned to control her own weapon.

"Imagine you've opened a closet." She focused on keeping her voice calm and soothing. "You reached in and pulled this sword out. It's time to put it away. The sword isn't solid; it's dust in your hand. Let it go and let the wind blow the dust into the closet. Once that's done, shut the door. Focus Gwynn. Try to see it."

His grip tightened on the hilt.

Shit, shit. She was losing him.

Try something else.

What did Gwynn care about? What might he value enough to fight back against the dark seduction of his weapon?

"Think about your family Gwynn." *Risky, Fuyuko. If someone said the same thing to you, you'd cut their head off.* "What about... What about Sophia?"

His eyes softened. "Sophia? My...family?"

"You went into that house after her, Gwynn." Fuyuko grasped onto this thread, found hope in it. "I heard the story. No one else had the courage or cared enough about her, to do it. But you did. You went in there because you had the courage, because you cared. Use that courage now, let the sword go before you stop being the boy who cares about Sophia."

Gwynn's gaze fell to the sword. His chest heaved. He slammed his eyes shut and held the sword out at arm's length.

"That's right Gwynn. The wind, feel it start to swirl around you. The sword is growing lighter, less solid in your hand."

Gwynn's arm wavered.

"The wind is a gale now. Let go and the sword will turn to dust and blow through the door."

Her heart beat in the back of her throat. If he pulled his arm back toward him without letting go, she would have to fight him. "Come on Gwynn, you need to go home."

Home.

He threw his fingers wide. The sword shattered into a million particles and dissipated.

Fuyuko sighed. "Now, the last thing, close the door. In your head, walk up to it and shove it closed."

A moment or two passed. Then, a slight loosening in her core—a tear closing.

Gwynn sank to his knees and gasped for air.

In her own mind, Fuyuko performed the same ritual she described to Gwynn. Her own spear dissipated, returning to the Veil.

Gwynn started to wretch.

Fuyuko turned her back and waited for the heaving to stop. When no more sound came, she said, "You okay?"

"Yeah." He gagged some more. "No... Uh, maybe."

"Good enough." She turned back and waited for him to find his feet. "Show me your right arm."

"What?"

Fuyuko was finished with mysteries. She strode toward him and grabbed his right arm. She pushed his sleeve back and gasped. She ripped the glove from his hand, revealing the glyphs extending to his fingers. She trembled.

"You're a Script?"

Gwynn shrugged. "I guess."

"Fuck." She spat the word out. Very unprofessional, but satisfying after weeks of frustration. "How long?"

"What?" Gwynn asked.

"How long since you first tore the Veil?" her voice teetered between rage and hysterics.

"Almost two weeks."

"Two weeks?" *Impossible.* "But you're seventeen?"

"So?"

"So? So, no Anunnaki has ever awakened later than ten. Scripts are always earlier; six, five even."

He sounded ashamed when he said, "I don't know why."

"Yet you know what a Script is?"

"A man met me at the hospital. He explained some things." Pain filled Gwynn's eyes. "Not enough, though."

Fuyuko drew a long, slow breath. She imagined it flowing through her like liquid, smoothing the heaving in her chest. Being out of control wouldn't solve anything. Besides, did this frightened boy deserve receiving the brunt of her own frustrations? For a moment, she tried to imagine awakening without someone for guidance. Maybe this was the mission?

"Look, I can help you." She shook her head. "No, I think I'm *supposed* to help you. Are you still suspended?"

"Yes."

"There's someone I need you to meet at the school. Can you meet me there when it's over?" she asked.

"I guess."

"In the meantime," she took his arm, "we should get you home."

"What about those?" Gwynn motioned to the carcasses.

"These?" Fuyuko walked over to the bodies and gave them a firm kick. They crumbled into dust.

"What?"

Fuyuko shrugged. "Curses. When they die, they go to dust. The popular theory states they come here through the Veil. When they die, the Veil takes back what belongs to it. All that's left is dust."

"But the thing in the Cameron house, they said it was a homeless man."

"Must have been a Taint. Again, the monster part goes back to the Veil, but the thing they were before stays behind. It's a messy business, hunting monsters."

The two walked in silence.

"This is me," Gwynn said pointing to a small two story.

"Tomorrow, at the school when it's over. Don't forget." She tried to keep her tone soothing but injected enough force to prevent negotiation.

"I won't."

He went into his house. When the door shut, she pulled out her cell phone, punched the number, and waited.

"Hello?" The voice sounded hoarse. She hadn't even checked the time.

"Hi, Dad. Sorry if I'm waking you."

"Fuyuko?" He cleared his throat. It must be late. She imagined him rubbing the sleep from his eyes and looking at the clock. "Calling twice in one night? What's happened?"

"I have an odd request dad." She cringed, but she had to know.

"All right. What do you need?"

Gwynn's sword. Would asking her father about a forbidden topic bring more scrutiny on Gwynn? How would she respond when her father asked why she wanted to know? Still, the similarities were too much. The stories the kids whispered to each other in the dorms in Suture and the spooky tales told by those who visited the lowest levels were forefront in her mind. Even if her concerns were childish, even if asking her father made her appear foolish, it would be better to know and have her mind at ease.

Fuyuko drew a deep breath. "I need you to tell me about the bogeyman."

The Workings of the Soul

Gwynn closed the door behind him, watching out the window until Fuyuko moved on.

Light spilled from the kitchen into the hall.

He drew a big breath. He was wrong. He flew off the handle. He needed to accept this and set things right with Jaimie.

She didn't greet him in the kitchen. Pridament sat at the table.

"Where's Jaimie?" Did his voice show the anxiety clenching his chest?

"Upstairs," Pridament said. "She's sleeping."

"What?" Gwynn couldn't believe it. After their fight, she gave up and went to bed. Maybe he'd missed his chance to fix things. Maybe she saw how much easier her life would be without him. "She didn't want to see me?"

Pridament held up his hand, "I needed to explain things to her Gwynn. I needed her to understand what you were going through."

"What did you do?" Gwynn's fists balled tightly.

"Nothing. I showed her a few things. She's fine, just a bit... overwhelmed. She asked if I could wait for you and let you know she's not angry anymore. She needed to get some rest."

Gwynn flopped into the other chair and rested his head in his hands. He breathed slow and long through his nose, counted, and let the air out through his mouth. He stretched the exhale until he reached ten. "I guess I can understand. This...thing, it's too much for me too."

"It doesn't have to be Gwynn." Pridament reached out with his hand. He stopped short of touching Gwynn and let it rest on the table. "I can help you. If you'll let me."

"I still don't know about that vortex. I don't think I can fix something like that." *I can't fix that.* "You say I have the power, but I don't feel it."

"Don't worry about that for now. What's most important is making you comfortable with your abilities. When things don't feel so foreign, then maybe you can decide what to do about the other things."

Gwynn shook his head. "There isn't time. I was in the park. I was..." he drew a breath, tried to think about whether he should mention Fuyuko or not, "attacked, by two creatures. I think you would've called them Curses."

Pridament's mouth went slack, but his eyes remained intense. When he spoke, he measured each word. "Was there a tear?"

Gwynn shook his head. "No. Not that I could see or feel," he added quieter, "I don't know much. I might've missed it."

"Let's assume you're right, and there was no tear. What are your thoughts?"

A chill ran down Gwynn's spine. In the midst of staying alive, it hadn't been something worth thinking about. Here, in the kitchen, safe, he recalled their eyes, the way they sniffed the air, and their determination to get him. Fuyuko was a nuisance in their way. "They were hunting. Probably me."

Pridament nodded. "Yes, I think you're right." The man's eyebrow lifted in puzzlement. "You were able to defeat them?"

"I did." It wasn't a lie. Fuyuko fought them, but in the end, he finished them both. Right? The details became wispy and escaped between his fingers.

"How?"

"You'll think I'm going insane." Gwynn was nearly convinced himself.

"Adrastia?"

Gwynn shook, and a cold sweat broke out on his brow.

Pridament nodded. "I heard you mention her name at the Cameron house. Right after you started channeling so much power you convulsed. I interrupted it."

"Do all Scripts see her?"

Pridament shook his head. "No. She's all yours."

Gwynn ran his hands through his hair, grabbing a handful, as though pulling out his hair might pull out the madness. "So I am going insane."

"No, I don't think so. I've known of Scripts who had similar experiences; they would have a vision of a person or thing offering them power. Most Scripts awaken at six or eight years of age. It's too young to gain near-godlike powers. By creating a gatekeeper who controls the power and doles it out at a manageable rate is possibly a way they cope."

"So this is normal?"

"Well," Pridament dragged out the 'l' a little too long, "I wouldn't say it's normal. But it isn't something that's never happened before either. So, in other words, it's a little odd, but you're not insane."

"That's not as comforting as I hoped."

"The point is you saw her. She offered you power, and you took it. And with that power, you defeated two Curses."

"No." Gwynn shook his head. "She said I wasn't ready for the power. She... sang."

"What did that do?"

"I don't know. It was like I could see clearly. The doubts, the fear, it went away. I tore the Veil, and it gave me a sword. Then I killed the Curses." Gwynn trembled. The word 'kill' hit him like a fist. "I killed. I used a sword and I... I killed."

"Things that would have killed you, Gwynn. Those creatures aren't of our world. You said it yourself; they attacked you. What you did was in your own defense."

"Still. I've never..." Something in him broke. The darkness, where his sorrow and the sword, lived, whispered to him. *That's a lie....*

Pridament put his hand on Gwynn's arm. It comforted him, grounded him. Like his father's had.

"Let it go, Gwynn. You're alive." Pridament smiled. "And the reason is that you defended yourself."

Gwynn's throat constricted with the choking back of tears. "I need you to show me how to control this."

Pridament squeezed his arm. "Good. Yes. We can start tomorrow."

"I should probably check with Jaimie," Gwynn sniffled.

"I told her you would need training. She said I could if you were willing. You still off school tomorrow?"

"Yes."

"Then I'll see you in the morning."

Pridament rose from the table and moved toward the front door.

"Do you really think those things were hunting me?" Gwynn asked.

Pridament looked outside. "We start your training tomorrow. Get some rest."

"That doesn't answer my question."

Pridament went rigid, his eyes sad. "My priority is to teach you to defend yourself. Does that give you an answer?"

***

Gwynn awoke to the ringing of his cell phone.

"Hello." His voice hoarse and cracked.

"Didn't I tell you we would start work this morning?" Pridament's voice said. "Get up."

Gwynn turned to the clock. It said ten. "Shit."

He tumbled out of bed and moved with the grace of a drunken stupor to the closet. He struggled into some pants and yanked a sweater over his head.

He opened his bedroom door. Down the hall, Jaimie's door was wide open. He found her room empty and the bed made.

Right, ten. She would've left for work a long time ago.

Gwynn trudged down the steps, his chest heavy. The sight of a piece of paper lying on the table made him feel a little lighter. He picked it up. For a brief moment, the terror crossed his mind this wouldn't be a good thing. He forced himself to read.

Gwynn, I thought after everything you went through yesterday, I should let you sleep. Your friend explained a lot. I'm sorry I was so angry; it wasn't all your fault. I'll be home around dinnertime. We can talk more then. Love you, Jaimie.

After he'd read it, the tension in his chest eased.

The doorbell sounded.

"Well, you look like crap," Pridament beamed. "Ready?"

"Sure," Gwynn grumbled. He opened the closet for his usual coat but found it missing.

"That thing was torn to shreds, remember?" Pridament said. He held a bag out to Gwynn. Inside, a new black coat waited.

Gwynn didn't know what surprised him more, that it fit, or he liked it.

"Thanks," he said. "I can pay you back."

"Don't worry about it. Consider it my way of starting to apologize for wrecking your life."

"It's not your fault. You didn't make me a freak."

A pained grimace flashed across Pridament's face. "No, no I guess I didn't. Thanks for not shooting the messenger."

Gwynn shrugged. "No worries. Let's go."

Walking to the car, Gwynn looked skyward. Overhead, the vortex growled. "How long will that thing last until, um, everything goes?"

"There'll be signs before the end."

"Like what."

Pridament stopped and turned to the sky, seeming to inspect the anomaly he couldn't see. "Horrors of biblical proportions."

"Do you mean that, or are you making a sick joke?"

Pridament sighed. "Honestly? Most of the people in town will turn to Taints, any bodies of water will boil, and there will be earthquakes that will turn this place into a crater. After that, similar events will repeat worldwide until the planet tears itself apart." Pridament raised an eyebrow. "Glad you asked?"

"At least I got a straight answer." Deep down, though, Gwynn began to understand why adults sometimes sheltered kids from the truth.

They were in the car traveling south on Kennedy, heading toward the industrial district.

"I know you're helping me by doing this, but could you try and drop me off by three at my house?" Gwynn asked.

"Do you have a date?"

Twinges of guilt pricked at him. Sophia in the hospital. She wasn't his girlfriend, but what if the events at the Cameron House hadn't happened? She might be. Somewhere inside her fractured mind, she might want that. No, he wasn't going on a date with Fuyuko. He just hoped to find out more. Maybe he wouldn't have to stop the vortex with only Pridament's help.

"No. Just meeting a friend about the work I've missed."

"I'll do my best. We're not doing anything too fancy today; I need you to learn the difference between drawing from your own power reserves and tearing the Veil. I also want to make sure you can seal any tears you create."

Pridament pulled into the driveway of a derelict warehouse. He traveled down a laneway running the entire side of the building and pulled around the back. He hopped out of the car to open a large door and then drove into the warehouse.

The space was empty, except for a table with a chair and a laptop.

Gwynn pulled his coat tighter around him. "Going to be hard to concentrate with this cold."

"I'll take care of it."

Pridament went to the table and reached underneath. A moment later, the hum of a small generator filled the space. Pridament stretched out some extension cords with heaters attached.

"It's not ideal, but it should help. See the circle on the ground, go stand in the middle of it."

Gwynn moved to where Pridament indicated the circle drawn on the ground. Getting closer, it turned out a cable formed the circle. In four places, the cable met with small black boxes. Separate wires ran from the boxes to a generator and the computer.

"What's this?" Gwynn asked.

"A Prometheus circle. It's used for training new Anunnakis. If your power starts getting away from your control, I can activate the circle, and it will negate any Anunnaki's powers within its perimeter."

"How's it work?"

"Honestly, the science is a little beyond me. Something about wave canceling or something. The only thing you need to know is you don't have to worry about things getting out of control."

Gwynn stood in the center of the circle. Despite Pridament's assurances, his throat tightened with anxiety. He kept scanning the warehouse, waiting for Adrastia to make an appearance. He wasn't sure whether he considered it lucky or not she had yet to appear.

Pridament sat at the table and punched a few keys on the laptop. An electric hum buzzed around the warehouse. He stood up and approached the edge of the circle.

"So, there's a few things you should know. First off, the Veil is everywhere. Right now, you and I are standing in an abandoned warehouse. Also in this same spot, dozens of men are working. As well, it's an open field where animals are grazing. All those things and countless more are happening right here, right now. The thing keeping us all from crashing into one another is the Veil."

"You said the Veil is also where our...souls live?"

Pridament nodded. "Right. Think of it as a battery. The soul of a living thing is energy. If energy cannot be created or destroyed, it must come from somewhere and then return there when we die, correct?"

Gwynn shrugged.

"Well, the Veil is that place. Its energies give life. It is the power source of every cell in your body. Put out your left hand."

Gwynn hesitated but then put out his hand as Pridament asked. In a shift movement, Pridament pulled a knife from behind his back and slashed it across Gwynn's palm.

"Fuck! What the hell did you do that for?"

"First lesson," Pridament replied. "Use the Veil to heal yourself."

The cut stung like hell. "How do I do that?"

"On Halloween, a Taint attacked you and broke several of your ribs which in turn punctured you lungs. Yet you walked out of the hospital without even a scar several days later. Yesterday, Elaios beat you nearly to death, but now you're standing her without a bruise. How do you suppose that happened?"

"You said," Gwynn replied, "it was because of my connection to the Veil."

"Right. So tear the Veil now and will its energies to close the wound on your hand."

He'd only torn the Veil in moments of desperation. How did he leisurely tear into it?

Sensing his hesitation, Pridament said, "Imagine the Veil as a waterfall right in front of you. Then, plunge your arm in, breaking the flow. The symbols on your arm are your pass. The Veil will respond to it and your intent. Remember, the energies of the Veil are the same energies living within you. Your desire, your will, is born of that energy as well. Now, heal your hand."

Gwynn took a deep breath.

Tear the Veil.

He plunged his right arm ahead of him. Was it the image Pridament placed in his mind, or had it always felt this way? Maybe he lacked the words to explain. It *was* like plunging his hand through water. At first, some resistance, then as his hand passed through, a chill ran along his arm. But once his hand pushed through, warmth brushed his fingertips. The energy of the Veil rippled up his arm.

Use my will...?

He imagined the energy moving from his right arm, passing through his torso and then down his left arm. The energy pooled there, prompting his flesh to knit back together. The sensation of pins and needles danced across his hand.

"Enough," Pridament said. "Use your mind. Tell it to sever the connection."

Gwynn focused his thoughts. *Withdraw. Close.*

The tingling in his left hand ceased, and the warmth against his right stopped.

Pridament grabbed Gwynn's left hand and raked his thumb over the wound.

"Wait... What?" He inspected his palm. Pridament wiped the blood away, revealing new, pink, flesh. All evidence of the laceration vanished.

"Good," Pridament said. "Now, what about that sword you used last night? Can you show it to me?"

Gwynn tried to remember what he did. He tore the Veil again, this time willing the sword to appear. A bead of sweat broke from his forehead and traced down his cheek and jaw. No matter what he imagined, begged, or swore, the sword wouldn't reappear.

"Stop," Pridament said.

Gwynn willed the tear to close. "I don't know what's wrong. I swear. I did it last night."

"Most likely you were acting on instinct, desperation. It's not uncommon. You're having a bit of performance anxiety today."

"So what's the Viagra for an Anunnaki?"

Pridament shook his head with a smirk. "Practice my boy, practice. You should also know the weapon an Anunnaki draws from the Veil is personal. Most believe it represents the Anunnaki's inner nature. Even though it appeared to be a sword, don't be surprised if it has other abilities the more you use it."

"Do our weapons...have a mind of their own?"

"Sometimes it can seem that way." Pridament smiled. "It might appear to impart knowledge and skills unique to itself, but in reality, it's revealing a hidden part of ourselves."

"Mine made me...scary."

"Then there is a part of you that is scary. You'll need to learn to control it. It'll require practice to control. But too much practice is dangerous. We walk a fine line using our powers. Too little, and you're an average person. Too much, and you risk losing yourself. Over time, you must learn balance. You need to learn the point where you feel stronger and the point where you feel like you're being overwhelmed."

"Okay. Don't overdo it. Too much of a good thing is a bad thing. So what next?"

"We'll do more practice. Try to speed up your process of drawing energy from the Veil. Get you used to finding your breaking point. Then you can try and draw that sword again."

Gwynn spent the following hours practicing drawing energy from the Veil. After several sessions, he had to rest, allow the energies to subside. Pridament kept a close watch on him, watching for any abnormalities.

"When you've strengthened your abilities, you can eventually allow parts of your body to change," Pridament said. "The more you draw from the Veil, the more you become an image of your other self. Perhaps you'll have a very powerful hand, or legs that can run faster. Anunnakis have honed these techniques for years. But *you* shouldn't even try it right now."

The problem lies with letting too much in without being able to control it. If you do, you might never be able to go back. Do you understand?"

"I guess."

"For now, know if any part of you starts to look different as you draw energy from the Veil, you need to stop. That's getting to the point of danger."

The hours wore on. Pridament held up his hand. "I promised you'd be home by three, so we should call it a day."

Gwynn's muscles ached. The constant give and pull of energies left him ready to crawl back into his bed. He hoped whatever Fuyuko planned would require him to sit.

When they arrived at Gwynn's house, Pridament opened his window before pulling away.

"We'll need to do some more work tomorrow. You go back to school, right?"

"Yes."

"Then I'll meet you here *after* school. That thing over our head isn't going to wait forever."

Gwynn gave a half-hearted grunt of agreement and waved goodbye. When Pridament pulled out of sight, Gwynn made his way to the school.

He had no idea the vortex already grew tired of waiting.

Places You Can't Go Back To

Fuyuko stood waiting for Gwynn at the corner of the school grounds. She gave an angry look at her watch.

"You're late."

"Sorry," Gwynn huffed. He'd run all the way.

"He should still be inside. Come on."

Gwynn scanned the grounds for any teachers or students who might notice him.

"You know I'm not supposed to be on school grounds during my suspension, right?"

Fuyuko shrugged. "This is more important."

Gwynn followed Fuyuko into the school. Even though classes ended thirty minutes earlier, the halls were deserted.

"So who are we meeting?"

Fuyuko sighed. In that single gesture, Gwynn understood. She would not answer all his questions. Instead, she would take him to someone who could stomach the torrent of quandaries Gwynn had. *She's from Suture.* He felt no doubt.

"We're meeting someone who's better equipped to answer your questions."

There it was.

Gwynn followed her through the school. He found it odd how two days had passed, yet this place seemed like a relic from another lifetime. He'd never been comfortable here, but now he felt removed, above it. Why had he ever worried about the petty politics and social maneuvering? A world existed with things none of them could begin to understand. But he had started to. He'd become a part of it. Not one, large world, but millions of worlds. A multitude of universes, opening wide for him to explore and draw strength from. This place *was* beneath him.

They came to an office door. Fuyuko knocked and waited. Gwynn stole a glance at the nameplate on the door.

"Mr. Baker? We're here to see my English teacher?"

"He's much more than that," she said with a wink.

Fuyuko knocked again. After waiting another minute, she eased her ear toward the door. Her eyes and nose crinkled into an expression of puzzlement and she opened the door.

The office was empty.

Not empty, deserted.

Fuyuko went behind the desk and started opening drawers. She moved from drawer to drawer, getting more flustered with each failure to find anything.

"I don't understand." Her voice filled with anxiety. "I just spoke to him. I was sure that's why he was here. There...there's nothing left. He hasn't even left his teaching notes. Other than the name, it's like he's erased himself." She spoke the last bit in an ever-quieting voice. Terror crossed her face. "No. Oh no."

Someone cleared their throat behind Gwynn. He turned and found the principal, Mr. Davis, standing behind him.

"Students should not be in a teacher's office unsupervised," Mr. Davis said. Then he clamped his hand on Gwynn's shoulder. "Especially students who are suspended."

Mr. Davis' voice started to change. It filled with the sounds of breaking stones and the finish of his sentence ended in a guttural growl. Gwynn stood transfixed. The man he knew changed. The skin in Mr. Davis' shoulders bubbled and expanded. His face elongated and his teeth became jagged and too large for his mouth. The grip on Gwynn's shoulder increased in pressure.

Gwynn grimaced in pain, much more and he expected his shoulder would snap. Still, he couldn't break his gaze from the horror happening in front of him.

"Gwynn," Fuyuko yelled.

The sound of her voice snapped his senses back into place. He struggled against Mr. Davis' grip. The thing that used to be Mr. Davis did the closest thing to a smile its disfigured mouth would allow.

Fuyuko's feet smashed into the thing's face. It released its grip on Gwynn and fell backward. Fuyuko rolled away and got back on her feet next to Gwynn.

"Move," she yelled, and shoved him out the door.

Behind them, the monster howled. Gwynn thought if its mouth and teeth weren't so deformed, it might have been screaming obscenities.

Gwynn and Fuyuko made it a few steps when the world exploded in a hail of concrete. The two fell to the floor and covered their heads as rubble fell on them.

Gwynn twisted to see the creature hulking out of Mr. Baker's office. Its eyes were red and murderous.

Fuyuko scrambled through the dust and debris. Gwynn followed her lead.

They ran at full pace, twisting around hall corners.

"Tell me again why we don't fight him?" Gwynn asked.

"Too close. We need more space."

Behind them, the sound of smashing concrete and savage roars signaled the creature's pursuit.

Gwynn tried to lay out a map of the school in his head. He plotted the exits, the nearby rooms. Space, they needed space... He turned to Fuyuko. She had the same idea.

"Cafeteria," Gwynn said.

"Yes."

The cafeteria lay at the end of the hall. To get outside would require a few more halls. Not to mention letting the creature outside could prove a disaster.

The air sizzled. Fuyuko tore into the Veil and drew her spear. He tried to do the same but stumbled and failed to produce any result.

"Problem?" Fuyuko asked.

How did he tell her he had never torn the Veil while moving before?

"Give me a minute," Gwynn said.

He slammed into the doors of the cafeteria and burst into the large room that doubled as an auditorium space. A few kids surrounded a table playing cards.

"Get out of here," Gwynn yelled.

"Fuck off," one of them said while the others snickered.

Gwynn tore into the Veil. The energy gushed through his system. If he was fatigued from running, he didn't feel it any longer. His muscles tightened and rippled. He spun and pounded his fist on the closest table. A shower of wood shards filled the air.

"I said, get out," He bellowed in a voice he didn't recognize.

The kids scattered.

I'll never be able to come back here again. He realized that didn't matter anymore.

From the other side of the cafeteria doors came the sound of oncoming destruction.

"You'll need your weapon," Fuyuko said.

Gwynn plunged his arm into the Veil once more. Despite trying to picture the sword he held the night before, the Veil refused to heed his call.

The cafeteria door buckled.

"It's not coming." Gwynn tried to keep the rising panic from his voice.

Fuyuko's eyes probed him. "Call out to it."

"What?" Why couldn't she say something straight forward? Did she miss the threat of a huge monster about to pulverize them?

"Try tearing the Veil and call out to Xanthe."

Gwynn meant to question her, but the doors burst open, revealing the hulking mass of death beyond.

He tore the Veil again. *Xanthe.*

Dark mist snaked around and out from his hand. It took shape and gained mass. It took seconds, maybe less, for him to hold the sword again.

The Mr. Davis monster lumbered into the cafeteria. Its shoulders were broad and high, with its head hung low. In shape and posture, it resembled a fur–less gorilla. It bellowed and seized one of the tattered metal doors. The creature tore the door free of the last of its hinges and tossed it at Fuyuko. She didn't flinch. Instead, she dropped low to the ground, allowing the door to sail above her. The door just cleared her head, and she was back on her feet, charging at the creature. It swung at her, and she jumped toward the wall. She propelled from the wall back toward the beast, catching it across the eyes with her heel. Her momentum carried her past the monster. She landed on her feet and swept her spear forward, striking the beast low on the legs and tripping it backward. Gwynn rushed forward, bring his sword down against the monster's chest.

Too slow.

The thing swept its massive hand forward and crashed it against Gwynn's midsection. He huffed as something in his side gave. He slammed hard into the wall and crumpled on the floor.

The beast regained its footing. It moved with speed seemingly impossible given its size. Gwynn caught sight of its clawed hand crashing toward him and rolled away. A searing pain erupted in his side. He scrambled to his feet. His coat hung in tatters, and warm, slick blood ran down his side.

Fuyuko jumped on the creature's shoulders, trying to stab it in the head with her spear. It swatted her aside like an annoying bug and returned its attention to Gwynn. It charged forward, a murderous bellow erupting from its mouth.

Take to the air. Did he think it, or did someone say it to him?

As the beast bore down on him, Gwynn followed the suggestion and leaped into the air, spinning as he did so. The beast passed under him, as his sword came crashing down on its skull. The black blade passed straight through without effort.

The monster's momentum carried it forward, and it crashed with a sickening thud against the wall.

Gwynn landed on his feet, but a wave of weakness swept through him and he fell to his knees. Fuyuko limped up to him.

"Are you all right?" she asked.

"I don't know." Something was broken, and his side still oozed blood.

Gwynn closed his eyes and let the sword disperse back to the Veil. Then he tore into it and drew its power into him. The warmth rushed from his arm and coursed through his entire body. The flow of energy swept him along with it, feeling each of his organs. He followed the flow of his own blood, passing through his beating heart out to the extremities of his body. Gwynn sensed the broken rib and wounds. He moved with the energy of the Veil, surged them into the damaged areas of his body. He envisioned the energy as a thick substance acting as a form of cement, sealing the breaks in his rib and plugging the holes in his flesh.

"Gwynn," Fuyuko yelled and shook him.

Gwynn snapped his eyes open, the disconnect from his body sudden and jarring. His head swam like he'd stood up too fast.

"Stop the flow, Gwynn. You're drawing too much."

The meaning of her words got lost in a haze. The continued rush of warmth from the Veil made him aware he had yet to sever the connection. He composed himself, shook his head clear, which rewarded him with a stabbing pain, and closed the Veil. He hazarded a deep breath and felt content to find no sign of pain. Gwynn ran his hand along his side. There was still the blood that had spilled already, but no sign of any injury. He grinned.

"Idiot." Fuyuko punched his shoulder. Hard. "You could've gotten Veil drunk and then what good would you be?"

Gwynn started to protest, but Fuyuko grabbed his shoulder.

"We need to go," She said.

She looked over his shoulder. He turned in that direction as well, but Fuyuko stopped him.

"Trust me. We need to go." Her voice softened. "And you don't need to see."

Numbness made his limbs heavy, but he got to his feet and followed Fuyuko back through the ruined cafeteria doors. They wound their way through the debris of the monster's onslaught until they reached another hall that branched off and would take them to the outside doors.

"I killed him, didn't I?" Gwynn tasted bile.

"You protected yourself."

Gwynn shook. What kind of monster had _he_ become?

"I don't get it," Fuyuko said. "I don't feel a tear nearby. How would he have gotten enough of a dose to change like that?"

Terror swept through Gwynn as he recalled Pridament's words; Horrors of Biblical proportions.

"It's the vortex," he said.

"The what?"

Gwynn told Fuyuko what he knew, which sounded minuscule. It was enough to shake her.

"That should mean a full deployment," Fuyuko cried. "There's no way I should be here alone. And now Justinian's screwed off somewhere? What the hell is going on?"

"Wait. You're here alone? There aren't more of you Suture people?" Gwynn asked.

"No, it's just me." She stopped and gripped his shoulder. Thankfully, not as hard as the monster. "Wait, how do you know about Suture?"

They moved away from the school and took shelter in a walkway.

"I'll explain later. Do you have a cell phone?"

Fuyuko handed him her phone. Gwynn rooted in his pockets and found Pridament's crumpled card. Another of Life's ironies—remember the card but not his own cell phone. He dialed the numbers and waited.

"Hello?" Pridament answered on the other side.

"It's Gwynn. It's happening. We can't wait anymore. Can you pick me up?"

Gwynn told Pridament where to meet them and hung up the phone.

"Who was that?" Fuyuko asked.

"The man I told you about; the one helping me."

"Who is he?"

"His name's Pridament," Gwynn said.

Fuyuko tore into the Veil and drew her spear.

Gwynn held up his hands. "What's that for?"

Fuyuko grit her teeth. "Pridament is one of the Fallen."

Questions of Trust

Gwynn looked to the end of the walkway in response to the high–pitched screeching of tires.

"Gwynn, what the hell—" Pridament said as he exited his car.

From the corner of his eye, Gwynn detected movement. He didn't think, just reacted. His hand shot out and grabbed Fuyuko's leg. He swung her down against the ground. The wind escaped her in a huff, and her spear fell from her hands. Gwynn tore into the Veil.

Xanthe.

The sword heeded his call, and before she could react, the tip pointed at her throat.

Fuyuko's eyes burned with hatred. "Do you know what you're doing?"

"No. I have no idea. Every time I turn around someone isn't what they say they are. Every time I think I have a handle on this, something changes. Everyone needs to stop and be straight with me." Gwynn shot a brief glance at Pridament; he wanted the old man to know he meant him as well.

"Can I let you up, or are you going to try and kill Pridament again?" Fuyuko stared.

"Stand down, Gwynn," Pridament said. "I can take care of myself if she chooses to attack me."

Gwynn stepped back and let Xanthe flow back into the Veil. Fuyuko made no attempt to move.

"Do you know why she was trying to kill you?" Gwynn asked.

Pridament stood motionless. Gwynn couldn't read anything in the man's expression. A deep breath and sigh broke the statue–like stance.

"Because I used to be a member of the Fallen."

"Was? No one leaves the Fallen." Fuyuko got to her feet.

"It's true, not many leave. The people who join them now believe in their cause to the point of fanaticism." Pridament's voice grew quieter, "It wasn't like that in the beginning."

"And you're different?" Every word from Fuyuko's mouth dripped venom.

The sound of sirens flying past drowned them.

Pridament glared at Fuyuko. "I joined the Fallen for my own reasons. When I realized what they were truly doing, I left."

"Too convenient."

Anxiety rose like acid from his gut. "Really, I don't give a shit. He's saved my life, and so have you. Right now, you stand about even in my books. What's more important is the fact my fucking principal turned into a monster and tore my school up."

"What?"

Gwynn gave Pridament a brief version of the events since they were last together. "It's happening, isn't it?"

Pridament was grim. "It sounds like it." He then said to Fuyuko, "You're from Suture?"

"Yes," she grumbled.

"So there's a team in place to stop this?"

A tremble passed up her spine. She remained silent, refusing to meet Pridament's eyes.

"I guess not," Pridament said. "I don't understand."

"What's there to understand? She's alone. Suture is busy or doesn't give a shit. So either we stop this, or we're all dead."

"Are you up to this?" Pridament asked Gwynn.

How did Gwynn answer? No, he wasn't ready. He had powers he didn't understand, let alone know how to use. But if Pridament told him the truth, if Pridament could even be trusted, only Gwynn could close the vortex.

"There's no other option," Gwynn said.

Gwynn turned to Fuyuko. "We could use your help."

Fuyuko looked beyond Gwynn to Pridament. She calculated and weighed her options. She turned her head and refused to meet Gwynn's eyes any further.

"Fine." Gwynn moved toward Pridament. "Let's get moving."

***

They sped down Dixie Road. Through Pridament's coaching, Gwynn studied the vortex above and spotted two tendrils extending down from it.

"Those will be the two tears feeding it. We close those, we close the vortex," Pridament said.

They were heading toward the first one now.

"I need your phone," Gwynn said.

"Who are you calling?"

"Jaimie."

With each passing ring, the knots in Gwynn's stomach tightened. If Jaimie left work already, it meant she wouldn't pick up again until she got home. One ring, then a second, then a third, Gwynn's finger hovered above the disconnect button when Jaimie's voice answered.

"Jaimie, it's Gwynn. Where are you?"

"About to leave work. Sorry, I was running late."

The knot in his chest lessened. "No, that's a good thing. Jaimie, you can't come home."

After a long pause, she asked, "Why? What's happening Gwynn?"

"I don't know how much Pridament told you, but trust me; it's safer if you stay away for a day or two."

"But—"

"Please," Gwynn's voice verged on a sob. "If you've ever trusted me, if you love me even half as much as I love you, please, you need to stay away."

"Gwynn, you're scaring me."

"It'll be fine. I'll be fine." Gwynn stung. He wanted to believe everything, including himself, would be all right. Saying it aloud felt like a lie. "There's something Pridament and I have to do. It would be a lot easier if I knew you weren't in town."

Another pause. He imagined her twirling a stray brown curl of her hair, her jaw set. "Okay Gwynn, I'll stay out of town. But I expect to hear from you soon."

"That's fine. Thanks, Jaimie, I'll call you."

Gwynn handed the phone back to Pridament.

"You think she'll listen?" Pridament asked.

"I hope so. If people are going to start changing into monsters, I don't want her anywhere near this place." As the full impact of what he'd said hit him, his stomach sickened. "Oh God."

"What?"

"Sophia." *How the hell did I forget Sophia?* "She's still here, in the hospital."

"I know you care about the girl, but she's in a locked down part of the hospital. I think she's as safe as can be staying there."

Gwynn chewed on his lip. "I hope you're right."

"Right now we need to focus on closing that vortex. No matter where people are if that thing stays open, they're all doomed."

"You're right," He said it, he knew the truth of it, but Gwynn still hated it. Knowing Jaimie was out of town made him feel better, but now thoughts of Sophia preoccupied him. He tried to get his mind to switch gears and searched for a new topic to discuss with the stranger who had become his mentor. "Hey, why didn't you tell me about the secret word to call a weapon from the Veil?"

"What do you mean?" Pridament's expression said, *you're talking crazy.*

"When I was fighting Mr..." No, he couldn't think of it as Mr. Davis. "That monster at the school, I tried to call the sword I told you about from last night. No matter what I thought or concentrated on, it wouldn't come. Then Fuyuko gave me a word to call it, and it worked."

Pridament frowned. "Unless that's some kind of Suture thing, I've never heard of it. Like I told you, an Anunnaki's weapon is a part of their soul. Most do have names, but they're personal and only known to the Anunnaki themselves. Are you sure you didn't call it by name last night? It's usually during the first summoning such a thing presents itself."

"I'm sure. I'd never heard the word Xanthe before Fuyuko said it to me. So you're saying Fuyuko told me the sword's name? How would she know?"

"I have no idea." Concern filled Pridament's voice. "Where did you meet her?"

Gwynn told Pridament about his experiences with Fuyuko.

"What are you thinking?" Gwynn asked.

"What do you mean?"

"The look on your face. You're thinking something, I can tell."

Pridament shot a quick glance at Gwynn. "I believe you were right. We should go see Sophia."

"Why the sudden change?" The change of plans should've made him happy—it was what he wanted. But the suddenness of Pridament's decision bothered him. "I mean, the end of the world versus visiting Sophia? I thought you said there was no choice."

"I don't think we're quite at the apocalypse yet." He didn't sound convinced. "I need to see something for myself. Hang on."

Pridament took a sharp turn and headed west toward the hospital.

"Can I ask the exact reason for your change of heart?"

Pridament's jaw set and his eyes were angry. "I told you before—I thought Sophia had a plan. She gained some foresight into events. Now, I have to wonder if someone else is using that information too. Someone's playing the game knowing everyone else's hand. It's time we got a peek at the deck too."

Shaping Reality

A dream held Sophia Murray captive. Or was it reality? The world was filled with dreamscape imagery, and dreams were too real to be comforting. So did it matter? How many years had dreams been real? When did she start rising from bed with the day's events already known?

The answer came easily—she was eight.

The first dream, the one etched into her memory, the one about the boy. The boy in the car. The crash. All that happened afterward. She woke from the dream exhausted and chilled from sweat. She lay in bed wishing for her head to stop throbbing and her breathing not to be so hard.

Why did I dream that? She said a little prayer she would never dream it again.

That morning, she sat at the kitchen table, pushing the last Cheerio around her bowl, contemplating whether it should suffer the fate of its friends or be the sole survivor of the breakfast massacre. She shuddered and pushed the bowl aside.

"Good morning, Princess," her dad said. As always, he wore a smile and moved with an easy grace suggesting he'd been awake for some time. She couldn't remember a single time her father rushed around in the morning. Had he conditioned himself never to be late, or did the time he arrived at the office not matter? She could never decide.

He paused to look at her, signs of concern replacing his smile. "What's wrong sweetheart? Did you not sleep?"

She told him about the dream. All of it. A stream of words tumbling forward of their own will. Even the worst of it, the part frightening her most, the part making her question how her mind even conceived of the thing, fell out. "I couldn't sleep after that," she finished. Years later, she would ask herself why she told him the whole dream. Why not say, "I had a nightmare and couldn't sleep?"

Her dad stood and regarded her for a few moments. He then sat at the table across from her, putting his briefcase on the floor beside him. His jaw set, pressing his mouth into a straight line. She could feel his probing eyes on her skin. "Have you ever dreamed like this before?"

"No." She shook her head emphatically.

"You say it felt real? When you first woke up the thing scaring you most was the certainty it happened?"

Sophia shifted in her seat. Her dad had always been so warm and supportive. The man across the table seemed different. His eyes held a hungry anticipation.

"Yeah," she said. "I guess so." *He thinks I'm crazy. That's why he's different.*

His smile returned, though his eyes were still wrong. "I'm sure it's nothing to worry about. You probably watched something you shouldn't have."

Sophia opened her mouth to argue, but something told her to let the conversation end.

"Sophia?"

"Yes, Daddy?"

"If you have any more dreams that make you feel that way; you know, like they were real? Let me know, okay?"

She nodded.

And she told him. They were less frequent at first. In the following two months, she had four more odd dreams. None of them made sense to her, but none frightened her like the one with the boy.

Five months after the first dream, she learned the boy's name, Gwynn Dormath.

She walked into her classroom and saw him sitting at the back. Instinct told her to run, but curiosity kept her there. Eight years old and here sat her nightmare given flesh. She spent the day glancing to where he sat. He made no attempt to be friends with any of his classmates. Even stranger, none of them seemed in a hurry to end the boy's silence.

When Sophia wasn't looking at Gwynn, she searched her classmates, wondering when one of them would force the boy to interact. But none of them approached him. The first day ended without incident, and she raced home.

Don't mention the boy, a part of her cautioned. But keeping it locked within made her feel nauseous. She hoped her daddy would have answers. She hoped he wouldn't think she lost her mind.

She found her father sitting at the kitchen table.

She couldn't recall if he went to work that morning or not.

"Daddy?"

"What's up, Princess?" He read a stack of papers. To Sophia, they appeared business related–eight–and–a–half by eleven, and white, filled with black type. He laid them on the table face down. A nagging doubt ate at her. *This is my daddy*, she reasoned with herself, *he'll know what's going on. He'll believe me.*

No matter how much she reassured herself, her voice still shook as she spoke. "Something happened at school today. I think, I mean, I'm sure, I saw the boy from my dream. You remember the one?"

For a brief moment, he wore an expression that disturbed her. If she hadn't been probing his face for any sign of reaction, she might have missed it. Now, so many years later, trapped in dreams, she understood. He wasn't surprised. He knew. He'd been happy.

The past faded and her mind returned to the world of the now.

They would arrive soon. About now, they would be at the hospital administration office, seeking to have her released to their care. They would succeed and come for her.

Tumbling, back to the world in the past.

The seventh grade with Gwynn and Eric Haze.

Haze had chased her for a while. He was pompous and often cruel to others he thought beneath him. But school involved politics and outright spurning its most desired boy equaled social suicide. So she played coy, dodging his advances with an athletic prowess besting Eric's grandest performance on the ball field. That day, the day when she started to understand her dreams, Eric wasn't playing. He cornered her in the hall with a frightening persistence.

"Not now, Eric," she said, giving eyes intended to make him fade back.

"No, Sophia, right now. You know you and I are perfect for each other. We rule this school already. C'mon, you aren't going to find anyone in this place better than me."

"Then I guess I better switch schools." It tumbled out. Those words, and the look in Eric's eyes, triggered her memory. She dreamt this a few nights before.

Eric grabbed her arm too hard. She let out a stifled cry.

"Let her go."

She knew who it would be.

"This is none of your business, Gwynn. Screw off."

"She said to leave her alone. Maybe *you* should screw off, Eric."

It was the longest conversation she heard Gwynn have with anyone in the school. It also followed the dream, word for word. She knew what came next. Not only because of the dream, but because of Eric's predictability. He didn't respond with words. His fist flew into Gwynn's face, and the boy crumpled to the ground. Sophia's impulse was to grab Eric, pull him away from Gwynn, like in the dream. And in the dream, Eric hit her. And then Gwynn...

Sophia held herself in place. She said a silent apology to Gwynn.

Eric leaned toward him. "So what do you have to say now, eh, hero?"

A voice bellowed from behind them. "Mr. Haze."

In the dream, the principal said something different. In the dream, his voice hadn't sounded angry; it was stretched thin and filled with horror. Gwynn still sat on the floor, blood flowing from his nose. She waited, but nothing happened. It hit her then; she controlled the outcome. Her dreams, as much as they seemed to see the future, were not set. She could change them.

The principal took Eric to the office. Gwynn waved off assistance and got to his feet. Sophia wanted to say something. She wanted to tell him about the dreams. About her pity for him—alone and not even knowing why.

"Thanks." It was all she could manage.

"You're welcome."

Gwynn said nothing else to her. He didn't even smile. Yet as he walked away from her, she felt pulled toward him. It wasn't until later, at home, alone in her room, she understood. Both hid a side of themselves. Both of them wore masks to conceal the horrors. Maybe he could sympathize with her situation. Lying on her bed, she let her mind drift to idle daydreams. In them, she and Gwynn were a couple. When she had a dream, she sat down and talked to him about it instead of her dad. He never had that hungry appearance in his eyes like her father now did. Instead, he helped her figure out what it meant. Together they used the knowledge her dreams contained to help people. Maybe she would one-day dream of a way to solve the world's problems. Maybe this curse might turn out to be a blessing. In warm daydreams of support and love, she fell asleep.

Sophia awoke some time later, soaked in sweat. As her eyes became accustomed to the dark of her room, her breathing slowed, and she made a decision. To avoid this dream from coming true, she couldn't be with Gwynn.

She shifted back to the present.

The men were at the double doors, her mother in the waiting room. Her mom would confront them, causing a few minutes of delay. But as always, she would relent. Sophia felt no anger toward her mother. If anything, she pitied her. Like Gwynn, something inside her mom was broken. Unlike Gwynn, her mother's injury made her compliant, a willing pawn in the greater schemes circling her.

Then, the world of the past.

Asking Gwynn out on Halloween made her feel conflicted. A part of her felt guilty—he would walk a difficult path because of her. But everything she dreamt told her one simple thing; Gwynn had to awaken. She almost relented when he said they could leave. Standing in the coffee shop parking lot, his simple offer reminded her why she wanted to be with him. The sound of his voice, the conviction, the sincerity. She could have left with him. Perhaps she was wrong. Maybe this one time her dreams lied. No. That only happened in fairy tales. Only one path led to the future...that she couldn't see. But because of what she'd done, and this last step, she knew it existed. That was enough.

Now, the occurring world.

The men arrived. The door to her room swung open. Two large men, dressed like paramedics, came inside. Sophia struggled through the haze separating her from the world outside her mind and focused on the man who came in behind the other two.

"Hello, Daddy."

19

The Blood of Others

Gwynn and Pridament arrived at the hospital.

"What the hell?"

The sounds of sirens filled the air. Police in full riot gear blocked every entrance they passed.

Gwynn's head swam. He was quick to agree with Pridament they should see Sophia, but now, everything seemed to be falling apart. "It's happening, isn't it?"

"I'm thinking so, yes."

"We should go close the tear. We'll never get in past the cops."

Pridament shook his head. "No. Sophia is a seer, I'm sure of it. I think she's been feeding information about her visions to someone who's been using them to manipulate events. I'd rather try and find out what's going on."

"So we find out after the vortex has been shut."

Pridament locked his gaze with Gwynn's. Something dark and dangerous filled his eyes. "Someone has set this up, Gwynn. Someone wants this to happen. What if Sophia's already told them we're coming to close the tear? What if we're walking into a trap? I'd like to find out first."

Gwynn searched deep in Pridament's eyes. He scanned for any sign of a lie. At the same time, he searched his own memories of the girl. Why did he feel drawn to her? Was she having visions of him? Had she been betraying him all these years?

Gwynn drew a deep breath. "So how do we get in?"

Pridament motioned for Gwynn to follow. The two made their way around to the side of the hospital where the walls were sheltered by a growth of trees.

"We need to fold."

Gwynn guessed his expression betrayed his lack of knowledge.

Pridament sighed. "Someday you'll know the full extent of your abilities, and you'll shake your head that you could ever be so ignorant."

To hell with the Veil, Gwynn fumed, *maybe I'll tear a new hole in you.* Ignorant? Damn right. Maybe he wouldn't be if people stopped telling him half the truth. The words hung on his lips when Pridament held his hand up, indicating Gwynn should remain quiet.

"I'm sorry." His voice was filled with sympathy. "Hear me out. The average person sees the world as a string of places with space between. In reality, the world is like a series of dots on a piece of paper. If you exert enough force, you can fold the paper, so the points that were apart now occupy the same space. Do you understand?"

"It's a little too Star Trek for me," Gwynn said.

"Never mind. Just don't let go of my hand, no matter what." The '*no matter what*' held a terrifying intensity.

Gwynn nodded and clutched Pridament's hand.

With his free hand, Pridament reached out into the air. With his arm extended, the sleeve of his jacket pulled back exposing a section of his wrist, allowing Gwynn to see some of the runes trailing along Pridament's forearm. The runes began to flow as fresh ink exposed to water. They shifted on Pridament's flesh until a new pattern of symbols appeared. Once they stopped moving and assumed a set shape, electricity prickled at his skin. Ahead of them, the world yawned open. He couldn't see what lay beyond, but the immediate layer below the tear crackled with bolts of light crisscrossing along the opening.

"You're kidding, right?"

"Remember," Pridament said, "Don't let go of my hand."

Not a chance.

Pridament inched forward. As his hand passed through the tear, it hissed and spat. Gwynn couldn't see Pridament's face but saw no indication of flinching or pain. The bulk of Pridament disappeared, yet Gwynn still felt a firm grip on his hand.

Pridament's grip increased to the point where the bones of Gwynn's hand would shatter. He cried out. But Pridament couldn't hear, and his crushed hand already entered the tear. His arm sank deeper, causing the pressure to dash ahead of it. Soon, it threatened to pass from his arm into his torso. Gwynn started to take gulps of air. Had he let go of Pridament's hand? What would happen if he did? The pain reached his chest. His rib cage threatened to buckle and collapse. A series of blinding colored spots crashed across his vision. He couldn't breathe. He couldn't scream. His stomach slammed against his throat and his vision darkened. He hoped he would live to see tomorrow. Despite Pridament's assurances, hope quickly evaporated.

***

"Hold her down."

Sophia thrashed.

"I've got it. Hold on."

Something jabbed her in the shoulder. She twisted her head to see a large needle withdrawing from her flesh.

"Keep holding her. It should take effect in a minute."

The visions began to clear. The realities of what passed, and what may yet come, began to melt away. At last, she had only the now.

"Daddy?"

Mr. Murray helped her up. "It's okay Sophia; we've come to take you somewhere they can help."

"What did you give me?"

"It's a new medicine. We're going to take you to the hospital that developed it."

Sophia drew a deep breath. He was here. Her father. As she planned. One more thing to do.

"Dad, is Mom here?"

"Yes, she's in the waiting room."

"Could I have a moment with her alone?"

His eyes filled with suspicion. She had to act quickly, or she'd lose her chance.

"Dad, you know Mom won't want you to take me somewhere else. Let me talk to her, show her how much better the medicine made me. It'll make things easier."

He paused. Had she said the right words? She couldn't remember the exact ones that worked in her dream.

Her dad patted her shoulder. "You're probably right. She can be difficult. I'll go get her."

Mr. Murray left the room. The two men dressed as paramedics stayed, discomfort evident in their eyes. How would they react if she told them what was going to happen? Would they run from the room?

Her dad returned with her mom.

"Just a couple minutes alone, okay?" her dad said.

The men left the room.

Sophia threw her arms around her mom's neck.

"Mom, we don't have much time. You need to listen very carefully."

Confusion painted her mother's face. "Sophia, is it really you? Are you all right?"

"I'm okay, Mom. Yes. Please, we don't have much time. If you love me, if you were only going to listen to me once in your life, now's the time. When Dad and I leave, you need to go into the waiting room and stay there until someone tells you it's safe to come out."

"What? I don't understand."

"Please, Mom, I'm begging you. Stay there until the police come and say 'It's safe to come out now miss.'"

"No. I'm coming with you. There's no way I'm letting them take you without me."

Motherly instincts. Of all times, why did she have to have them now?

I could hurt her. Say all sorts of hurtful things that make her leave me alone. She took a deep breath. *Is that how I want things to end between us?*

"Do you love me?" Sophia asked.

Her mother's eyes were wet. She stroked her hand along Sophia's cheek.

"You know I do sweetheart. That's why—"

"Do you believe in me?"

Her mother looked stricken. "I...do. Yes, always."

"Then do what I'm asking you to do. I love you too, and I need to know I can trust you."

Her mother sighed. "Okay. I will." She didn't sound happy about it, but Sophia felt convinced she would keep her word. "What about you? Why wouldn't it be safe?"

"I'll be fine." She took her mother's hand. "*I'll be fine*. Just do what I ask. Please?"

"Okay sweetheart." Her mom kissed her forehead. "I love you."

"Love you too."

Sophia knocked on the door. Her dad and the other men came in. "All good?" her father asked.

Sophia nodded. She squeezed her mom's hand tight. "I'll see you soon mom."

The paramedics guided Sophia to a wheelchair. As she and the men went down the hall, she turned. Her mom went back into the waiting room. The pieces fell into place. She should be frightened. Instead, a sense of calm came over her. Her plan was working. Just a little further.

They passed through the doors of the psych word. Sophia counted the paces. Maybe another hundred feet. Step by step, moment by moment. A couple more.

A roar.

They were here.

***

Gwynn lay on the ground sputtering. He still held Pridament's hand in a viselike grip. His insides were on fire and dry, heaving, coughs, racked his whole body.

"Yeah, I should've warned you kid; the first time sucks."

In his mind, Gwynn ran through a myriad of curses and expletives he should spout but managed only a whimper.

"Try tearing into the Veil and draw a little energy out. That should help."

Gwynn stretched his fingers and flexed them. He summoned an image of the Veil, a tangible curtain, and plunged his fingers inside. A rush of power flowed into him. His limbs, feeling starved, were nourished.

Nausea passed, and Gwynn managed to sit up without barfing.

"Where are we?" he asked.

"Utility closet. I scoped out the hospital for a possible entry point. This was the best I could find."

"What did you do?"

"Folded. It's somewhat unpleasant to do, but it's useful. The trick is, you have to know exactly where you're going, or you could get lost in the Veil."

"And if that happened?" Gwynn asked.

A grim look painted his face. "If you enjoy living, don't do it."

Pridament moved to the door and eased it open a crack. "We should get moving. Sooner we speak to Sophia, the sooner we can figure out how we're going to close those tears."

Pridament slid out the door into the hall. Gwynn eased his way back to his feet. He prepared for a wave of nausea, or weakness in his limbs. Much to his delight, he found his body responded in a more than admirable way. He followed Pridament out into the hall.

Weakness flooded his limbs.

Not from the folding, but from the destruction facing him.

Large gashes exposed the innards of the hospital walls. Sparks flew from the ceiling lights, many of which hung by frayed wires or were smashed on the floor. A city of several hundred thousand people. A single hospital to serve them all and not a person in sight.

Swear. Cry. Ask a million questions. Gwynn's mind and mouth worked hard trying to reconcile an appropriate response. Neither could agree.

"They're here," Pridament replied to Gwynn's questioning expression. Two words. Two syllables.

It explained everything.

"Call your sword," Pridament said.

Xanthe.

The reassuring weight of Xanthe filled his hand, answering his call. The sword's consciousness slithered up his arm, a serpent carrying the fruit of knowledge. His fear evaporated. The tools to deliver death granted. Pridament drew his staff from the Veil.

Pridament motioned for Gwynn to follow.

The hall ended with a choice of directions—left or right.

To their right, sounds of monstrous roars and clashing of weapons. To the left, the way to the psych ward and Sophia.

Pridament probed Gwynn, a question in Pridament's eyes, *Go help, or go to Sophia?*

Gwynn motioned to the right. What was the sense of seeing Sophia if he couldn't look her in the eye?

They inched their way down the hall, the sounds of monsters and men growing louder.

The air filled with familiar electricity.

"Anunnakis?" Gwynn asked.

Pridament shrugged, but his pace quickened.

Drywall, dust, and metal rained down as a wall exploded next to them.

A creature similar to Mr. Davis' transformation stood amidst the ruins and let out a roar.

Pridament's staff caught the beast across the jaw, sending it stumbling backward.

"Gwynn," a voice called. A soft, familiar, feminine voice.

He saw her on the other side of the wall. Sophia. His desire to see her, to protect her, drove him forward. Xanthe, the manifestation of the darkest parts of his soul, guided him. He moved low and fast along the ground, the tip of Xanthe catching the monster below its waist. With a quick upward flick of his wrist, Gwynn ended the menace.

He ran to Sophia.

An unseen force slammed into him and shoved him backward.

"Sorry Gwynn, not the time for reunions," the familiar voice of Mr. Murray said.

Another of the beasts lay at Mr. Murray's feet, while two men dressed as paramedics fought with another.

"Justinian," Pridament called.

Mr. Murray regarded Pridament. "Who let the Fallen in?"

"You know I'm not, Justinian."

"Of course cousin, I know very well who *you* are." With a nod toward Gwynn, he added, "Does he?"

No time for answers. The ceiling shattered above them in a hailstorm of dust and plaster.

Instinct, perhaps born of Xanthe, yelled, *Move.*

Gwynn hurled himself back onto his hands and propelled backward ten feet. A clawed hand crashed through the air his head previously occupied.

Back on his feet. Steady, breathing slow and controlled.

Strike.

With a cry, Gwynn plunged into the fray. Xanthe sang as it hacked through the air, claiming the arm with lethal intent.

Something howled in the haze.

No stopping. Low, out of reach of the other hand shooting out searching for a target. No injury now, just the end. Xanthe bit deep into flesh. There seemed little resistance as Gwynn dragged the blade upward, cleaving the beast in two.

Do not stop.

He twisted to the left, avoiding a killing blow as another beast descended. A quick spin and the monster's head fell free.

Gwynn stumbled on something on the floor. He paused long enough to see it was the torn remains of one of the men dressed as a paramedic.

No matter what Xanthe pumped through his system, he couldn't help but feel convulsions run through his stomach.

A momentary pause.

A human reaction to human death.

Mistake.

The back of a hand caught Gwynn in the midsection slamming him back first into the wall.

The air in his lungs rushed out of him. Stars filled his vision. Because it screamed for him to hang on, he managed not to drop Xanthe.

Something else hit him. Softer. Nothing murderous in its actions. As he tumbled away, claws raked across the wall he previously leaned against.

Whatever, whoever, had slammed into him still hung on. Time dropped to a third of its normal speed. His body spun. No helping it, his fingers loosened around Xanthe, and the sword fell away, returning to the Veil.

Time returned to normalcy as his body hammered into the floor. He met the wall with a bang, the extra weight of his savior helped to increase the velocity.

Lying against the wall, feeling battered and broken, the person against him stirred. "Are you okay Gwynn?"

"Sophia?" He croaked.

Her face came into focus. "Hi."

Gwynn stroked a stray strand of hair from her face. "I'm sorry. I should've come for you sooner."

She shook her head, the smile never leaving her face. It was her. Sophia. His Sophia. Whatever visions plagued her before seemed to have fled. In their place, they left tranquility.

"Nope. You came at the time you were supposed to."

Her warm, soft lips touched his. The feeling of her gentle tongue entwining with his sent chills rocketing through his battered body. For the first time he could recall since death stole his parents, he felt alive and at peace.

Sophia leaned back, breaking their connection, so he could see her face. She wore a radiant smile. His angel, come to deliver him from this life of pain. She reached up and stroked her hand from his temple down until she held him on his cheek.

"Gwynn. I'm so sorry. This isn't going to be easy for you. This is important. What happened to your parents wasn't your fault. You need to remember it, believe it. When you take her hand, you'll know you're ready."

Was she talking gibberish again? Her words made no sense to him. "I don't understand."

"You will." She gave him a quick kiss on his cheek. "Know, no matter how painful, how hard this world is, in another world, you and I are happy and in love. When you don't think you can go on, remember. Remember you alone have the power to protect them."

She stood up. Her skin seemed to glow. "Gwynn, know all those years you looked my way, I always looked back. I just wasn't confident enough to challenge fate."

She smiled, her eyes fixed on Gwynn.

She didn't break eye contact or stop smiling until the massive clawed hand smashed her into the wall. Her head made the sound of a pumpkin tossed from a height against concrete. When the monster released her, she crumpled to the ground like a rag doll, her once golden hair streaked with crimson.

"Sophia?" Gwynn croaked. "Sophia?" A sob tore his throat. Which then rose into a howl.

The monster turned its attention to Gwynn.

The howl turned into a roar.

And the roar tore the world to shreds.

***

Blood splashed across the wall feet from where Pridament stood. A wave of energy slammed into him. If he hadn't already drawn so much from the Veil, he knew he'd be dead. He struck the end of his staff against the ground and tore into the Veil. He drew energy, radiated it out from the staff, forming a defensive bubble around him. Once protected, he hazarded a glance to try to see the source of the devastation. Gwynn, kneeling over the broken body of Sophia Murray. His heart ached. First love should never end in tragedy.

Gwynn lost all control. His skin rippled. Anunnaki glyphs covered his flesh. The boy's eyes were blood red and shone like they were burning. He bent forward; his back bulged and swelled. Blood shot on the wall behind Gwynn as two leathery wings folded up and away from his back. Gwynn roared, and flame consumed the ceiling above him.

Sweat poured from Pridament's brow. No matter how powerful his shield, Gwynn would soon overwhelm his defenses and destroy him.

Gwynn screamed, howled and roared all at once. A cacophony of sounds of anguish tearing at the fabric of the world.

"You'll need to show him the truth."

A girl now stood next to him. How had she entered through his defenses? How had she gotten this close without the energies Gwynn unleashed destroying her?

She glanced at Pridament. Her eyes were green, alive with experience belying her seventeen-year-old appearance. A pale hand reached to him and rested on his shoulder.

"Force won't stop him now. Only something that shocks his mind will break this. You can do that, right?"

Pridament nodded.

The girl stepped forward, her black ruffled skirt flowing like a living thing around her. On top, she wore a white old Victorian style blouse. She passed through Pridament's shield unscathed and no matter the destruction raining down around her, she did not waver or come to any harm.

"Adrastia," Pridament called. She turned back to him and smiled. "Who are you?" he asked. She responded with a smile and shook her head 'No.'

She knelt in front of Gwynn and wrapped her arms around his neck. One hand crept up and caressed the top of his head.

"You'll be okay Gwynn." Pridament had the impression she whispered, yet he still heard her. "Someone's here to help. Someone you've been longing for. You need to look now Gwynn. You need to see who has come."

Over her shoulder, she said to Pridament, "Now."

For the second time in as many days, Pridament willed himself to return to his true form. Years ago, he adopted this face and became Pridament. Living became easier as someone else—a better way to run from his old life. Now, he hoped his shame might serve some good.

His cheekbones rose, and his chin narrowed. The world shifted in appearance as his eyes slid into a new position. Even his scalp tingled as the color of his hair changed. The first time was painful and frightening. But that day lay many lifetimes ago. Now it was nothing—another thing his body could do like breathing or clenching his fist.

The transformation complete, he looked to Gwynn and tried to hold the boy's eyes. It took a moment. Adrastia restrained Gwynn, keeping him from looking anywhere else. The world stopped. Had Pridament been right in trusting her? When Gwynn realized who stood in front of him, would it heighten his desire to destroy?

Gwynn's eyes widened. The moment where memory and reality collided evident in his face.

"It's all right Gwynn," Pridament said in a different voice. His true voice. "You can relax now son, let it go."

Tears started to stream down Gwynn's face. "Dad?"

The boy collapsed.

So Close, Yet Worlds Apart

A veil of haze obscured the world. Pain, stabbing pain, crashed through Gwynn's head. *Am I dying?*

Somewhere in the distance, a voice called him.

The blurs of color began to coalesce into shapes. The sounds were less distant.

"Gwynn, wake up."

Pridament's face came into focus. *His* face, the one Gwynn recognized as Pridament. But another existed. A face both frightening and warm.

"Have I been dreaming?" Gwynn asked.

"What part?" Pridament kept his tone soft as if he feared to push Gwynn's boundaries.

"We were in the hospital. I... I saw my dad and..."

The memory of Sophia hit his gut like a fist. He fell over the edge of the bed he lay in and wretched. Convulsions wracked his body. He emptied himself until nothing further would come. Even then, he still spasmed for some time.

"God, that's nasty," another voice. Female. For a moment, he dared to believe the impossible.

No. Dreams weren't coming true. He hoped his disappointment wouldn't hurt Fuyuko's feelings.

"I thought you abandoned us?"

She wouldn't meet his eyes—out of shame or revulsion?

"She heard about the commotion at the hospital," Pridament said, "and decided to check it out. Good thing for us too. I didn't have the strength to fold us out. She did it."

Gwynn mumbled his thanks. He rolled onto his back and recognized the ceiling. "Are we in my bedroom?"

"Yes," Pridament said. "Fuyuko folded us to the backyard."

"So it all happened." He turned on his side and his knees folded up under his chin. "Sophia is really..."

Neither of them answered, but the truth of it lay in their expressions.

"And you?" he asked Pridament. "Did I imagine you as well?"

Pridament turned to Fuyuko. "Do you think you could give us a few minutes?"

She hesitated. Gwynn couldn't imagine what might be going through her mind. But whatever she saw in Pridament's eyes convinced her.

"I'll be out in the hall if *either* of you need me." Her eyes made it clear she meant it mostly for Gwynn. "If he's able, we should do something about those tears. And soon."

When she left the room, Pridament turned to Gwynn. "Tell me what you remember about the day your parents died."

Gwynn tried to read Pridament's face. His eyes burned with the intensity of knowing some earth–altering secret. But like all those types of secrets, it weighed on him.

"We were moving. My mom and dad finished packing the car. The movers had already left. I said I wanted to take one last look at my bedroom."

"What did you do once you were in your room?"

"I locked my door. I tried hard to come up with a plan how I could stop them. I didn't want to leave. I had friends, a school I liked and where I felt I belonged. That house was my whole life."

"So what did you decide?" Pridament's anticipation appeared to grow.

"I went to my bedroom window. I opened it. I thought about running away. There was an old forest behind our house. I figured if I ran fast enough, I'd make it to the trees before my dad got into my room."

"But you didn't run away, did you?"

"No." Gwynn felt miserable. "When my dad came to the door, I hesitated. I mean, I sat there, torn what to do. But, I was afraid. I'd never been in the woods alone. I knew how angry my dad would be. I opened the door, and I went with them." Gwynn drew a long, ragged breath, "They died. I lived. But that's not what happened, is it? I mean, I saw it, didn't I? You... You're somehow my dad, right? Or was that a trick?"

Pridament sat back, his gaze falling to some distant point on the wall. "Let me tell you how I remember that day. Gwynn said he wanted to see his room one last time. I knew how upset the move made him, so I said he could. I waited a while, as it turns out, longer than I should have. I went to his room and knocked on the door. He didn't answer. I knocked again, called out to him to open the door. But there was nothing. I kicked the door open. He wasn't in the room. Instead, his window was open. I figured he'd run to the forest. It was the only place he could've gone without someone seeing him. I ran out, calling his name. His mom came with me. We searched for a while, and then called for help." A sob caught in Pridament's throat. "We never did find him."

"So what are you saying? You're not my dad?"

"Remember what I said about the world splitting? For whatever reason, the world split at that moment you sat in your room. In one world, you went with your parents, and their car crashed. In the other, you ran away and disappeared. I guess what I'm saying is," his shoulders sank, "I believe up to the point you were eight, I *was* your father. But for me, my son disappeared. I've been searching for him ever since."

"My parents died." Gwynn sat up straight, his fists gripping the sheets. "I've blamed myself. From what you're saying, it was my fault. If I'd run away, you both would've survived."

Pridament grabbed Gwynn by the shoulders. "Don't you dare say that. Don't you think I would gladly trade my life to know my son was safe and growing into a fine man? Yeah, your mom and I survived, our marriage didn't. On the second day, I found the tear in the Veil. I couldn't see it, but I felt it. It was huge, stronger than any I'd ever encountered. I begged Suture for help. They sent a Script who confirmed there was a tear, and from what they determined, Gwynn fell through it. My son was lost out there in some other world. I pleaded with them to help me search, but they didn't care. Their mission, as they told me, was to protect their world and only their world. When they refused to help, I turned to an organization called Ark. They were a group of Anunnakis who were crossing the Veil into other worlds. They were contracted by some wealthy men and women to search for a world they could escape to, should their current world become endangered."

"Ark? Let me guess—they became the Fallen."

"Yes. I had no idea. I helped them survey other worlds. I was ideal for the task because I could change my appearance. It meant I never worried about meeting myself or someone recognizing me in another world. All the time they led me to believe they were searching for my son while they carried out their mission. Soon though, it went bad. I found out what they were doing. I fled through the Veil, and I've been running ever since."

"Until you found me."

"At first, I thought maybe you were my son. Then I found out about your past, saw you were living with Jaimie. I knew then what happened. I mean, you have the same scar on your abdomen—"

"From when I got caught on the barbed wire at the Wilson's farm. Johnny had to see the abandoned house in the middle of the field."

"Right. And you wear this." Pridament pulled a chain from out of his shirt. There hung the same St. Christopher's medal that belonged to Gwynn's father.

"I don't know what to do now," Gwynn said. "I mean, you're my dad, but you're not. Where do we go from here?"

"I never meant to confuse things. I didn't know what else to do. You lost all control. You were...changing. I shocked you out of it. For now, I think I'll stay Pridament, your friend. Is that all right?"

Gwynn didn't know. How could he forget this? Still, he mourned his father for almost ten years. What type of son would he be if he substituted this other man? What Pridament said made sense. Gwynn lost his father like Pridament lost his son. And if they delayed any longer, this whole world would be lost. He quelled the churning in his stomach and steadied his voice.

"Yes. Stick with what we know. For now at least," Gwynn said.

Pridament nodded. He turned his head toward the door. "You can come in now Fuyuko," he called.

A moment passed, and then the girl returned to the room. "Are you finished?"

Was she listening? Suspicion was evident in Pridament's expression. Would he press her on it?

Pridament said nothing.

Even if she listened, would it matter?

"Can you stand up?" Fuyuko asked Gwynn.

Gwynn swung his feet over the side of his bed. He still wore the clothes beaten and dirtied in the fight at the hospital. He took care to avoid the puddle of sick he left on the floor. He needed to clean that, or Jaimie would kick his ass. He put some hesitant weight down, then a bit more, and then went for broke and stood erect. It never ceased to amaze him the damage he could sustain and yet some energy from the Veil repaired it all. Still, his back itched and burned for some reason.

"Sure," Gwynn said. "I can stand. Though walking might still be a problem."

"I'm going to get something to clean that floor. Jaimie'll kick your ass if she sees that," Pridament said. "You might want to change those clothes of yours too."

"I'll be downstairs," Fuyuko said. They both left Gwynn alone in his room. He looked at the bare walls. Why had he never seen the coldness of it? And Sophia... When it seemed things were going to happen between them. Did he still want to save this world when it felt as cold and barren as his room?

But Sophia knew. When she kissed him. When she stood up, she knew she would die. She orchestrated things for him to arrive at this moment. She hadn't sacrificed that much so he could give up.

He squared his shoulders, took a deep breath, and searched his closet for clothes suitable for saving the world.

***

Fuyuko waited for them in the kitchen. The gloom outside the window seemed too bright to be nighttime.

"Exactly how long was I out?" Gwynn asked.

"About thirteen hours or so," Pridament replied. "Fuyuko and I took shifts. She stayed with you for a few hours while I slept, then I finished out the night."

"So what's our next move?" She asked.

Pridament pulled out a chair and sat. "We resume the original plan. Find the last two tears feeding the vortex and shut them down." He turned his eyes on Gwynn. "Are you up for that?"

Gwynn pushed hard past the lump in his throat. "Because of them, Sophia's dead. Damn right I'm up for it."

"Then we're going to need some transportation. My car's still at the hospital, and I don't think we should be anywhere near there right now."

"I've got a car," Fuyuko said.

"You do? I always see you walking."

She blushed. "They insisted I take it. But, um, I'm not the greatest driver."

"No worries." Pridament rose from the chair. "I'll take the wheel. Gwynn, you're the navigator. Is the car at your place?"

Fuyuko nodded.

Gwynn turned from one to the other. "You two are suddenly getting along?"

"Don't worry about it. Let's just say we learned we could work together," Pridament said.

"C'mon," Fuyuko seemed almost excited. "I can fold us right into my living room."

Gwynn held up his hands pleadingly. "Can't we walk? I mean, please?"

Fuyuko and Pridament were not pleased with walking, but they didn't press Gwynn too hard.

Fuyuko sighed, "At least it's not that far a walk."

Fifteen minutes late, the three arrived at Fuyuko's house, loaded into the car, and took to the road.

Gwynn leaned forward so he could see the vortex out the front window.

"Head south on Dixie. When we get closer, I'll let you know."

"Will he be able to guide us there?" Fuyuko asked Pridament.

"Ever chase spotlights? Same thing."

It was more complicated than Pridament made out. First off, they were all exhausted. It took a few drives through the industrial complex to find the right building.

"This the one?" Pridament asked.

"Uh huh."

"Well then, I guess it's the three of us to save the world."

"Wait," Gwynn said. He turned to face Fuyuko in the back seat. "What about Mr. Baker? Were you ever able to get a hold of him?"

Pridament and Fuyuko exchanged a look.

"What is it?"

Pridament rested his hand on Gwynn's shoulder. "The man you saw at the hospital, Sophia's father? His name was Justinian. He was an Anunnaki with a unique ability. He could mimic any Anunnaki's power. The face changing bit he stole from me."

"Is that why he called you cousin? You're related?"

"No, not by blood. In any case, Fuyuko and I've talked. It turns out Justinian was also your teacher, Mr. Baker."

"I don't understand. Why?"

Fuyuko chimed in. "We're still not certain. Since Sophia was a seer and you're a Script, he could've been watching either one of you. Given the things we suspect Sophia told him, it's likely he was watching *both* of you."

"So what? Suture's behind everything?"

Pridament cleared his throat. "We're not sure if he was working for Suture, the Fallen, or even a third party. The only thing we know for sure is either he was orchestrating some larger scheme, or at the very least, he was a component of it."

"He's dead, isn't he?" They hadn't said it, but their voices made it plain. Not regret or remorse, but the frustration answers were beyond their grasp.

"I tried to save him, but one of the other Taints got in my way," Pridament said.

"Maybe that's a good sign."

Both Fuyuko and Pridament stared slack-jawed at Gwynn.

"Would you like to explain?" Fuyuko asked.

"It means Sophia didn't see everything. Or, even better, she didn't tell him everything. Otherwise, he wouldn't have been in that hospital."

"So you think Sophia covered for us? You think she knew what was coming but hid it so we could finish this without interference?" Pridament appeared skeptical.

"I know. It's a long shot. Maybe I'm hoping it's true because it means she cared about me. But I can't believe Justinian would be there if he knew he would die. So either we're in the clear cause she lied, or because she didn't see this far."

Pridament drew a deep breath, and his knuckles whitened as he gripped the steering wheel. "Well, hope's kept me going this long, why give up on her now?"

The three left the vehicle and went up to the warehouse. No signs of life or activity. The parking lot stood empty, and large shades blocked the office windows.

"There's something the two of you should know before we go in there," Pridament said.

"What?" Fuyuko and Gwynn said in tandem.

"It's the way the Fallen work. The tear at the old Cameron house was a naturally occurring tear. These two, though, they've been created within a particular relation to that tear to create the vortex."

"Are you saying an Anunnaki opened a tear on purpose?" Fuyuko asked.

"Yes."

"Wait." Lightning struck Gwynn. "If they opened those tears themselves and left them open, then they've been connected for a while like I was. That means—"

"They're not exactly human any longer. Truth is we have no idea what's going to happen when we enter that building."

Gwynn's resolve wavered. A deserted building and an Anunnaki mad with the Veil's power. But at the corner of his mind came a voice—soft and loving. It reminded him of two people who were in love, and he alone could protect them. Whether true or not, it reminded him of the one thing that mattered, the one need able to propel him to the lowest levels of hell if need be. Vengeance.

"Let's go."

The door to the main office complex was unlocked. Not good. Pridament and Fuyuko agreed. They eased their way into the building. The door slammed behind them, and they plunged into darkness.

The Truth Too Hard to Face

Gwynn asked, "Did anyone think to bring a flashlight?"

Silence answered him.

"Pridament? Fuyuko?"

Still nothing.

Gwynn called out again.

He yelled.

Nothing.

Gwynn started moving forward. The ground seemed odd, uneven.

A few more steps.

He stumbled, falling face first to the ground.

Instead of hitting cold concrete, his hands rested on soft grass. The smell of earth filled his nostrils.

"What the hell?"

A faint light illuminated the ground around him. The light filtered through what appeared to be trees. He scrambled to his feet and did a three-sixty. He appeared to be in the middle of a wooded area. From ahead, a brighter light cut through the trees. Gwynn moved toward it.

He climbed an embankment and found himself on a road—the bright light an oncoming car's headlights.

No, no.

The lights cut across him. Tires squealed, and metal tore. But he didn't wake up.

Minutes passed. Then movement where the car left the road. A small figure grappled its way up. In the moonlight, it took Gwynn a moment to recognize himself.

He wanted to call out to the boy. Was this how it happened? He couldn't remember leaving the car.

More movement caught his attention.

His father.

The older man called out to the younger Gwynn. "Stop, Gwynn. Come back. Your mother's hurt."

The boy turned around. From this distance, Gwynn shouldn't have seen the boy's eyes. But he could. They held nothing but cold rage.

"I don't care. Good. That's what you both get for making me leave my friends."

Gwynn could only imagine what the words were doing to his father, but they struck *him* like a knife in his chest.

His father advanced on the younger Gwynn. The man reached out to grab the child by the arm.

An explosion of light.

Gwynn slammed his eyes shut. It was like movie depictions of an atom bomb. He expected searing heat and his flesh torn from his bones. Instead, he felt nothing.

When the intensity of the light outside his eyelids subsided, he dared to open them.

At his feet lay his father. Broken. Dead.

The younger Gwynn stood motionless, white fire filling his eyes.

"No," Gwynn screamed. This wasn't how it happened.

He stole another glance at his father. When he turned back, his younger self stood in front of his face.

"This *is* how it happened," the boy said. His voice echoed and boomed like thunder. "Didn't they tell you? They found your father outside of the car. So were you. How do you suppose that happened?"

"No." Gwynn gave his head a violent shake, denying the horror in front of him. "No. This isn't what happened. I could never—"

"Stop lying to yourself. This is the truth you've hidden from all these years. You could never admit this reality. Why do you think you always woke up just after the crash? Why do you suppose you would never allow yourself to go forward? Because you couldn't face this. Now that you know, perhaps you'd like to do something about it?"

Gwynn didn't know what his younger self meant. Then he felt a familiar weight in his right hand. Xanthe.

"You should do the right thing. You are a murderer after all. End yourself, before anyone else has to suffer like your father."

***

Fuyuko fumbled around in the dark for hours.

She'd long given up trying to find Gwynn and Pridament. Initially, she turned around to open the door that should've been right behind her. But it wasn't. Now she blundered along, blind, alone, and forgetting why she even came to this place. She just wanted to find a way out.

Lights started going on around her. Bright, powerful spots. She braced herself.

"You seem to be failing this exercise, Fuyuko," a male voice said.

As he stepped from the shadows, she gasped.

"Paltar?"

"Who else would be evaluating you?"

Fuyuko's eyes grew accustomed to the lights. Not just Paltar, but the entire Ansuz team, including Jason, were present.

The sight of Jason made her heart leap. She wanted to tell him about everything that happened. Her need to have him hold her and say everything was fine verged on desperation.

But Jason did not seem pleased to see her.

Nor did anyone else.

"I don't understand," Fuyuko said. "What do you mean 'evaluating'?"

"This has been a test. Sending you out on your own, having you chase after that boy. Even having you end up here, all part of it. But you haven't scored too well. Especially since you've spent hours wandering around in the dark. I mean, did you ever think of trying the Veil for some aid? Or maybe that if you are attacking an enemy's stronghold, you should be prepared with things like a flashlight?"

"It all happened so fast. None of us—"

"Of course none of you did. The two men you came here with weren't going to come up with that. They were waiting to see what you would suggest."

"Why would they—"

"Because they were in on it. Do you honestly think something like this would happen without Suture being heavily involved? I mean, really, a vortex about to collapse the world and you believe we would send just *you*?"

"I thought it was odd, but a test?"

"Well, we don't let just anyone onto the Ansuz team. You need to prove yourself."

"I *have* proven myself." She lowered her voice, fighting back tears. "I went through all the training, completed five field missions, I even pulled a rabbit out of the hat."

"Yes, I heard about that." His expression said he didn't believe it. "I'd like to see it for myself."

Fuyuko looked at her teacher for a long time. He was there when she did it. Hadn't he been the first to pat her on the back? No. Maybe not. Her mind felt muddled. But she endured too much and pushed herself too hard making the Ansuz team. She wouldn't let it go.

She tore into the Veil.

Pulling a rabbit out of the hat, their slang term for materializing an actual being across the Veil. It was difficult. No, it verged on impossible. Unlike Curses, which were creatures who came through a tear of their own volition, these creatures were often extensions of the Anunnaki's abilities and, if done right, obeyed them.

She pushed harder into the Veil. Tearing the Veil as an Anunnaki was easy. To push all the way through, to tear deeper than the surface so the creature could come forward, required intense concentration.

Fuyuko willed the tear to widen and deepen. At the other end, something began to pull at her mind. Most failed at this point. One of three things happened; you severed the connection, you pulled the rabbit from the hat, or you lost your mind. Fuyuko wouldn't lose. In her mind, she pictured herself pulling on a fishing pole, reeling in the creature from the other side.

It resisted her.

She pulled harder.

Its consciousness touched her own—feral and angry. She didn't remember it being so mad before—as if she were doing it some great harm or injustice.

The tear extended from her arm down to the floor and up above her head. It yawned open, and the beast lumbered forth.

It hunched forward on its knuckles—roughly the shape of a gorilla though double the size. It snorted through large nostrils and regarded Fuyuko with huge yellow eyes. It shook—its long white hair moving in waves and ripples across its skin. Then it roared.

Fuyuko filled with horror. She wasn't in control.

The beast leaped away from her and tore into one of the Ansuz team. Someone screamed. Bodies scrambled anywhere for safety.

Paltar stood his ground. He tore into the Veil and drew his battle-axe. As the beast approached, he twisted in a smooth motion and cleaved its head in half.

The moans of the injured and the weeping for the dead filled the room.

Paltar approached Fuyuko. "Not only are you not worthy of the Ansuz team, but you also are not worthy of Suture. Perhaps you should do the honorable thing and fall on your spear."

Fuyuko couldn't remember pulling her spear from the Veil but now felt its weight in her hand. The sharpened tip beckoned to her, and she readied herself to answer the call.

**

The room went dark for a minute.

When the lights came back on, Pridament found himself alone. He made a quick scan of the space. No windows and no door behind him where it should've been.

He resisted the urge to call out to Gwynn or Fuyuko. Somehow, they were folded away from each other—most likely sent to differing areas of the warehouse.

Pridament tore into the Veil and called his staff. The heft of it helped to drive away some of the dread he felt for his lost companions. He gripped the staff tighter and drew a deep, slow, breath.

He was in a long, low-ceilinged, room littered with boxes. The fluorescent light in the ceiling flickered and sputtered, casting chaotic shadows across the walls and floor.

Pridament took slow, measured, steps toward the door at the other side. He paid particular attention to his balance, his gaze sweeping from one side of the room to the other.

He stopped. A deep hiss came from the right side of the room.

A shadow moved on the left.

Ahead of him, a stack of boxes fell.

Pridament swung his staff.

Behind.

Catching the Curse in the head, sending it flying hard against the wall.

Pridament twisted the ends of his staff in opposite directions and drew the two halves apart. Thin blades extended from either side. He waited for the Curse to make a move. Boxes flew in all directions where the creature landed. Something scuttled across the floor, sounding like a million cockroaches fleeing a fire.

The shadows shifted to his right.

Pridament attacked to the left.

The Curse howled as one of the blades slashed across its face.

Pridament took a clawed hand to the side—dagger–like nails digging trenches in his abdomen. With the warmth of blood coursing down his side, he cracked the Curse in its skull with the other end of his staff and threw himself away from its grasp. Pridament dashed for the door. Boxes tumbled all over the room. The room shook and tilted. He struggled to maintain his balance.

With a hiss, the Curse flung itself at him. Pridament ducked down and shoved his blades into the air, catching the Curse in the torso.

Momentum carried the monster forward. The blades cut a deep trough down its center, splashing the walls and Pridament with black tar. It crashed into the opposite wall and crumbled into a heap. Pridament sat on the floor puffing. When his heart ceased its threat of leaping out his throat, he stood and took a hesitant step toward the Curse. He kicked it hard and the thing crumbled to dust.

Pridament reassembled the staff and reached to turn the knob to exit. His heart stopped beating for the long moment between twisting the knob and finding out if the door would open. A satisfying click signaled his escape from the room.

Pridament found himself in a hallway. He hadn't inspected the building while outside, but based on the length of the hall, he assumed it ran the entire length.

Pridament inched his way along. Apart from the door he used to enter, one other door led off the hall. At the end, a set of stairs went up. When Pridament got to the door, he reached out to the knob. An electrical jolt bit his skin when he touched it. His gut seemed to react. He looked down the hall toward the stairs. After a minute of mental tug–o–war, he left the door alone and continued to the stairs.

From the bottom of the stairs came the soft whir of machinery.

He ascended, keeping his back toward the wall and his staff in a defensive position. The top of the stairs opened into a large room. His stomach tightened. He couldn't see the tear, but he could feel it.

A single machine occupied the room. It consisted of a large pod connected to several monitors. Pridament hazarded a glance in the pod and gasped. He tore at the cords and cables and fumbled his hand along the edge searching for some kind of release mechanism. A moment later a click and swoosh rewarded his efforts, and the pod lifted open.

"Gwynn," Pridament called.

The boy lay inside the pod, his upper torso stripped bare. Wires from the pod ran to numerous sensors attached to him. Pridament took quick stock of the boy. He was breathing, his skin color appeared normal. He had the scar on his abdomen.

But he wasn't wearing the St. Christopher medallion.

"Gwynn," Pridament shook him.

The boy's eyes fluttered for a moment and then crept open.

"Who are you?" Gwynn croaked.

"It's me. Pridament."

"I don't know you."

"What?" Pridament searched the boy's face. Had something happened to his memory? Or maybe... His heart pounded in his chest. Hope. He let his defense slide, revealing his real face.

"Dad?" Gwynn asked. "Oh my God, Dad?"

Gwynn sat up and threw his arms around Pridament's neck.

"All these years." There were tears in Gwynn's voice. "I'm so sorry. I'm so stupid. I ran away, I never meant to go far. I never wanted to be gone so long."

Tears flowed down Pridament's face. "It's okay son, I forgive you. Everything's going to be all right. We need to get you out of here, close that tear, and find our way home. All right?"

Gwynn's eyes filled with fear. "It's too late Dad. We need to get out of here now."

Gwynn stumbled out of the pod. He drew a breath and then tore the Veil.

"C'mon Dad, we can leave this way." Gwynn held out his hand. "Take my hand, and we can be a family again."

Acceptance

Gwynn looked to Xanthe and then to the crumpled body of his father. He just needed to fall on the sword. No more suffering, no more hurting the ones he cared for. An end.

"You know it's the right thing to do," his younger self said.

He felt a light touch on his left shoulder. No one was there.

A familiar scent of blended fruits carried on the wind. It tugged at Gwynn's memory. Like an old VCR, the tape of his mind clicked and whirred in reverse. Sophia, smiling, telling him when he looked her way, she looked back.

"I was too afraid of fate," she said. She told him to take her hand. She said, "No matter what, always remember, what happened to you parents wasn't your fault."

The evidence lay in front of him. He killed his father.

"No matter what," the wind seemed to reply.

Gwynn gave his head a shake. The younger version of him stood stone-faced a few feet away.

"Somewhere, you and I are in love, untouched by all this madness." He would never forget her smile. "You need to protect them, Gwynn. Only you can."

Another soft touch on his right shoulder—different from the other. He turned, no longer alone.

"Adrastia."

Her lips curled into a smile, but her eyes showed disappointment. "Yours is not to be defeated by phantoms." She raised her arm and pointed.

They were further down the street. From this angle, Gwynn saw a tear in the Veil near the road. Something came out. A Curse.

The car came around the corner, catching the Curse in its headlights. Tires squealed, and the vehicle went spinning into the ditch.

A few minutes passed. This time, Gwynn didn't come out of the ditch first, his father did.

The older man limped, and blood streamed down the left side of his face. He gripped his abdomen.

The Curse hissed and charged.

The older Dormath tore into the Veil and drew a familiar staff. Was this why Pridament's staff seemed familiar?

A fight ensued. But with his injuries, Gwynn's father couldn't prevail.

Gwynn turned away, unable to witness the creature's killing blow. An agonized scream echoed along the pavement. He turned back to see his younger self watching from the side of the road.

"I...saw?"

The Curse scrambled along the road toward the young boy. Instinct kicked in, and Gwynn moved to defend the child. Grips on both his shoulders restrained him.

"There's nothing you can do. This is an echo, a memory long forgotten," Adrastia said.

The Curse readied to strike down Gwynn's younger self when the same light he saw in the other vision erupted.

In the flash, Gwynn made out the Curse bursting into dust.

With the Curse gone, his parents dead, the younger Gwynn lost consciousness and fell to the pavement.

"But I didn't wake as an Anunnaki until now. How did I do that?"

Adrastia moved in front of him. "You're wrong. You awoke then. Because of the trauma of it, the pain, you subdued it. It lay inside you, waiting for the time when you would call on it again."

"So what is this? Why am I dreaming this?"

"It's not a dream," Adrastia said. She nodded behind Gwynn. He turned to see the other version of his younger self, eyes ablaze with white light. "You're being manipulated, your memories pulled and twisted."

"Why?"

"Why don't you ask it?"

Gwynn called out to it. "What do you want? Why have you brought me here?"

With no emotion, it said, "Do everyone a favor and finish yourself."

"So it brought me here to drive me to suicide?"

"It's an effective way of dealing with enemies. Use their own memories against them."

Gwynn strode over to his younger self with the blazing eyes. "I'm done with this game." He brought Xanthe down on the boy, shattering it into a million pieces like a smashing mirror.

Gwynn blinked and found himself in a new room. Pridament and Fuyuko were beside him. A cloaked figure stood at the opposite end. Three threads extended from the hood and attached to Gwynn, Pridament and Fuyuko's foreheads.

Gwynn slashed upward with Xanthe and severed the thread. Then he spun and cut the threads connected to Fuyuko and Pridament, who crumpled to the floor. The person in the cloak hissed. It bounded from floor to ceiling and crashed through a door at the other end of the room.

Gwynn rushed to Pridament and Fuyuko. Gwynn shook Pridament by the shoulders and called out to him.

Pridament came around, and Fuyuko soon followed. Gwynn explained the cloaked man and the dreams meant to destroy them.

"So we should follow the wizard behind the curtain?" Pridament asked.

"I guess that's where the tear must be," Gwynn replied.

"OK," His eyes were a mix of anger and longing, "fair enough. Let's go."

The three inched along the office area toward the door the cloaked figure used to escape.

Cubicles cluttered every inch of available floor space. With each step, Gwynn scanned the tops, waiting for an attack. When they made it to the door, Pridament eased it open with the end of his staff.

Three threads hit the door with a loud 'Thock, thock, thock' sound.

"Looks like our friend hasn't gone too far."

Pridament went to one of the desks and grabbed a chair. "When I count three, I'm going out the door. When I do, I want you two to dash out and take that bastard down, clear?"

Fuyuko and Gwynn nodded.

Pridament counted. "One, two... Three."

The older man plunged through the door with the chair held in front like a shield. Pridament staggered as the threads hammered against the seat. Gwynn and Fuyuko charged through the door.

They were in the main warehouse area. Fuyuko leaped over Pridament and ran in a zigzagging manner toward the source of the threads. Gwynn followed on her heels. A second volley of threads cut through the air toward them. Gwynn slashed forward with Xanthe. The sword reached out, slicing the threads to harmless ribbons.

Fuyuko's spear stabbed toward the figure and deflected with a metallic clang. The cloak slid down, revealing the man's arm encased in steel extending to a lethal point at the end. Gwynn attacked from the other side, but the man used his other arm to deflect Xanthe.

The three began a deadly dance. Every advance Fuyuko or Gwynn made, the man's armored arms turned aside. In the heat of battle, the cloak fell back revealing a man from the nose up, but his mouth resembled a spider's mandible. The man threw himself back against the wall and scurried into the ceilings.

"Damn," Fuyuko huffed. "That guy is fast. Did you see his face?"

Gwynn tried to catch his own breath. "Trying to forget it, thanks."

A staff slashed through the air above their heads, knocking several threads aside.

"Pay more attention you two," Pridament yelled, "He's above us."

More threads came down. These ones smashed bits of concrete as they struck the floor.

"Not trying for subtlety anymore," Pridament said. "One of those hits you; it'll split your head like a melon."

Instinct hit Gwynn and he threw Xanthe above his head. The sword deflected the threads, but the reverberations on the steel sent painful shock waves through Gwynn's arms. "We need to get him down from there."

Pridament shook his head. "No. We'll never win that way. Gwynn, guide us to the tear. Hopefully, he'll have to come down to try and stop us."

Gwynn scanned the warehouse floor. There were no boxes or shelves, just wide–open space. Yet he couldn't see anything.

"It's not here. I mean, not that I can see."

"Feel your way to it. My gut's saying up," Pridament said.

"Me too," Fuyuko chimed in. "Is there another level?"

Gwynn tried to focus. Thwack. Pridament's staff deflected another thread. Up. Try looking up.

Let my gut guide me?

He tried to remember the night at the Cameron house with Sophia. He'd felt something then, hadn't he? Some sensation lured him up to the attic. He tried to ignore the mental image of his head splitting like a melon and focused on the feelings in his body. A moment passed. Queasiness started. Then, the tugging. Yes, the tugging sensation in the center of his body, drawing him forward. He searched in the direction where it pulled him.

"I've got a ladder," Gwynn said.

Pridament batted another thread aside. "Go."

Gwynn dashed for the ladder. He trusted Fuyuko and Pridament were not far behind. Thwack, thwack. The threads grazed his shoulder. Warm wet traveled down his back. Gwynn reached the ladder. He turned in time to smack several threads aside with Xanthe. Fuyuko and Pridament joined him.

"We'll never get up this ladder without him getting us," Fuyuko said.

The first night he'd held Xanthe, it was born from the darkness and regret in his soul. How deep did the pain go? How far could his misery reach? How much more had the past two days added? Gwynn tore into the Veil and drew more energy. "Start up the ladder. I'll cover you."

Fuyuko seemed ready to argue. She had no reason to have faith in him. Those she worked with were trained and understood their powers. He lacked in those areas, but he knew his pain, sorrow and the dark places inside of him. It would reach. Gwynn channeled his energy into Xanthe. With a howl, he lashed out at the direction of the threads. Xanthe screamed through the air, its blade elongating and slithering like a serpent. It hammered into the ceiling causing dust and debris to fill the air.

"Go," Gwynn bellowed.

Fuyuko and Pridament let their weapons fade back into the Veil and started up the ladder. Gwynn watched for threads. No, he wasn't watching, he sensed them. Slash, debris. Slash, threads cut down from the air. The minutes passed like hours. He kept drawing on the Veil to power Xanthe. His arm throbbed. Gwynn hazarded a quick glance—his skin started to scale. Too much. The Veil was starting to invade him.

"Gwynn," Pridament called down. "Come on."

They were up and through a hatch in the roof. One last push. Gwynn drew from the Veil and sent Xanthe skidding across the ceiling. As the debris fell, he let Xanthe fall back into the Veil and threw himself up the ladder. No hesitation, no second-guessing, he skipped several rungs at a time. A thread grazed his leg as he gulped the fresh air of the roof. The pain shocked his foot loose, and he slipped.

Strong hands grabbed him under the arms and yanked him through the hatch onto the roof.

Gwynn grasped his bleeding leg. He drew on the Veil again, focused the energy to his wounded leg and shoulder. The pulsating of his blood escaping lessened and stopped. The throbbing in his arm increased. He didn't bother looking at it. Press on and finish the job.

Gwynn searched the area. "There." He pointed to the center of the roof. The tear was there, though it looked larger than any he saw before. Black, wispy tendrils stretched out from it and reached into the sky. Gwynn followed them up to where they joined with the vortex spinning with a dark hatred above.

The hatch exploded, sending Gwynn spiraling across the roof. He scrambled, reached out for Xanthe. Too late. Threads, dozens perhaps, flew toward him. Then splayed outward. Gwynn looked behind to see Pridament with his staff in the ground, an intensity in his expression.

"Shield," Pridament said. "I've got this, close that tear."

Fuyuko grabbed Gwynn by the shoulder, hauling him to his feet. "Hurry."

The two ran for the tear. Metal striking metal from behind signaled Pridament engaging the Anunnakis.

After running what seemed the longest marathon in his life, Gwynn reached the tear. He reached out with his right arm and let his fingers brush the surface. Ice ran up his arm and pain shot through his chest. His breaths came in ragged heaves.

"It's rejecting you," Fuyuko said. "Push back Gwynn. Remember, your mind over its matter. You are in control. You have the keys."

Gwynn imagined himself pushing on a door. Someone, or something, on the other side, pushed back. He envisioned drawing strength from the Veil, pushing harder against the door. Back and forth, a battle of wills.

"She believed in me," Gwynn said. "If only because of that, I'll never give up."

He kept pressing until the other side gave. Seizing the opportunity, he slammed the door shut and locked it for good measure.

Gwynn stumbled back. The tear closed. The tendrils feeding the vortex faded and fell away.

A high-pitched screech pierced the air—inhuman, terrifying. The man-creature bore down on him. Fuyuko tried to stop it with her spear, but it swatted her aside. Gwynn rolled away from the thing's onslaught. He called Xanthe, pulling the sword from the Veil in time to block bladed arms.

The thing hissed at Gwynn, and its mandibles began to work. Holding the deadly arms back left Gwynn pinned. Any moment, it would spit threads at him. He was helpless.

Two thin blades tore upward through the creature's torso. Its arms went slack against Xanthe. The person behind it lifted and tossed the body aside.

"Told him," Pridament puffed. "I wasn't through with him. It feels different up here. Did you close the tear?"

Gwynn nodded. "Thanks."

Fuyuko joined the two of them. "Do we need to climb down now?"

"Afraid so," Pridament replied. "Might as well get to it."

One ladder and a warehouse length later, they stood on the ground outside.

"We still have one more?" Fuyuko asked.

Gwynn nodded. It was almost too painful to think they had to do this again.

Two black helicopters screamed overhead. They turned and spun around, moving in closer and slower. The wind picked up and whipped the ground as they set down on the road in front of the warehouse.

"Is this trouble?" Gwynn asked.

"Maybe," Pridament's voice sounded grim. "It's Suture."

The Family He Never Knew

Many black-clad individuals jumped from the helicopter's open doors. Their uniforms reminded Gwynn of a SWAT team.

Several ran past Gwynn, Fuyuko, and Pridament, and went into the warehouse. Three approached. The one in the center was huge, six-foot–five at least and built like a linebacker. He removed his helmet. Fuyuko gasped.

"Paltar, sir." She snapped to attention.

"Fuyuko, report."

"Sir?"

"What is going on here, Fuyuko? We received a report of a vortex, and as we approach to close one of the feeder tears, it collapses. What are you doing here? Who closed the tear?"

"I'm here following the orders I was given, sir. I've been assisting this boy, Gwynn. He closed the tear, sir."

Paltar regarded Gwynn with the same disdain he'd give a cockroach. "Him? A Script?"

"Yes, sir."

"Who are you affiliated with young man?"

"Excuse me?" What did this guy mean?

"Which branch of Suture do you work for?"

"Me? None."

Gwynn hadn't thought it possible, but Paltar took on an even greater air of disgust. "Humph, a free agent? That won't do. And who are you?" He asked Pridament.

"In another world, you would have called me brother," Pridament said.

Paltar inspected Pridament. A brief bit of surprise passed over his face. "The brother you claim to be is dead." Paltar straightened, his eyes angry. "You're nothing but an impostor. Get these two out of my sight."

"What?" Gwynn exclaimed. A hand gripped his shoulder.

"Gwynn, don't," Pridament said.

"After everything we've been through, after everything we've done, they're just—"

"Enough," Paltar's tone ended Gwynn's protests. "I will not have some amateur and an off-worlder getting in the way of my operation. The professionals are here boy. Leave this to us. Fuyuko."

"Yes, sir?"

"Go with them. You're relieved of duty until this mess is sorted out and I have a full report."

Fuyuko wanted to protest but bit her lip.

The two Suture members flanking Paltar stepped forward and stood guard over Gwynn, Fuyuko & Pridament until a van pulled up. They were ushered into the vehicle and encouraged to remain silent.

Minutes passed, and they pulled up to a hotel. The agents swept them into a back door and into a service elevator whisking them to the top floor.

"You two, wait in here."

The Suture members shoved Pridament and Gwynn through a door. Nausea swept over Gwynn, and he swallowed back some sick.

"Prometheus circle," Pridament said as way of explanation.

Gwynn inspected the room but couldn't see any sign of the black boxes or wires.

"They wouldn't lock two Anunnakis in a room without inhibiting their powers. We'd fold our way out, or fight." Pridament said the last bit with a slight smile.

Gwynn went to the washroom and splashed water on his face. When he came back, Pridament had claimed one of the beds.

"I don't get why you didn't do more. I mean, you just let them cart us off to this place. Is that guy really your brother?"

Pridament sighed. "First off, yes, he is my half–brother. Which makes him your uncle. Second, since he is my brother, I knew there was no point in fighting with him. In fact, if I pushed him any harder, we would be in even bigger trouble. They're the ones who do this for a living, Gwynn. Relax and let them use their training."

"My uncle." He tested the word. It felt strange. "I go from only Jaimie to having a father from another world and now a wrestler–sized uncle. Do I have any other relatives I don't know about?"

"A number." Pridament sounded bitter. "For instance, your grandfather happens to be the head of Suture."

"Which Suture?" Gwynn thought of the question Paltar asked him. "My uncle made it sound like there was more than one."

Pridament swung his legs around, so he sat on the side of the bed. He looked at Gwynn long and hard. "There is one Suture, but it has several branches. Their major locations are in North America, South America, Greece, and Egypt. Each branch has a religious pantheon as its base. Egypt and Greece should be self–explanatory. Same with South America. Here in North America, it's the Norse."

"Norse religious pantheon? What?"

"You know, Odin, Thor and the like."

"I'm lost."

Pridament rubbed the bridge of his nose and up into his tear ducts. "Remember how I said throughout time, Anunnakis have sometimes been seen as gods? And the various pantheons, such as the Olympians and Egyptian gods, were Anunnakis that grouped together?"

Gwynn nodded. So much had happened, but he vaguely recalled the discussion.

"Wherever they were worshiped, they remained. When Suture was created, it formed a blanket organization for the different factions to unite under."

"So my grandfather runs it all?"

"I suppose you could say that."

"Where is he?" Then a bigger question occurred to Gwynn. "*Who* is he?"

Pridament *hmphed*. "Last I heard, he was somewhere on this continent. Who is he? Well, let's say the Norse pantheon claimed North America as the Vikings were here first."

Gwynn shook his head. "Please tell me you aren't forgetting the Native North Americans."

"I'm not. But their religious pantheon didn't include Anunnakis. Those who were born with powers among their people became shamans, religious leaders, and chiefs. They didn't seek to be gods. They wanted to make life better for their people. Therefore, this area remained unclaimed by an Anunnaki pantheon. It boiled down to the fact the Vikings brought that here first."

"Norse. So my grandfather is... No. Really?"

"The All–Father himself."

"So who are you?" Gwynn asked.

Pridament flopped back on the bed with a sigh. "No one. Just an unwanted, bastard child."

"Is that who Mr. Murray was working for? Is that who he was taking Sophia to?"

Pridament shook his head. "I don't know. I think Justinian went rogue and was working for himself. He was able to get Suture to send Fuyuko here, so they sanctioned part of what he was doing. I have no idea how deep their involvement went."

"This is insane."

"Kid, you don't know the half of it. Lie down and get some rest. I think it's going to be a long night."

***

Paltar grew impatient.

"Jason, tell me again, there's still a vortex over our head?"

"Yes, sir."

Jason was the Ansuz team's Script. He was younger, much younger, than Paltar and been with Suture since he turned six. Under Paltar's tutoring, he had grown into a man. And now took his first awkward steps of love with Fuyuko. Paltar chuckled at how Jason and Fuyuko tried so hard to hide their feelings from everyone. First love, full of secrets and joy. It reminded Paltar of his own past. Loves gone too long ago. Youth and the powers of a Script. It was difficult not to harbor some resentment. As a Script, the boy could see the phantoms Paltar fought based on faith alone.

The returning group of the Ansuz team disturbed Paltar's reverie.

"Sir, we've done a full sweep of the warehouse. There's a body on the roof. We believe it belongs to the Anunnaki who held the tear open at this location. There's no one else in the building, and there doesn't appear to be any contamination from the tear."

Paltar called up to the front of the helicopter. "Call the Ehwaz unit. Tell them this location is secure. All they have to do is some cleanup. We're moving on to the next target with the Purisaz team. Jason."

"Yes, sir."

"You're navigating up front."

Paltar hopped back into the chopper. When his team all boarded, he swung the door shut and the helicopter lifted into the air.

There were too many questions. How could Justinian have been here so long and be ignorant of the world killer above his head? Why had no one at Suture detected it earlier?

Over the past two weeks, the Ansuz team saw home for only a handful of hours. They received dispatches to every corner of the continent to combat tears and Curses. Maybe only a third of those were emergency situations. It felt wrong.

"We're here," Jason called from the front.

Paltar looked out the window. "Really?"

"Yes, sir."

Paltar sighed. A high–rise office building in the middle of the city. It was going to be a long night.

"Can you see the tear, Jason?"

"No. We've passed over a few times. I can see the tendrils feeding the vortex, but it looks like it's coming from inside the building."

"Roof access?"

The pilot spoke up. "There might be a hatch, but I wouldn't set this thing down on that roof. It's not likely to be reinforced enough to handle the weight."

"Repelling lines?"

An awkward silence. "Not packed sir," the pilot finally said.

"Fine," Paltar fumed. This operation was a complete mess. "Set us down at the closest entry point."

The aircraft jostled and settled. Paltar opened the door. The second chopper landed as well and disgorged its occupants.

"What's the plan, brother?" Hodur asked.

Hodur. Not the strongest of his brethren, nor the most talented in a fight. But he compensated with his steadiness and dependability. While he expected some of his brothers to crash into a battle with reckless abandon, Paltar could always count on Hodur to be at his back.

"We'll send our point men in first. Considering the warehouse Intel I received, it looks like the Fallen are employing Anunnakis to hold these tears open. I don't need to tell you how dangerous that makes them."

"No, I remember the feral one the South American branch called us in to help with. Nasty bastard," Hodur shuddered.

"My other concern is if this area's been tainted. By the father's name, right in the middle of the city. And yet..."

Hodur gave the area a once-over. "This place is deserted."

"Precisely. The middle of town. Where is everyone?"

Hodur slapped Paltar on the shoulder. "Consider it a blessing, brother. Can you imagine the number of Taints we might come across otherwise? I look at a deserted area and all I see is our job just got easier."

Paltar gave his brother a smile. When his other siblings asked why he always brought Hodur, he tried to articulate to them the various reasons. He always mentioned the man's ability to see the positives.

Paltar assembled the Ansuz team. They were composed of kids. Such young faces. His appearance was youthful too, but he long lost the ability to see it. Too many years. Too many battles. Some of his family, and those they adopted over the years, seemed to thrive on it. But Paltar would've been content to leave it behind. These young men and women around him, he trained every one. Like Jason, he'd watched them pass through their childhood into adolescence and into the early years of adult life. And on an increasing number of occasions, he sent them into situations that could end their short life. It wasn't a fair existence.

"Brandt and Caelum, you two are up front; weapons out, all eyes. We haven't been subtle about our presence; there's no point. With the collapse of the other tear, they're aware we're after them."

"Respectfully. Sir, why not hit the building balls out," Brandt said.

A typical Brandt suggestion. The kid was a hot head, one of the ones who thrived on chaos. If the boy had his way, the choppers would be equipped with full armaments, and they'd leave every location they visited a smoldering crater.

"Have you bothered to assess the situation, Brandt? We're in the city center. We blow a hole in this building; we're encouraging whatever is inside to come out. From what I gather, there have already been an unacceptable number of civilian casualties. I'm not going to increase that number."

Paltar delivered it all with a look that would cause the greatest of bravado to shrink. He worked hard to suppress a smile when it had the desired effect.

"Now, Brandt, Caelum, get ready. Purisaz team, I want you broken into smaller groups and covering exit points. Nothing gets in or out, clear?"

With assignments handed out, the Ansuz team made for their entry point. Paltar usually opted for the straight–ahead approach. They'd go in the front entrance. Apart from the obvious, no one ever expected it, in this case, it meant having an easier time finding the stairwell. There was no way they'd be lucky enough to locate the tear on the ground floor.

Brandt and Caelum entered the building. Paltar sensed the tension in the rest of the team as they waited. Two minutes passed. Caelum's voice came over the radio. "All clear to enter."

The remaining members of the Ansuz team breached the building. The lights were all on. An ornate reception area with marble and natural woods greeted them. The rest of the floor consisted of several offices and cubicles. Brandt and Caelum stood in the center of the space motioning them forward.

"How far did you go in?" Paltar asked.

"Just this floor and the first flight of stairs. The stairwell's at the rear," Caelum reported.

The team swept through the office complex. Satisfied nothing would come at them from the rear, Paltar gave the order to move into the stairwell.

No scouts this time, only a steady stream of Anunnakis pouring through the door and to the second floor to await further orders.

Paltar and Hodur were the last through the door. "Hodur, is it just me, or is this far too easy?"

A stabbing pain shot through Paltar's lower back. It dug and burrowed through his torso until a spear tip punched through his sternum.

"Oh, I don't know," Hodur hissed in his ear. "I think it's about to get very difficult."

Mythology

Gwynn paced. Despite Pridament's insistence he rest, he couldn't. Every attempt at sitting or lying down sent painful spasms through his legs.

"How long have we been here?" Gwynn asked.

"No idea. Some of us are trying to take a nap."

"I can still see it out the window and feel it in my gut. The vortex is still spinning. Suture hasn't been able to shut it down. Shouldn't they have been able to manage that by now?"

A knock came at the door. It unlocked, and Fuyuko entered.

"Fuyuko, What are you doing here?" Gwynn asked.

She refused to meet his eyes.

"She's here because her team is either dead or missing."

Pridament hadn't shifted from where he lay on the bed. When the words came out of his mouth, a shudder passed through Fuyuko.

"He's right, isn't he?" Gwynn asked.

"I...was supposed to stay confined. I couldn't take it. So I snuck out, went to the command post where I heard the radio traffic. The last transmission was..." She whimpered, "Sounds of battle, screaming, then... nothing."

"But there's a backup, right? I mean, Suture has to have more than one team, right?"

Fuyuko shook her head. "Everything's happened at once. Everyone they could spare was already here. There are tears and Taints everywhere, occupying all the other units. There are a few people from Ehwaz team, but they lack battle experience. And, they don't have a..." Her eyes fell away from him.

"A what?" Gwynn asked.

"They don't have a Script," Pridament said. "There's no sense in sending them in because even if they get there, without a Script, they can't close the tear."

"So are you asking, or is Suture?" Gwynn asked.

When she turned back, there were tears in her eyes. "I am. Please, those are my friends. There's no one else who has a hope of helping them."

"We'll do it, right Pridament."

The older man swung his legs over the bed and looked at them. His eyes were so tired. "I don't know if we should Gwynn."

"What?"

Pridament drew a deep breath and let it out slow. Moisture glistened at the edges of his eyes. "Gwynn, I lost you once. And over the past few days, I can't keep track of the number of times you've been in danger. Paltar and his team are the best Suture has. If they've failed, I don't see what hope we have."

"If we don't stop it, then this world dies."

"You think I don't know that?" Pridament got to his feet, his voice raw and ragged. "You think I don't carry the guilt of every world I've watched the Fallen destroy? You're the closest I've come to finding my son, Gwynn. This is a suicide mission. I can't let you do it."

"So what? We run? How many worlds will we let die before we make a stand? Or do you think we'll keep going until we're dead? Please, Pridament." Then Gwynn said quieter, "*Dad, we have to do this.*"

Pridament stood motionless, his eyes full of sorrow. Nothing in the room moved.

Gwynn's heart pounded in his chest, and his body shook.

Then Pridament moved to Gwynn. He rested his hands on Gwynn's shoulders. "Are you sure?"

"It's the only way I'll be able to live with myself." *Because she believed in me.*

Pridament looked over Gwynn's shoulder. "Fuyuko, we're going to need out of here."

The girl nodded, joyful determination on her face. "Right. Give me a minute to shut down the Prometheus circle and, umm, persuade the guards."

She didn't lie. Within a minute, she returned.

"When this is all over, and Suture finds out what I've done," She said sheepishly to Pridament, "I might need you to take *me* to another world."

Pridament grimaced. "Don't worry about it. Either we come back heroes, or we don't come back at all."

Out the door and down the hall, they used an exit door to enter the stairwell.

They rushed down the stairs, Fuyuko in the lead.

"Has anyone thought how we're going to get there?" Gwynn asked.

Ahead, Fuyuko dangled some keys.

"The van that brought us here?" Gwynn asked.

She shot him a quick, mischievous smile.

"I think you're enjoying this a little too much."

They exited through a door out into the last dying moments of daylight. Fuyuko took a quick scan of the parking lot. "Over there. Here," She said handing the keys to Pridament, "you drive."

"Do you know where they are?" Pridament asked.

"I heard something about a large office building or something. They were talking about it being in the center of town."

"It's a small town. Not too many large office buildings," Gwynn said. "We can start out that way. If I see the tendrils feeding the vortex, we'll know we're on the right track."

The trio loaded into the van.

"How'd you know what Fuyuko was coming to see us about?" Gwynn asked.

"You just finished saying the vortex was still there. One look at her face and I figured what happened. Are we headed in the right direction?"

Gwynn leaned forward and searched the sky. "It looks like it. There's a ton of tendrils, more than I remember, but they're all coming from the same spot."

"Downtown?"

"Definitely."

The minutes passed like hours. Each ticking second raised the anxiety levels in the car to tangible levels. Gwynn snuck a glance at Fuyuko in the back seat. She fidgeted, staring at her lap, never lifting her eyes to see out the windows.

Two blocks from the building, nausea hit Gwynn as if he'd slammed into a wall. "Damn. The last one didn't feel like this."

They turned a corner, and the office complex came into full view. Gwynn gasped.

The building was engulfed by an angry green and black, sparking and crackling, light. It reached up into the sky, where numerous tendrils stretched away and into the vortex.

"Can you see this?" Gwynn asked.

"I see something. What are you seeing?" Pridament asked.

"The entire building is drenched in this green and black energy. There are dozens of tendrils coming off it feeding the vortex. It's like a bunch of tears are open in this one place."

"That explains what I'm seeing. The building is phasing. It's slipping from this plane of existence. We need to get in there and stop this, now."

Having left the car, Gwynn approached the wall of energy. He scooped a stone from the ground and threw it. The rock passed through and bounced off the building on the other side.

"Well, rocks can get through it. I'm not sure about people."

Pridament inspected the building. "It shouldn't hurt us. It's probably because of all the dimensional energy inside. I'm more concerned about what's going to be inside."

"Curses," Fuyuko said

"Lots of them. And they're going to be even stronger because there's more instability here."

Fuyuko inspected the grounds.

"What are you looking for?"

"Purisaz team. The standard operation would be to have them outside covering exits. Even if something did happen inside, they shouldn't have all gone in."

Maybe something happened out here too, Gwynn thought. Seeing the worry on Fuyuko's face, he kept it to himself.

"In either case, we need to go," Pridament said. He approached the entrance and reached out a tentative hand.

The energy rippled and snapped outward as Pridament touched it.

"Dammit" Pridament gasped. "No way we're going to walk through. It's pushing back."

"Let me try," Gwynn said.

Gwynn reached out his right hand. The energies swirled and retreated from his hand. He drew on the Veil and pushed his hand further. His arm tingled. The symbols on his hand danced across his flesh, a human decoder trying to find the hidden message. The opening widened. "Go in under my hand."

Pridament and Fuyuko ducked under his arm and entered the building. Gwynn closed his connection to the Veil and dove through the opening as it closed.

***

The air clung to Gwynn like wet clothes.

"I feel like I've gained fifty pounds," he said. "It's hard to move."

Pridament slapped Gwynn on the shoulder. "Give it a minute. It's all the tear energy in here. Once your system adjusts, you'll feel a little closer to normal. What do you think Fuyuko? How should we proceed?"

Fuyuko scanned the lobby. "I'm going to guess the tear isn't on the first floor. They would've taken the stairs. Elevators can be tampered with too easily."

Pridament nodded. "Okay, so we need to find the stairs. I'm going to take a wild guess and say they're back that way."

"How do you figure?" Gwynn asked.

The older man chuckled and pointed to a sign hanging from the ceiling. "Follow the arrow."

Pridament drew his staff from the Veil. Gwynn and Fuyuko drew their weapons as well. The trio edged down the hall, casting a wary eye toward every door. The fluorescent lights and dying gloom of daylight outside did nothing to stop Gwynn's hairs standing on end and his pulse quickening.

At the stairwell, Pridament motioned for Gwynn to pull the door open. "On three," he mouthed. Pridament held up a fist. One finger went up, two, three and Gwynn pulled the door open.

Pridament plunged into the stairwell. Several heartbeats later, he emerged. Something had him shaken.

"Fuyuko," Pridament said. "I think you're going to want to prepare yourself. I don't know what it means, but it can't be good."

The color drained from Fuyuko's face. She took hesitant steps to join Pridament at the open door. She gave a stifled sob. No longer able to bear waiting, Gwynn entered the stairwell.

Words escaped him.

Blood. So much blood. On the floor, stairs, and walls.

Fuyuko stood next to Pridament, who held her shoulders to keep her from collapsing.

Pridament's voice was hushed, reverent, as though the stairwell had become hallowed ground. "What do you feel Gwynn? Do we go up?"

Gwynn closed his eyes to the horror of the stairwell. He tried to find the tugging sensation. His stomach churned.

"I don't know. It's like I'm being pulled everywhere all at once. I'm sorry."

Pridament shook his head. "It can't be helped. The whole building is saturated. Okay, well there's nothing on this floor, so we go up and check each floor."

"How many floors are there?" Fuyuko's voice sounded hollow.

"The directory at the door showed ten."

One by one, they ascended the stairs, picking each footfall to avoid the blood.

"How many people in the Suture team?" Gwynn asked.

"Standard is eight. I wasn't there, so they would've had seven in Ansuz and eight in Purisaz."

"So fifteen people. Do you notice we're halfway to the second floor and there's no more, umm..."

"Blood?"

Gwynn gave Fuyuko a sheepish look. "Yeah. Sorry."

She straightened her back, squared her shoulders, and set her jaw. "It's okay. That's a good thing. At least, that's what I'm telling myself."

"Enough chatter," Pridament growled, "keep moving."

They paused at the door to the second floor.

"Anything?" Pridament asked.

Gwynn shook his head. "Still feel the same as I did downstairs."

"Stay here."

Pridament eased the door open and slid through. A moment later, he returned, and they continued upward. The same pattern happened on the third and fourth floors.

When Gwynn hit the landing marking the halfway point between the fourth and fifth floors, he doubled up, slammed against the wall, and heaved.

"What's wrong?" Pridament asked.

Gwynn ran his sleeve across his mouth and tried to ignore the stinging acid in the back of his throat. "I feel like I got punched."

"This must be the place then. You going to be all right?"

Gwynn drew in some deep breaths, letting them flood his innards. On an inhalation, he straightened, flexed his hands, twisted a little, and even gave his toes a wiggle in his boots. "Yeah, I'm good."

At the fifth floor, Pridament signaled they should have their weapons ready. He went through the door first, followed by Fuyuko and then Gwynn.

Thick cables snaked along the floor; they throbbed and pulsated, almost alive. From the main bundle in the hall, individual cables branched off into the various rooms. Pridament flattened himself against a wall and moved to one of the open doors. He crouched down and peered inside. He stood up and motioned for Gwynn and Fuyuko to follow.

Fuyuko gasped.

Inside the room, the cables coiled themselves like boa constrictors around two boys no older than Gwynn. The parts of their bodies still visible revealed they wore Suture uniforms.

"You know them?" Pridament asked Fuyuko.

"Not well. They're from Purisaz team. What is this?"

"What do you see Gwynn?"

Gwynn looked closer at the two boys. The coils around them emitted a faint glow. The cables pulsed and jumped over their bodies like they were drinking.

"It seems like...the cables are draining them?"

The words just left Gwynn's mouth, and Fuyuko twisted and hacked the cables with her spear.

A screech sounded somewhere down the hall, and a noxious fluid spurted from the severed cables. The coils around the boys fell to the floor slack sending Gwynn and Pridament dashing to catch the two Purisaz team members.

Out in the hall, two cables rose from the mass.

"Gwynn, the door," Pridament called.

Gwynn threw himself across the room, slamming the door shut as the cables pounded against it. The door shook and thundered.

Fuyuko and Pridament arrived with a desk they shoved in front of the door.

Sweat fell from Gwynn's brow. "What the hell are those things?"

"I think we're in a lot of trouble," Pridament said.

Groggy moans sounded behind them.

Fuyuko approached the boys. "What happened?" she asked.

The one boy, whose hair was a nearly white color of blond, started to regain consciousness. The other still lay motionless.

"What?" he asked in a ragged and cracked voice.

"I said, what happened?" Fuyuko grasped the boy around the collar and pulled his face to within three inches of her own.

Pridament placed one hand to support the boy's back and with the other took firm hold of Fuyuko. "Go easy on him."

Fuyuko's eyes were wild with desperation.

"Let him go Fuyuko. He'll answer in a minute." It amazed Gwynn how anyone could sound tender yet leave no room for argument. Jaimie could do the same thing. Despite the many times she lamented the lack of a manual for raising a child, it seemed to Gwynn some abilities came with time and experience.

The door continued to rattle and buck against the desk. Gwynn leaned all his weight to aid the desk against the door. "If we're going to do something, we should hurry up."

Pridament leaned over the blond Suture member. "Listen to me kid, what did you see?"

The boy's voice was weak and full of disorientation. "We heard commotion on the radio. The chain of command broke down. We moved to the front door to breach. Then...we saw something at the doors. We thought it was a Curse. But, a face..." The boy trembled. "I remember looking and then, nothing."

"It's going to be okay. You'll be fine." Pridament eased the boy down to the floor. "Get some rest. You'll feel better in a few minutes."

"You're more bothered than usual," Gwynn said to Pridament.

"Because I know what we're dealing with. It's a Gorgon."

"That's a legend," Fuyuko said. "A silly myth made up to entertain children."

Pridament shook his head. "Don't they teach you anything? Almost every myth, monster, or deity has some root in truth. In most situations, it's because of Taints, Curses, or Anunnakis. In the case of the Gorgon, it's a Veil beast."

"And that is?" People kept talking like he should understand what they meant. It pissed him off.

"A Veil beast," Fuyuko piped in, "is a being living within the Veil itself. What we see is a small portion of the actual creature. Often the portion visible in our realm is a minor component of the beast, and so they are often considered immortal."

"Damn near textbook," Pridament said. "The Gorgon is such a creature. Like the myth, looking at its face causes paralysis. A lesser-known fact is it could steal the power of gods. I guess that's what is happening here. Elaios must be using the Gorgon to drain the energy of the Suture teams to feed the tear and keep the vortex growing."

"But those things need to be summoned," Fuyuko tried to argue. "Not to mention trying to control it."

"How do we kill it?" Gwynn was tired of feeling left out.

Fuyuko and Pridament looked at him as if he spouted Pig Latin.

"Weren't you listening?" Fuyuko's tone was incredulous. "You can't kill this thing."

"Fine, how do we *beat* it?"

Fuyuko stared at Gwynn. She had no idea.

"There's one way," Pridament said. "We need to force it back into the Veil."

"Impossible."

"Really Fuyuko? You think so? You've never faced yourself, have you?"

Fuyuko looked stricken. "It's forbidden."

"Maybe to you. Thankfully, I've never been one for rules."

"Stop," Gwynn roared. "I don't know what you're talking about and I don't care. If Pridament has a plan, then that's what we should do." He asked Fuyuko, "Do you have a plan?"

She shook her head.

"Right. Tell us what you need."

"Okay. Gwynn, Fuyuko, get tight against the wall beside the door."

When they were in place, Pridament joined them. With a shove, he moved the desk. The door flew open, and the tendrils moved in. Pridament restrained Fuyuko from interfering as they wrapped themselves around the two Suture members.

"They'll be free when we finish this," Pridament whispered.

He then stepped out into the hall. Gwynn and Fuyuko edged out after.

"The plan?" Gwynn asked.

"We find the Gorgon and then hope I have a stronger will than it does."

"I'm starting to hate this plan."

Pridament ducked across the hall into a washroom. They heard a muffled crash, and he emerged with several pieces of mirror. "Here. Like I said, some parts of myths are true."

The trio made their way down the hall. Each room they passed contained ensnared members of the Suture teams. When they reached the end of the hall, Pridament held his piece of mirror to peer around the corner.

"All clear."

They rounded the corner. This stretch was divided in two by another hallway branching off in the middle. Thinking of the floor plan below, Gwynn assumed this central hall led to the elevators. The coils all seemed to originate from that central hall. Closer, the sound of breathing—like a combination of the braying of a horse and the crushing of bones. Pridament held up his mirror.

"It's there. I'm going to go in front of it and bring up a shield. Once I do, you two need to severe the coils. Hopefully, I'll keep it occupied, and that'll give the Suture teams a chance to recover."

"How will we know you've succeeded?" Gwynn asked.

Pridament gave him a weary smile and gripped his shoulder. "If I walk away."

"I *really* hate this plan."

Pridament gave a wink. Then he walked straight out into the center of the hall. He struck the floor with his staff and a pulse of energy waved out as his shield formed. The Gorgon hissed. Tendrils flew at Pridament, but the shield turned them aside.

Through gritted teeth, Pridament yelled. "Cut them, now."

Gwynn dashed across the hall, dragging Xanthe along the ground and severed the tendrils. It took every ounce of control to avoid looking at the Gorgon. The creature shrieked a fearsome sound that stabbed right to Gwynn's core.

An invisible weight fell on his shoulders and forced him to his knees. Fuyuko struggled as well.

Is the Gorgon doing this?

But Pridament still stood. He lifted his staff and struck it on the ground. Wind spun in a visible mass around Pridament's shield. With a roar, he flung his arms forward, and the wind slashed toward the Gorgon. A form appeared behind Pridament, anchored to him by several tendrils. Was this Pridament's true self; that part of him living within the Veil?

Gwynn inched forward and held his mirror at an angle to see around the corner. The Gorgon stood eight feet tall. Unlike Hollywood versions, the monster bore little resemblance to having been a beautiful woman. Huge tusks protruded from its cheeks curling in a deadly arc ending below fierce gold eyes. Ripples in the space behind it reminded Gwynn of air above pavement on a sweltering day.

The rippling air behind the Gorgon and the form attached to Pridament rushed forward and slammed into each other in a percussive explosion that sent Gwynn flying backward.

When he regained his footing, he inched back to the battle. Whatever war waged between the hidden forms of the Gorgon and Pridament, its effects on the combatants were visible. At times, the

Gorgon would wince, and parts of it would fade from view. Likewise, Pridament fell to his knees, sweat pouring from his brow. Gwynn's heart hammered as Pridament became a ghostlike version of transparency, and then solidified again. He leaned on his staff. Without it, he'd be face flat on the floor.

It dawned on Gwynn he was not watching a battle of wills—he was witnessing a literal battle between two souls. How could one calculate the strength of one soul against another?

Then Pridament blinked out of existence.

Gwynn screamed. Longer than a blink went by. Seconds, minutes, hours, days, time itself lost meaning to Gwynn. An eternity seemed to pass, and still, Pridament was gone.

Hot tears burned Gwynn's cheeks and coursed down his throat on his heaving chest. He lost his parents, Sophia, and now Pridament. When would the universe be satisfied with his losses? How much blood would spill to allow his continued existence? Breathing was getting difficult.

"Do you remember what she told you?" Gwynn found Adrastia leaning against the wall behind him.

"What? Who do you mean?"

Adrastia shook her head. She appeared one part disappointed and another part sympathetic. "For having been in love with her, you paid little attention to what she told you."

"Sophia? What did she tell me that could help here?"

She cleared her throat. "Blood taken through betrayal will summon the monster. Blood given shall drive it back."

"What?"

The girl knelt down in front of him. Her gem green eyes bore down into his soul. "What did you see in the stairwell?"

"Blood."

"And is there a monster standing in front of you?"

Gwynn nodded.

"So if blood was taken to summon it..." She rolled her hand to prompt him to finish her sentence.

"Blood given..." he said. "Will banish it."

Gwynn dragged his hand across the tip of Xanthe. Red crimson stained the obsidian colored blade. His flesh stung. It didn't matter.

He charged around the corner, keeping his eyes low and focusing on the core of the beast.

Tendrils struck to intercept him. A number wrapped around his ankles, forcing him forward, crashing toward the floor. He willed the sword to fly, the same as in the warehouse. Like a lightning strike, Xanthe extended, snaking a path through the tendrils until it struck the breast of the Gorgon.

The tendrils fell limp, but Gwynn kept his iron grip on Xanthe. He regained his feet and pushed harder against the sword.

"Back to where you belong," Gwynn hissed.

Like a blanket, the Veil wrapped itself around the Gorgon and pulled it back. A moment later, Xanthe returned to its normal size and the hallway was empty.

"How'd you do that?" Fuyuko asked.

Gwynn ignored her.

Instead, he walked to where Pridament stood—the floor marred where his staff struck its surface.

He released Xanthe, which disappeared back to the Veil. Gwynn took a few ragged breaths. *The Veil is everywhere.* Pridament told him. *It sits right in front of you and hides entire universes under your nose.* He imagined Pridament drawn into the Veil, still in this very spot, just hidden by the curtain of creation. Gwynn ran his right arm down the space where his mentor once stood. He imagined it as fabric, long and cumbersome, blacking out the light on the other side. All he had to do was open the point where the curtains met each other. Pull open the curtain, and Pridament would be there on the other side.

He plunged his arm into the Veil.

It wasn't like the other times. Before, he asked for a bit of energy, or to contact something he belonged to. Now, he was forcibly trying to take back something the Veil claimed. It did not take to his intrusion kindly.

His arm burned. As he tried to draw Pridament back, the Veil attempted to pull both he and Pridament into it. Convulsions ran up his spine. He couldn't remember his last breath.

I'm part of something larger. Somewhere in the Veil, there's a part of me that could help. Please, I know you can hear me. I don't know what cosmic laws apply, but I need him. I can't finish this without him. I won't give up. I'll keep pulling. I need you to push.

The tear he created was the size of a grown man. Inside, nothing but formless light.

A shadow rushed by within the light. Something huge, powerful in a way he could never hope to comprehend. Then the tugging on the other side of the Veil ceased. Gwynn seized the moment and pulled with all his might.

"Pridament... Father, come back to me."

Gwynn stumbled backward, and Pridament fell from the tear into his arms.

Both of them crumbled to the floor. Gwynn sealed the tear and attended to Pridament.

The older man lay unconscious. Gwynn leaned his ear next to Pridament's mouth and looked at his chest. It was faint, but he heard the sound of inhalations and saw a slight rise in Pridament's chest.

"Is he okay?" Fuyuko asked. A single question, but the tone of her voice contained a million more.

"He's breathing."

He gripped Pridament with both hands.

"C'mon Pridament. Wake up."

Several yells and shakes later, Pridament's eyelids crawled open. "Quit yelling kid. My head is pounding." His eyes opened wide, and he sat up too fast, inducing fits of coughing and wincing. "Did I win?"

"Gwynn did," Fuyuko said. "Though I'm not sure how."

Gwynn turned to where Adrastia stood. He wasn't surprised to find her gone.

"Sophia told me. It made no sense at the time, but I remembered now. She said blood was taken would summon the beast, but blood given would banish it." He held out his lacerated hand.

"I think you were right, Gwynn. She was helping us."

The hall filled with Suture members.

"What happened?" being the most common question.

"Fuyuko?" One of them said.

"Jason." Fuyuko threw her arms around him. The boy seemed embarrassed, but he did nothing to break her embrace. "Do you remember what happened?" she asked him.

Jason's eyes said he did.

"We were betrayed. Hodur. He...killed Paltar."

Fuyuko's eyes went wide. Pridament shook.

"The stairwell," Gwynn said.

"Considering what Sophia told you, we can guess how they summoned the Gorgon."

"Gorgon?" Jason asked. "Is that what it was? I was near the front, behind Brandt and Caelum. I heard a scream. When we came around the corner, there was something there. That's all I remember."

A 'ding' sound filled the hall.

"Was that the elevator?"

The doors on each elevator opened and the hall flooded with Curses

25

Facing Betrayal

The air crackled with the summoning of weapons from the Veil.

Despite their incapacitation minutes before, the Suture teams surged forth against the Curses. Gwynn sensed no fear, hesitation or questioning. This was their job and purpose. To suggest they shouldn't fight was like saying they should give up breathing.

A firm grip on his shoulder dragged him around the corner away from the fray.

"We need to keep going," Pridament said.

"Shouldn't we help? Won't we need *their* help?"

"No time. We move. They'll catch up."

They headed for the stairwell. Fuyuko blocked the door.

"Where do you think you're going?"

"Up," Pridament said. "We can't waste any more time. That tear has to be closed. Go help your friends, then join up with us."

Fuyuko shook her head. "No. I threw my lot in with you when I broke you out. I'm seeing this through with the two of you. They can take care of themselves from here."

"Fine." A noticeable air of relief was in Pridament's voice. "Let's get going."

They burst into the stairwell and ascended to the sixth floor two steps at a time.

"Where are we going?" Gwynn asked.

Pridament stopped mid–stride. "Probably the top floor. Now that the Gorgon's gone, I hoped you'd get a better fix, and we could skip searching every floor."

"Maybe. Give me a minute."

Gwynn closed his eyes. Sounds of battle raged a floor away. He concentrated on his abdomen. Five, ten heartbeats passed. There, the familiar tugging sensation. Pridament was right; it was like a thread attached to his midsection pulling upward.

"Okay," Gwynn said. "We go up. Slower though. I might miss the change if we go too fast."

Pridament and Fuyuko nodded.

At the ninth floor, Pridament held up his hand, halting their progress.

"You two keep going. There's something I need to do here."

"What?" Gwynn's insides trembled. "We need you."

Pridament turned to face Gwynn, his expression pained. "Gwynn, I want to stay with you, to see this through and keep you safe. But if I don't do this, there's a good chance none of us are going to survive. Trust me. Trust Fuyuko. Remember what you've accomplished. No matter what comes, you'll be okay. I believe in you."

Pridament said nothing else. He spun and went through the door.

Gwynn was one step from following him when Fuyuko grasped his shoulder.

"Don't. He said it was something he had to do."

"I... I don't think I can do it without him. The one time he left me alone, Elaios almost killed me."

Fuyuko's face crumpled into a mask of disdain. "Really? I seem to remember another time you were without him you saved my life."

"Luck. I didn't know what I was doing."

"Then that's your answer. Don't think so much about it. Just act. Your connection is to something old and powerful. Trust your real self to see you through."

"Maybe."

She punched him hard in the shoulder.

"Keep talking like that and Fallen will be the least of your problems. Now call that crazy sword of yours."

Gwynn looked at his empty hand.

When did I return Xanthe to the Veil?

He called, and it returned.

Gwynn sensed the sword always rested in his hand, whether visible or not—the weight and balance felt too natural to be a coincidence. What else might surround him the Veil kept shielded from his vision? Would it be there for him when he needed it?

Fuyuko pushed past him and moved toward the tenth floor.

Gwynn skipped a couple steps to catch up. When they came to the door, the tugging at his core increased. Instead of tugging in an upward direction, it now urged him forward.

"It's here," he said.

Gwynn reached for the doorknob, but Fuyuko swatted his hand away.

"Do you think we should charge in there?"

Gwynn shrugged.

Fuyuko flattened herself against the wall. "On three, pull it open, but stay behind the door. Clear?"

She counted one, two, and three. Gwynn opened the door.

Nothing happened.

Fuyuko took a hesitant peek inside. With catlike grace, she slid through the door.

Gwynn rounded the door to follow, only to have an explosion of movement shove him back.

Fuyuko fell out the door, her spear a flurry of blocks and strikes. The Anunnaki she fended off carried curved blades in each hand.

She twisted and shoved the man away. "Gwynn, go."

"But..."

The Anunnaki lunged at Gwynn, but Fuyuko turned him away with her spear. "Close the tear. Everything gets easier once that's done. Go."

Spurred by the ferocity in her last word, Gwynn flung himself past their sparring and through the door.

***

The ninth floor hadn't been finished; an open space with girders and wiring in the ceiling exposed. Only the outer walls and where the elevators pushed through were drywalled.

"Hodur," Pridament called. "I know you're here. I think you and I have things to discuss."

He waited. How long had he known Hodur? His whole life. Such a long time. He tried to convince himself this wasn't his Hodur. This was a different world. Perhaps something happened in the almost-ten years since their worlds divided turned Hodur away.

But ten years meant nothing in a god's long lifetime. No, deceit of this magnitude would've taken decades, centuries perhaps, to germinate. The frightening reality was his world's Hodur might've already made a similar move.

A figure stepped out from the cover of the elevators.

"I knew it would be you," Hodur said. "Why don't you take off the mask so I can face you for real?"

Pridament allowed his form to revert to its natural state.

Hodur gave a small chuckle. "I've seen you do that a thousand times. I never get used to it. Justinian stole that trick from you, did you know?"

"I found out recently. I thought he'd been forbidden to take the powers of Odin's blood."

"Ah, but you're dead in this world, brother. Your body barely graced the ground, and he started using your little trick. I suppose he copied it years ago and was waiting for his opportunity."

Pridament spat. "Were you the one he was working for? Has this been your plan from the start?"

Hodur shook his head. "Sadly, I can't take all the credit. Did I summon the Fallen here? Yes. Did I ensure Suture remained ignorant of the vortex until the last moment? Yes, I did. But you? Gwynn? No, I had nothing to do with that. Why would I? If anything, the two of you have been thorns in my side."

"So what did they promise you?"

"Simple. A world where *I* would be the All-Father. And death to every world the progeny of Odin ever touched."

Pridament's heart ached. "Why? Have you always hated us so much? We used to play as boys. Paltar always believed in you."

"Please. Paltar thought I was a simpleton. His 'respect' was nothing more than pity. I'm through being the shadow. It's time for me to take my proper place upon a throne."

"So what?" Pridament spat. "You killed Paltar and used his blood to summon the Gorgon?"

"Brilliant, don't you think?" Hodur wore a hungry smile. "If the Greeks were here, it wouldn't have been so effective. But those trained by Asgard were little prepared for it. I admit I'm curious how you defeated it."

"Turns out the blood of a god not only summons the monster, but it can also banish it."

Hodur regarded Pridament suspiciously. "How could you know? That's magic older than Asgard."

"It doesn't matter. I'm guessing the Fallen told you. Did they find out during their travels perhaps?"

Hodur shrugged. "Perhaps. Does it matter? The fact is the Gorgon saturated the vortex with energy. Nothing will stop it. All that remains is for me to end you and the boy. Once that's done, I'll leave for my new home and begin my reign."

Pridament summoned his staff. He flipped it from hand to hand, making a show of his effortless control. "If I recall, you might have a hard time backing up those words."

Hodur's hand reached behind the elevator and came back with a spear. "Oh, I think this might even the odds a little."

"Since when did you use a spear?"

A burning evil filled Hodur's eyes. "Not just a spear, brother. This is ages old, the slayer of gods. How do you think I managed to kill Paltar? No weapon of man or Veil has ever managed to scratch him. But this, yes, this will make all the difference."

Hodur launched at Pridament, the sharpened blade of the spear glistening in its desire to mete out death.

Pridament sidestepped, bringing his staff upward to knock the spear's razor tip aside. Preoccupied with the spear, he left his side open, where Hodur's delivered a savage kick. Pridament stumbled. Hodur spun. Pridament threw his staff behind him turning the spear away from his spine. It cut through the fabric of his coat. Pridament dropped his arm from the coat and tried to catch the spear in it.

Too slow.

Hodur pushed the spear upward, glancing it along Pridament's cheek.

Pridament stumbled back, the left side of his face burning. Warm blood trickled down and followed the line of his chin. He threw the coat off.

"First blood," Hodur said. "Times have changed, haven't they brother?"

Pridament took four steps further back. He brushed against the Veil, drawing on its energies to heal his wound. His heart pounded against his throat when the blood still flowed.

"No sense seeking the Veil for help," Hodur hissed. "I told you, this spear is a god slayer. No matter how much you draw from the Veil, no wound will heal faster than its time."

Hodur took a large step forward and continued the spear around his body. Pridament held his staff to the side, blocking the spear. The strike landed so hard it reverberated through his arms into his chest. Blocking the spear did nothing to stop Hodur continuing forward, his fist smashing into Pridament's cheek.

Pridament stumbled backward, striking the wall containing the elevators.

Hodur brought the spear down in a death arc toward Pridament's head.

Pridament brought his staff up to block.

Hodur leaned his weight behind the spear, forcing Pridament to his knees.

"So how close is your world to this one?" Hodur asked.

Pridament grit his teeth. "Best I figure, almost ten years."

Pridament fell to the ground and rolled. The spear struck the ground sending a fountain of debris into the air.

Hodur's reinforced combat boot caught Pridament in the side, sending him sprawling across the floor.

"Ten years," Hodur said. "About the time my brother in this world died. That would mean Gwynn was your son at one point, right."

Pridament swung his staff at Hodur's feet. The man took an easy, relaxed step over it. Another boot to the midsection.

Bits of drywall rained down on Pridament as he slammed into the far wall.

"That would also mean you ran away from Asgard. You should've seen father. I mean, I've seen him angry, but nothing like that."

Pridament ducked, the spear striking the wall where his head had been.

"This is almost therapeutic," Hodur exclaimed. "All the things I wanted to say, all the questions I've had. In this world, you died before I could ask. But now..." The spear glanced across Pridament's shoulder. "...I can finally have some answers."

Pridament rolled away. He slammed his staff into the small of Hodur's back sending his brother sprawling against the wall.

Pridament backed away, his shoulder on fire and numbness crept downward into his arm.

Hodur charged. Staff, spear, staff, spear, the constant dance of assault and parry.

White searing pain erupted from Pridament's side, like shards of glass radiated from the impact and tore through his torso.

"You've been slumming on Midgard too long, brother." Hodur's breath was hot and foul. "It looks like this is over."

The Children of Odin

Gwynn followed the tugging at his core. The air of the tenth floor crackled and nipped at his flesh. Perhaps the windows were tinted, or the barrier blocked out the light, or Gwynn lost the sense of time, but the outside world appeared dark and evil.

"I knew you would come," a woman's voice said.

Gwynn faced toward the right of the building. Her stance was relaxed, catlike. Her silver hair in a ponytail and glowing with a preternatural light.

"Elaios," Gwynn said.

She tut-tutted behind her teeth. "I suppose if I asked you to let me put you down like a rabid dog, you would protest."

Gwynn gripped Xanthe harder.

"Only a few days and you're stronger already. Impressive. Most Anunnakis can't draw anything from the Veil for years. Yet here you are, sword in hand, having vanquished a Gorgon."

"Where's the tear?" Gwynn did his best to keep his voice steady.

Elaios laughed—a high-pitched shriek. Underneath it ran a mocking tone that sent a pang of despair through Gwynn.

"You're too late. It's already closed."

Gwynn ran to his left, the closest outside windows furthest from Elaios. Outside the vortex spun faster, darker, and hungrier. Her piercing laughter sent waves of heat and anger through him.

"What you should have done," Elaios said, "was forget this whole world and run away with Pridament. You would've survived a little longer then."

Gwynn turned to face her. Elaios' face hardened.

"So why are you still here?" Gwynn asked.

"One last, most important task." The air sparked as her fists burst into blue flame. "You need to die."

***

Hodur twisted the spear. Waves of pain crashed through Pridament's body.

"Before we end this," Hodur said, "I want to know one thing. Was it worth it—throwing away a godhood?"

"I only have one word for you," Pridament rasped. He coughed and tasted blood in the back of his throat.

"And that would be?" Hodur's eyes filled with a delighted greed and desire to mock whatever he might say.

Pridament locked his gaze on Hodur. "Mjollnir."

Hodur's eyes widened in horror. A loud thunderclap sounded, and lightning erupted from Pridament's right hand, throwing Hodur across the floor.

Cool steel pressed against his skin and the familiar weight in his hand. It sent a joyful energy through him. He tore the spear from his side. He knew he should be in pain, but a thunderstorm tore through his veins that would rob even death of its sting.

"Impossible," Hodur stammered. "You had a seal placed on you when you deserted Asgard. No one breaks a seal of Odin."

Pridament hefted the hammer, its electric blue glow filling his vision. "You forget brother, I'm dead in this world, and the seal died with me."

The air smelled of ozone as Hodur drew two battle-axes from the Veil.

"That's more like I remember," Pridament said. "Enough trick spears. You want to take me down? Then see if you can with your own power."

Hodur charged. The battle–axes sliced through the air. Pridament stepped aside with ease. Hodur's momentum carried him a step further. Pridament slammed the hammer into Hodur's back, rewarding him with a loud crunching noise.

Hodur stumbled and fell to the floor.

"You want to know why I left Asgard?" Pridament asked. "You want to know if it was worth it?"

Hodur huffed; his chest heaved with every breath. "I told you," he gasped. "I wanted answers."

Pridament moved to Hodur's side and knelt down to see his eyes.

"I left because I loved my family. I left because of the bitch you're working for."

"Elaios?"

"That wasn't always her name. I'm sure you remember who and what she was before becoming a Fallen."

Hodur coughed, his eyes dazed. Was he in any shape to recall?

"A Vala," Hodur groaned. "A seer."

"Not any Vala. The one who told Odin of Ragnarok."

"She was the one who saw the end of the gods?" Hodur spat blood. "As if any such thing could happen now. What did she do to you?"

Pridament drew a long breath. It found all the wounds refusing to heal, sending shivers of pain through him. Mjollnir was mighty, but it didn't prevent Hodur from healing himself with the Veil. How long would he play the game of having mortal injuries? Still, it didn't matter. A weight lifted from Pridament. How long had he wanted to explain? Too many years passed by with him carrying his burden alone.

"She did nothing to me. Only told me a prophecy. One she gave me proof enough to believe."

"That made you abandon us?"

Warm tears built up to rush down his face. "Elaios told me I would be responsible for starting Ragnarok. I thought if I left I could avoid it and save everyone. I was wrong. The end is coming anyway."

Pridament drew a deep, ragged breath. He stood and took five paces backward. "You can stand up Hodur; I know you've all but healed yourself."

Hodur turned his head toward Pridament, a sly smile crossing his lips. The battle-axes faded back to the Veil and he stood, brushing himself off.

"The possum defense never was much use against you, was it?" Hodur said. "Is it true, what you're saying? Could she really have convinced you, you would start Ragnarok?"

"She did. I'm still convinced. All I can do now is try to stop it."

Hodur shook his head and let out a dry and humorless laugh. "Well, I have my answer. It's a shame it changes nothing. If you actually feel you're the cause of the twilight of the gods, then lie down here and die with this world. That should prevent the curse from troubling the rest of us."

"It's not that simple, and you know it. If Ragnarok *has* started, it'll play throughout the entirety of creation. No world will be safe."

"Thanks for the warning brother. But when the spawn of Loki come knocking, I'll have a whole world ready to end them. It helps to be a single and great God. Stay here. Your end will be far less painful and bloody."

Pridament reached out, but a wave of energy slammed into him and smashed him against the wall. Squinting against the intensity of the white light, he saw wings enfold Hodur. A final flash forced him to turn his face away, and heat pricked his skin and his open wounds burned. A minute passed before the floor plunged into darkness again.

Pridament was on his hands and knees. Warmth spread across his abdomen where blood continued to spill from his wound. Maybe Hodur was right, maybe it would be easier to lie down and let the end come. After all, there might be another him. Maybe that version managed to get life right. Maybe he found a lasting love and held tight to his child. Here in the quiet dark, it was easy to see the disaster of his life. Surrender seemed so simple.

A sound like an explosion came from above, sending cables and debris spraying from the ceiling.

Maybe he lost his son. Maybe the him who lived in this world abandoned his son for the embrace of death. But fate brought them together—the orphaned son and broken father. Perhaps this was his hope for salvation.

Pridament searched for the spear. When he held it, he pushed open the stairwell door and went to save the son that wasn't his.

***

Fuyuko slammed the Fallen into the rail. From the corner of her eye, she caught Gwynn make it through the door.

The Fallen shoved. Fuyuko's feet left the ground, the sight of descending stairs passed beneath her. She reached within herself and touched the part of her within the Veil. The cold vastness opened within her.

In the times when she severed herself from the Veil, she felt so small, closed, and powerless. But the enormity of the resource in the Veil—that was somehow also her—seemed limitless. She drew on it, focused the power into her arms and her spear. She rammed it into the wall, halting her descent. Momentum continued her moving. She swung around the shaft of the spear and came to rest crouched on it.

The fallen stood motionless, stunned.

She wanted to gloat and laugh at his underestimation of her. She wanted this moment to be a story she would talk boisterously about when she returned to Suture.

She wouldn't do any of those things. That would be dishonorable.

She didn't do this for fun or thrills. She did it out of a sense of duty and birthright. The moment you took too much pleasure in it—when pride blotted out common sense—was the day something put you to an end.

She swung down to the floor, pulling the spear free. The Fallen made for the door to pursue Gwynn. Fuyuko dashed up the stairs and drew on the Veil. The familiar chill filled her core. She imagined it coursing through her, up to her hands. Such intense cold, she often marveled at the fact it didn't burn her. Fuyuko curled her fingers as though she were holding a ball. In that space, she focused the energies coursing from the Veil through her. The moisture in the air froze. Years of practice compressed complex actions into fractions of a second. A moment later, she hurled the ice dagger toward the Fallen, who stumbled back to avoid it.

She reached the tenth-floor landing and slashed with her spear. The Fallen leaped over the rail and landed with a thud on the stairs on the other side.

Fuyuko slammed the door to the tenth floor shut, filling the lock and gap around the door with ice.

The Fallen charged up the stairs toward the midway landing beneath Fuyuko. Before his feet touched the landing, he jumped upward and pushed off the wall, sending him propelling toward Fuyuko, cleavers first. She used her spear as a pole and vaulted up and over the Fallen. As she did, she swung the spear downward, producing a satisfying strip of crimson across the man's back.

Fuyuko landed in a crouch. The Fallen stood above her. Despite her impression she inflicted severe damage, he gave it little notice.

The air crackled. The cloak concealing the Fallen danced and shred apart. The Fallen stood revealed, his flesh a red and purple bruise. Fuyuko's stomach gave a lurch as the man's muscles rippled, expanded, and split as sharp metal protrusions forced themselves out of his skin.

The Fallen howled and flung his arm forward. Several razor shards hurtled toward Fuyuko.

She twisted to her right to avoid one, and then fell backward to the floor dodging another. More projectiles intent on shredding her, sent her rolling across the floor. She leaped to her feet as a dozen blades flew toward her. She ran back toward the wall and used it to propel herself up and over the shards. She flipped over and tucked her arms in as she fell straight down the central shaft of the stairwell. Fuyuko let her spear flow away and then drew on the energies of the Veil. She reached out and grabbed a rail to cease her descent. *Her* arms would've ripped from their sockets, but the arms holding the rails were not her own. Instead, they were a bluish tinge, large and muscular. She only ever allowed the Veil this much of her body, and only in the direst of circumstances. As much as the thing in the Veil might also be her, she feared it having too much control.

Fuyuko flipped herself up onto the stairs. Below, the battle between the members of Suture and the Curses continued. Above, the massive Fallen crashed its way down the stairs toward her.

She laid her hands on the stairs in front of her and prayed she had time to do the job right. Just the right layer of ice would work. The Fallen approached, maybe too close to get the job done.

Fuyuko sensed the moisture in the air above the stairs. *Maybe enough.*

She pushed harder.

Maybe another ten seconds.

No eight, five.

The Fallen stood above her. She didn't stop or hesitate. She let loose with a melee of ice daggers. She didn't need to hit him, just force him closer, and distract him from looking at the steps. Another foot. Maybe six inches. The energies she dragged from the Veil started to weigh on her. If this didn't work, maybe there would be nothing left but to give herself completely to the other. Maybe it would have the strength to finish the job. But would she be able to come back from that? Still, it was preferable to defeat.

The Fallen stumbled. His foot hit the ice, and he fell forward. She breathed, felt the movement of time—waited for the right moment.

The beast rushed downward. Fuyuko tore into the Veil and spun, putting all her momentum into the spear's downward swing, passing it through the Fallen's neck. The body slammed into the wall with a sickening thud.

Fuyuko ran up the stairs, her feet sure and secure on the ice, as the stairwell behind her was painted red with the Fallen's blood.

Fuyuko made her way back to the tenth floor. She sensed movement and struck out with her spear. It met another, much older, spear.

"Glad to see you're still alive," Pridament said.

Fuyuko nodded. "You too. You're wearing that different face. Finish what you needed to do?"

His eyes were distant. "Not really. Gwynn?"

"Upstairs, closing the tear."

"Chances are he's not alone. We should hurry."

The Dragon that Fed on the World

Gwynn batted a ball of flame aside with Xanthe. "Why? What makes me so important?"

Elaios drew a deep breath and ceased her assault. "Why? You don't know, do you? Tragic, to have so much weight on your shoulders and not even know. Fine. The truth is, before I joined the Fallen, I was a Vala, one who could see the future. So powerful and accurate were my visions Odin himself sought my counsel on when he and his kin would meet their end. Have you ever heard of Ragnarok?"

A chill coursed through Gwynn's spine.

Elaios didn't wait for his answer. "Chances are you have. All the small details are irrelevant. What matters is the dragon. Did you know when the dragon appears, it would be the harbinger of the end? It's not only the Aesir that has that in their end times prophecies. Christianity and numerous others have seen the dragon as the bringer of the end times. Tell me, Gwynn, have you faced the part of you residing in the Veil? Have you gone that far in your development?"

"I don't know what you're talking about."

She laughed. Mirthless, mocking. "Pridament hasn't explained it all, has he? Crafty, that father of yours. He's already lost you once. He won't risk you falling through the cracks again. It's how you cross the Veil. You need to draw into the part of you existing there. You must become part of it and then be strong enough to separate yourself again. Most Anunnakis who try it go mad; numerous others become lost in the Veil, never being able to regain themselves. Facing yourself, the thing that is the true you, it can teach you more about yourself than anything else. You boy, I've seen your true face in visions decades ago. You are the dragon. You will bring ruin to everything. There's no place for the serpent in Eden. You must end here."

Gwynn shook. "Liar. I would never do that. I'm here risking my life to save everything."

"The greatest evil starts with the purest of intentions. Lucifer fell because he loved God so much he refused to bow to flawed humans. I wonder what will finally have you expelled from Heaven. Maybe the memory of your sweet blond friend having her head pulped by a Curse?"

Gwynn roared. He charged forward, Xanthe lashing out to close the distance between foes.

Elaios grabbed Xanthe's blade and held it firm. Gwynn continued and crushed his fist into her face.

Needles of pain shattered through Gwynn's hand. Elaios spun on her heel, and swung Gwynn off his feet and sent him crashing against the far wall.

The air hammered out of his lungs, and his hand let loose its hold on Xanthe. With their physical contact severed, the sword faded back into the ether. Gwynn heaved himself onto his knees. His hand was red, raw and swollen.

"I focus the flames out my hands," Elaios said in a casual, lilting tone. "But the fire runs beneath the surface of my whole body." She looked at her hand. For a moment, it blazed so bright Gwynn had to shield his eyes. "Fire. It purifies and fights away the darkness. I know you think I take pleasure in this, but I don't. If you could see the bigger picture, you'd give yourself to this. The Fallen are cast as villains, but we are seeking to create a better world. All we want to do is purge the sins of our ancestors and return to the land God made for us."

"You're insane," Gwynn coughed. He drew sparingly on the Veil, focusing the energies into his hand—enough to dull the pain.

"The typical defense of the ignorant. We are saner than any of you lemmings. We face ourselves in the Veil and then use it to find and purge the sinful parts of ourselves."

"What does that mean?"

"The Fallen are pure. Before we are given our angelic name, we must first eliminate all sinful versions of ourselves."

"You mean you go to other worlds and kill yourself?"

Elaios smiled. "The first time is difficult. Then you realize these aren't real people, they are shadows of yourself. We do them a favor by delivering them from the burden of their sins."

"You are insane."

Gwynn never took his eyes off her. But one moment she stood across the floor, the next, she smashed her fiery fists into his sternum and sent him spinning across the floor.

He tasted blood.

Was there any point to this? The tear closed, yet the vortex still spun, ready to devour this world. He should run. He should find Pridament and find a new world. Maybe they could take Jaimie. Maybe Fuyuko would come too.

Elaios didn't press her attack. "I can see it in your eyes, the desire to run. The first time I realized my visions came true, I wanted to do the same. Some of our kind would have you believe our powers are a gift, but they're a burden. You're a teenager, and yet you carry the fate of a world on your shoulders. Even if you run, even if you manage to avoid being hunted down by the Fallen, you will never escape the weight of your failure here. And if my visions are right, and I've yet to be wrong, you will cause loss of life on a catastrophic scale. Whatever crimes you accuse we Fallen of, you will commit worse. We seek to return humankind to paradise; you will rob them of it. Is that what you want? Let me purify you. Let me make your end as quick and painless as possible. You will be a martyr, celebrated instead of becoming a villain, reviled and hated."

Gwynn drew a deep, painful breath. He closed his eyes and hung his head.

"Good. I see why your father is so proud of you."

Gwynn waited for the end. Would it hurt? Was he doing the right thing? Did that matter? It was too much to bear. He didn't want to live with the guilt. He didn't want to question every decision and wonder if it would steer into an apocalypse. Soon he'd see his mother and father. He hoped they wouldn't be too disappointed in him.

Firm hands gripped his shoulders.

"Gwynn, what the hell. Are you all right?"

Gwynn opened his eyes. Before him stood his father. He wasn't wearing Pridament's face. It was the square–jawed ruggedness he remembered from his childhood. The eyes looked much older, but everything else fit his memory.

"Dad?"

"It's Pridament now, Gwynn."

"Where's Elaios?"

"Fuyuko's trying to hold her off. She needs our help."

On the other side of the floor, Fuyuko and Elaios performed a deadly dance. Fuyuko parried Elaios' attacks with a shield, which to Gwynn appeared made of ice. Each blow Elaios landed on the shield battered and chipped it, making it clear it wouldn't last. Elaios was relentless, leaving Fuyuko little chance to counter attack with her spear; what few attempts she made Elaios deflected.

Pridament got to his feet and made for the two women. As he did, Fuyuko lunged at Elaios with her spear. Elaios grabbed it in her hand. Time seemed to slow. Fuyuko's eyes filled with confusion. Elaios appeared triumphant, smug. Her hands burned brighter, and she twisted and smashed Fuyuko's spear to pieces.

Fuyuko's eyes widened in horror, and the remainder of her ice shield melted away. Pridament yelled. Ripples of heat burst from Elaios, throwing him back. Pridament hit the ground, the severity of his injuries apparent. He turned back to Fuyuko and Elaios. Fuyuko was a broken doll—fear and loss painted across her porcelain face. Elaios wound her fist back preparing a deathblow.

Something in Gwynn snapped.

He *could* die. Maybe he *should* die, but he wouldn't watch someone he cared about die again. His father. Sophia. He wouldn't add Fuyuko to his list of failure.

He shot out his hand. He didn't call it, and he didn't wait for it to materialize. Instinct said it would be there. Fighting the Gorgon taught him everything he needed always stayed with him, hidden out of sight.

Xanthe's dark blade cracked out like a whip. With no effort, the blade severed Elaios' hand holding Fuyuko.

Gwynn didn't wait. Even as Xanthe crossed the distance between himself and Elaios, Gwynn was on his feet following it. He swept across the space and hammered his shoulder into Elaios as she screeched.

The wall shattered as Elaios crushed against it. Gwynn held Fuyuko in his arms.

"Fuyuko, can you hear me?"

A glaze fell over her eyes.

"Bastard." Elaios rose to her feet with a growl. "You took my hand."

Gwynn turned. He raced to Pridament and shielded him, and Fuyuko as Elaios' flames flashed out of control. Glass rained down on them as every window shattered. Gwynn hadn't been able to touch her without burning. He clamped his eyes shut and waited for the flames to incinerate them all.

The floor scorched around them, but something shielded them from the flames. Gwynn opened his eyes to see leathery wings spread out on either side of him.

The heat ceased.

Gwynn stood to face Elaios. The wings responded by folding behind him; their movement natural and instinctual—like another pair of arms.

Elaios' eyes were two dark pits. She was a fallen angel with flesh and wings of flame.

"And here stands the proof," she bellowed. "The dragon all but revealed."

"I don't care what you say, I will save this world."

She mocked him with laughter. "You think so? Let's see you try."

Elaios threw back her head, and a fountain of blue flame erupted from her mouth tearing a hole through the ceiling. Her eyes challenged Gwynn, and her fiery wings carried her up and out.

Dark burns covered the entirety of the level. Pridament and Fuyuko were unconscious, injuries from previous battles apparent. Gwynn looked to the path Elaios used.

"You should go."

He turned enough to see Adrastia out the corner of his eye.

"How can I?"

She gave a stifled laugh. "You do know you have wings, right?"

Gwynn tightened his fists. Through his clenched jaw, he hissed, "As if I know how to use them."

She touched his shoulder.

"If you won't trust yourself, then trust what she told you."

"Who?"

"The seer. The one who loved you."

Gwynn's chest tightened.

"She said when you took her hand, you would be ready."

"How can I take her hand when she's...dead."

Adrastia gave him a pity–filled smile. "Think of what you did to Elaios. What did you take from her?"

Gwynn turned back to the hole in the roof. "She believed in me, didn't she? Even though I couldn't save her, she trusted me to protect everyone else."

"Because she saw it. She knew what would happen to her. She chose that path because it would save you and this world. She sacrificed herself, the same as you need to right now. Kill the doubt in yourself. Sacrifice the broken child restraining you. Shed your nightmares and take flight. She believed in you, Gwynn. She trusted you to do this when the time came. Don't let her down."

Gwynn closed his eyes and drew a deep breath. He summoned a memory of Sophia. She smiled and reminded him there were people he needed to protect. A world existed somewhere in which the two of them were happy and loving each other. Again, Gwynn sensed the greater part of himself within the Veil. His wings weren't new. They were always with him. Nothing in his powers was new or foreign. Xanthe, his wings, whatever else might come to him when he needed it; they were always present, just hidden. His wings were here now because he needed them. If he needed them, if they came to his aid, then the knowledge of their use should be there as well.

The wings didn't feel foreign; instead, they were a natural weight on his back. He spread them out, tested flapping them. His feet left the ground.

I can do this...

Gwynn stepped beneath the hole in the roof. Elaios, flying in front of the dark vortex, burned like a star.

Elaios yelled, "Come blood of Odin. Even if I die, I'll show you the monster you are."

"Ignore her," Adrastia said. "She's hoping to throw you off. She's afraid. She knows you'll defeat her. She knows if you live you'll be strong enough to stop all the Fallen. Fulfill your destiny. Write the first chapter of the new gospel. Take flight, Gwynn!"

He crouched down and drew strength from the Veil. He leaped up, through the ceiling and into the sky. As his body would've responded by walking if he wanted to move from one place to another, so too did his wings.

He swept up to Elaios' level.

"Look upon this form boy," Elaios said. "None who have seen it have lived to tell of it." From the Veil, she drew a scepter and charged at Gwynn.

The scepter clanged against Xanthe. Elaios' momentum pushed Gwynn back down toward the building.

Gwynn folded his wings behind him and rolled to his right. He passed through the flames of Elaios' wings, sending her spinning. His wings folded along his back protecting him from the blaze. Once she passed him, he spread them out and soared higher into the sky.

A plume of flame grazed his shoulder sending a shock of pain throughout his core.

Elaios rushed toward him, an angel of death—beautiful, horrifying.

Sword met scepter in a flurry of blows. The scepter's blows were so heavy—each parry sent painful shockwaves through Gwynn's arms. Elaios wielded it with ease and grace despite having one hand. His knuckles whitened as he gripped Xanthe with both hands against the punishing blows.

Gwynn's arms strained up into his shoulders as he held back the scepter. Daggers of pain stabbed into the center of his brain as Elaios crashed the flaming stump of her severed hand into his face.

He fell—the world a painful blur. He smashed into the pavement below and collapsed in on himself. But the Veil had him, and it wouldn't let him die. As his body collapsed, a rush of energy, like a tornado filling a balloon, pushed through him and kept him whole.

Gwynn staggered to his feet. He kept drawing on the Veil. Bones snapped back together, and he puked up fluid that shouldn't have been loose in his system.

Move! Something shouted in his mind. He fell to the left. Something struck where he previously stood, sending chunks of asphalt into the air. A nearby car exploded.

He caught sight of Elaios. She swooped down between the buildings and charged straight at him.

Projectiles of flame shattered windows and destroyed vehicles around him. Gwynn let Xanthe fly. The sword clipped Elaios across her arm, but she didn't react.

Xanthe snapped back in time to clash against Elaios' scepter. The asphalt buckled beneath him as Elaios' momentum pushed him down.

"Why fight this?" Elaios howled. "Only minutes ago you were ready to lay down your life."

Gwynn grit his teeth. "Someone reminded me of a promise I made."

Elaios wore a smile as many parts madness as it was hungry. "What good are promises made in this world? Soon it will be wiped from existence."

"Then at least I'll die with a clear conscience. Can you say the same?"

Elaios drew back her scepter for another strike. Gwynn kicked off the ground and flew above her. She twisted and glared at him, her face a mask of disgust and hatred.

"I told you. I've cleansed my sins. Because you're ignorant, I don't expect you to understand. But we are doing righteous work. Nothing but glory awaits us."

Xanthe struck out and bit deep into Elaios' abdomen.

She swatted the blade aside, her wound healing in a small blaze of bluish flame.

"Do you have any idea how old I am?" Elaios screeched. "You may bring the apocalypse. You may not. But there is nothing you can do that will destroy me."

"Tell that to your hand."

Xanthe danced through the sky, landing numerous strikes against Elaios. Each wound closed as fast as he made it.

Elaios' laugh verged on hysterics. "Do you see? What is the loss of this hand? Given enough time, the Veil will give me another."

Gwynn dove. *Let's see how you do without your head.*

Elaios didn't move. She stood still, her eyes locked on his. As Xanthe bit into the flesh of her neck, she was gone.

Something hammered into his side and sent him sprawling against a far wall. Masonry fell around him as the wall crushed under his force.

Gwynn stumbled to his feet. Elaios stood unscathed in the road.

"When will you accept it?" she asked. "There is nothing you can do. You've kept your promise. You've fought valiantly. At some point, isn't it better to go quietly into the darkness instead of kicking and screaming?"

Gwynn kicked into the sky. He flew upward, trying to keep distance between them. He came up over the building where the Gorgon and tear had been. Through the devastated roof he saw Fuyuko, still unconscious, and Pridament, injured, bleeding. He scanned for Elaios. She stood on street level, watching him.

This is a game for her now. She's humoring me.

He touched down on the roof.

"Gwynn? Did you beat her?" Pridament called.

"No," Gwynn sobbed. "She's toying with me now. I'm not fast enough. And anything I do she heals right away."

"Take this." Pridament threw the spear he held to Gwynn.

In his hands, it hummed with age and history.

"She won't be able to heal any wound you make with that," Pridament said.

Gwynn swung the spear behind his back. He inched toward the edge of the roof. He yelled to the street below, "Are you coming, or are you going to wait and see the end of the world with me?" The words were ragged and torn.

Elaios lifted off from the street at a leisurely pace.

Gwynn waited—sweat dampening his brow. He couldn't be off by even a second...

Now.

He swung the spear around and charged forward.

It plunged deep into Elaios' chest.

Her eyes widened and blood spurt from her mouth.

Gwynn pushed on. Up, over, and smashed her down onto the roof. He roared as he pushed so hard the ceiling collapsed and they fell to the level below.

***

Pridament cradled Elaios in his arms. Despite all she became, he recalled a time when she was a trusted adviser. Fanaticism left her shattered.

"Why Elaios? Why go to this?"

Blood trickled from the corner of her mouth and her eyes dulled. "A new world. A better place. I've seen the future of this world. We need to change course."

"You said my son would bring on Ragnarok. Did you mean Gwynn?"

Elaios coughed. "That is what I saw."

"But which Gwynn? I'm still searching for my son. This is this world's Gwynn."

She gripped Pridament's hand. "Two of them? No. Impossible. Fate's hand would only have one."

"So then my Gwynn is dead."

"No. Alive. I'm sure."

"Then which one? Which Gwynn is the harbinger?"

A moment passed without an answer. "Elaios?" The emptiness in her eyes meant she would never respond.

"Gwynn," Pridament said, "is the tear closed? Are we safe?"

Gwynn hung his head. "The tear collapsed when we defeated the Gorgon. But...the vortex is still going. I thought if we closed the last tear it would stop."

Pridament coughed. A rattle in his chest infected his voice. "Guess we left it too long."

"So what now? We wait and watch the world die?"

Pain racked Pridament's body. He'd been in this situation once before. He'd buried the guilt of running away long ago. He searched for an answer, but none came. Finally, defeated, he admitted the truth. "I don't know."

Gwynn looked up to where the swirling mass waited to devour the world. "It's a large tear, right?"

"I guess."

"So a Script should be able to close it?"

His gut twisted. He hesitated to answer. If Gwynn meant to do what he suspected, there had to be a way to stop him. Pridament had already lost one son; he didn't want to lose another. But the more he searched, it became obvious no other answer existed. Would he burden this boy, no, man, with the same burdens and sins he shouldered? Sometimes, even defeat was preferable. He said, "In theory, I suppose a Script could close it." Guilt stabbed his chest. He would lose Gwynn again. "But there's no way of knowing if it'll work. Even if it does," Pridament's voice cracked, "you might not survive it."

Gwynn remained silent, his gaze never falling from the sky above. After a minute had passed, he said, "You know, I never asked to be a hero."

"That's what makes people heroes—they're never asked. They just do everything they can when they need to."

Gwynn's wings flexed. He crouched in preparation to bound out through the ceiling.

"Gwynn," Pridament yelled. "No matter what happens, remember people are waiting for you to come back. Don't lose yourself, kid."

"Thanks." Gwynn smiled. "I'll do my best."

Gwynn kicked off and launched into the sky. For a brief moment, Pridament caught a glimpse of the mysterious girl, Adrastia. She gave him a faint smile and disappeared.

Pridament dragged himself to the hole in the ceiling. Gwynn became an increasingly indistinct spot in the sky until cloud cover obscured him.

Pridament waited, his heart pounding in his chest. A small part of him registered the arrival of the members of Suture, yet he refused to remove his attention from where he lost sight of Gwynn.

Seconds passed like hours. Time became a vile enemy, keeping all their fates secret.

A bright flash.

For the briefest of seconds, daylight exploded from the clouds. Pridament waited, searching the skies for Gwynn.

Closing Doors

The doorbell rang.

"I've got it," Pridament called up the stairs.

He opened the door to a man whose height and musculature cut an imposing figure.

"Fath—"

"Unless you preface that with 'All,'" the man said, his lone blue eye cold and piercing. "You will refrain from calling me that."

"You should know I'll not call you that. You're still just a man."

He rubbed his temple. "Perhaps I didn't form humanity with my hands, but I've shed enough blood and flesh to earn the title. After all, are two people who adopt a child and raise it to adulthood any less its parents? I don't know who put us here, but He left, and it's been up to us to pick up the pieces."

"Fine, fine." Pridament had no desire to listen to further ramblings. "Still, I'm not calling you that. What name do you go by now?"

"Woten. And you are?"

"Pridament. To what do we owe the honor?"

Woten regarded Pridament for a few minutes. "You do know who is upstairs, do you not?"

"If you mean your grandson and the sister of his mother, then yes, I know who they are."

"Is it so hard for you to accept I would check in on my grandson?"

Pridament shook trying to keep control of his tone. "Since you didn't check on your son for over a century, yes, it's hard for me to believe."

Woten's expression softened. "If I recall, you were the one that left."

Pridament tried to protest, but Woten waved aside any arguments

"Regardless," Woten said, "I have never abandoned my grandson. How do you think Jaimie found such a good job and this lovely, sold for less than market value, house? Why do you think Justinian was here in the first place?"

"As it turns out, he was here to betray you."

Woten's eyebrow rose. "You mean the seer? I knew of her power. After all, through her visions, we first learned of Gwynn`s existence."

"Did you know he assumed the role of her father? Have you been briefed on the whole story? Do you see everything he did was based on the seer's predictions and aimed at awakening Gwynn's powers?"

Woten's voice rose. Not enough to rouse everyone else in the house, just sufficient to strike a familiar fear in Pridament. "I have been betrayed by one son and lost another to that same betrayal. Can I not grieve the loss of my adopted son without you marring his memory as well?"

"I only hope you are objective about what's happened. Gwynn's safety might depend on it."

"I've already told you, I have watched out for my grandson's well-being from the moment I learned he existed."

"I'm glad to hear that," Pridament said. "There's one thing I would like to ask you."

"And you expect I'll answer?"

"It's my hope. Gwynn said Fuyuko told him the name of his Veil weapon. Have you developed some generic code name for such a thing?"

Woten probed Pridament with his single eye. "No such thing exists. We've come a long way, but certain laws are unbreakable."

"Then how did she know?"

Woten sighed. "Well, I suppose when she's recovered, we'll have to ask her. I'm surprised you didn't interrogate her earlier about it. You were never one for skirting an issue."

"There was no time. Besides, we needed her. I was afraid my usual... tactics, would turn her against us."

"My, my," Woten made a tut-tut sound with his tongue against his teeth. "Perhaps I was wrong about the usefulness of living among normal humans. It's taught you a care and control you lacked. You seem very attached to my grandson. Not far removed I assume?"

"Maybe nine, almost ten, years."

"Hmmm," Woten nodded. "Not far. Still, what brought you here?"

"On the night our worlds split, the Gwynn of this world lost his parents. In my world, I lost my Gwynn. He fell through the Veil, and I've been searching for him ever since."

"So how is *my* Gwynn?"

Pridament chewed his lip. "Not sure. Caelum says physically he's stable, but the psychological trauma, who knows? Thank you though, for Caelum. He's been a big help."

"He's a good boy. Wish I had a dozen more like him. Especially now. I risk the entire North American branch being Veil drunk to tend the worst of their injuries. We have to do it in shifts."

"What about Fuyuko's recovery? How is she?" Pridament asked.

"She had a piece of her soul shattered. Who knows? She hasn't said a word since we lifted her out two days ago. My only Script won't leave her side, and I've lost three sons all while the world is plunging into chaos because people have learned monsters exist. I don't think any of us are making it out of this unscathed."

The sound of footsteps came from upstairs. Caelum appeared on the stairs. "He's starting to wake up." Caelum's eyes widened. "Sir, I didn't realize..."

"It's fine Caelum," Woten said. "I understand you've been helpful."

"I'm glad to help, sir."

Pridament was already moving upstairs.

To say Gwynn woke seemed a slight over–exaggeration. His eyes were open, but he'd not regained his senses. Jaimie sat by his bed. She'd only left his side for washroom breaks.

A mountain of a young man with orange hair leaned against the far wall. The others called him Brandt. He'd refused to allow Caelum to remain alone.

"Did we make it?" Gwynn groaned.

Jaimie stroked Gwynn's head. "Yes, Gwynn. It's OK. We're here."

Gwynn did a slow scan of the room. "Where's Fuyuko?"

Woten spoke up. "She's been taken to Suture headquarters. I'm told she'll be fine."

"Gwynn, this is your grandfather," Pridament said in response to Gwynn's questioning look.

"I..."

Woten held up his hands for Gwynn to remain silent. "It's fine. We can talk at length another time. For now, know everyone is very proud of you and glad you seem to be doing well."

"I did it." Gwynn's eyelids and voice sagged. "Me. Huh, I saved the world." And he slept once more.

***

Another three days passed before Gwynn was up and moving around. He still ached and found his memories of closing the vortex hazy.

"So my grandfather," he said to Pridament. The two sat alone in the living room. Gwynn convinced Jaimie she should go back to work after her following his every movement for the past two days.

Pridament's gaze focused on some faraway point. "Yeah. I thought I'd have a chance to explain things a bit more before you met him. I noticed the two of you talking yesterday before he left. If you don't mind me asking, what did he say to you?"

"He invited me to join Suture."

"And what did you tell him?"

Gwynn sighed. "I said I wasn't sure. I mean, I thought I should talk to you first."

"You know Gwynn, as much as I might have once been your father, you don't owe me anything. In this world, you've lived without me for nine years. You're your own man. What do you want?"

"But that's the thing." Gwynn got to his feet, his body restless. "I don't know what to do. I've been watching the news. I prevented the world from being destroyed, but from what I see and what my grandfather told me, things aren't exactly roses. There's an increase in tears, and people turning to Taints. Curses are even attacking openly. It seems like there's a lot of work that still needs doing."

"So what's holding you back?"

Gwynn locked his eyes with Pridament's. "You are. It's clear to me you don't want anything to do with Suture. So I wondered what you were doing."

Pridament rubbed the bridge of his nose. For a moment, he wouldn't meet Gwynn's eyes. He rose to his feet. "I'm leaving."

"What?"

"Elaios wasn't the only Fallen. To be honest, I don't know how many there are. They work alone, so it could be months, maybe years, before they realize she's dead. I need to start taking the fight to them. I need to be the one they're hunting. Otherwise, they'll descend on this world, and they won't stop coming until you're dead and they've finished what Elaios started."

"Let me come with you."

"Gwynn, I can't—"

"Yes, you can," Gwynn pleaded. "You need me. What are you going to do if you need a Script?"

Pridament clasped Gwynn's shoulders. "Listen to me. You're not coming. I won't need a Script because I'm not going out there to save worlds, I'm going to keep them away from this one. I'm going out there to kill as many of them as I can find. This is no place for you Gwynn. The whole point is to keep them away from you, not make you a larger target. Besides, somewhere out there, my Gwynn is still lost. I found you. I'll protect you, but I can't forget him. I need to keep searching."

"When are you leaving?"

Pridament released his hold on Gwynn. "Now. I only stayed to make sure you were okay."

"What about those things Elaios said about me being the end of the world? How am I supposed to deal with that?"

"I ran away from myself for a long time because of what that woman said." Pridament shook with bitter rage. "When I found out your mother was pregnant, I can't begin to tell you how frightened I felt. Doctors said she couldn't conceive. We never even considered it. When she got pregnant, she thought it was a miracle. I saw it as proof fate would prove Elaios right. But when I saw you born, when I watched you grow into this amazing boy so full of decency, I knew she was wrong."

"Did you see what I did? What I became?"

"You were who you needed to be. You did what you had to. Our actions and dreams define who we are. What you do with this life is determined by you Gwynn, not by the ramblings of some fallen prophet."

Gwynn collapsed on the sofa. His body felt untrustworthy, like it conspired against him. "There's so much I don't understand. What about Adrastia? I keep seeing her, and she's always talking about some grand destiny."

"She is a mystery you might never solve. When it comes to her, though, be careful. I know I told you she was a vision you made up, but I've seen her too."

"So what does that mean?" Gwynn asked.

Pridament shook his head. "To be honest, I don't know. For now, she's helped you—even saved your life. Until that changes, I guess you roll with it. Eventually, you'll find the answer."

"I could use your help."

"I don't have all the answers. The truth is, you're going to have to find answers for yourself. You were right; I'm not a big fan of Suture. But that's more about my family issues than it is Suture itself," Pridament sighed. "Honestly? I think you should take your grandfather up on his offer."

"You mean join Suture?"

"It's a win from all points. You will be working with people who will train you on how to control your abilities, who will be equipped to help you find the answers you're seeking. And at the same time, you can aid in healing the world you saved."

"What about Jaimie?"

"Gwynn," Pridament said, "Jaimie has known you might be different from the day she took you in. Your grandfather told me he helped get Jaimie on her feet. She's had some knowledge of Suture for years. When I talked to her, she said she understood soon you would go to Suture, because it would be the right place for you. It's your decision. No one can force you, and no one can make the decision for you."

"I just got used to having a father again."

"And I was proud to have a son. But this is for the best. I know where you are. I'll find you again." Pridament turned toward the back door. "Now come and say goodbye."

The two walked out into the backyard. A dull, gray winter afternoon sky greeted them. Their feet crunched on the light, freshly-fallen, snow.

"You might want to look away; this can be kind of bright."

Gwynn threw his arms around Pridament. "Thank you. For everything."

"I'll see you again. Soon."

Gwynn stepped back. Pridament gave a wave, and a curtain of lightning engulfed him. Gwynn turned away. A moment past and the flash ceased.

Pridament was gone.

Returning to the house, Gwynn crashed onto the couch. He sat in silence for ten minutes, rolling around options in his head. He half–expected Adrastia to appear and tell him what he should do, but even she apparently decided to leave this up to him.

He reached into his pant pocket and pulled out the nondescript black cell phone. Gwynn flipped it open and shut, passed it from hand to hand and finally popped it open again.

A single button stared at him. His finger hovered over it.

He drew a long breath. As he let it out slowly, he pressed the button.

He put the phone to his ear and waited.

"Hello, Gwynn," his grandfather answered.

"I've thought about what you said."

"And?"

"I think you're right." *I've gone as far as I can here.* "I belong with Suture."

Gwynn's adventures continue in...

THE BLEEDING WORLDS

BOOK TWO

SUTURE

Suture. An organization created by immortals who once walked the Earth as Gods. A place containing eras worth of secret agendas.

Gwynn joins believing he will learn about his abilities, assisting to protect the world from the Veil.

Instead, he finds an ancient evil stalking him. A face from his past shows up in an unexpected place. And ghosts that prove to be very much alive.

Faith, friendship, family. All are tested within Suture.

Acknowledgements

Despite many solitary hours spent toiling away at words, I doubt any book has been created entirely in a vacuum. This book owes its existence to several people.

My wife suffered through my blathering on about ideas, plots, and frustrations. She provided great insight into the times when I should dial it back, and other times when I needed to hold no punches.

When the frightening time came to release these words into the world, Carolyn, Sabrina, and Dani, were my guinea pigs who gave me encouragement, suggestions, and pointed out my grammar and spelling faux pas. Their input greatly helped shape the book.

Also, I'd be remiss if I didn't thank the wonderful writing community on Twitter, most of whom I met through use of the hastag #amwriting. On those days when I wanted to give up, or felt like the words would never come, they kept me going and shared their own stories of overcoming their doubts and fears.

Since people always *do* judge a book by its cover, I'd like to thank Starbottle for her wonderful work.

Finally, a thank you to *you*, the person reading this book right now. Being a writer is that one itch/dream that's stayed with me since childhood, and your reading this right now is making that dream a reality. Thank you so much!

About the Author

Justus R. Stone's writing combines his fandom of light novels, anime, video games, and mythology. His first series, The Bleeding Worlds, is a very anime-esque retelling of the Norse end-times myth Ragnarok.

In addition to writing, he runs a YouTube channel (https://www.youtube.com/user/JustusRStone) dedicated to his love of light novels (the source material for numerous anime and manga). He posts several videos, including news, reviews, and podcasts, on a weekly basis.

Justus R. Stone was born, raised, and still lives in the Greater Toronto area in Ontario, Canada. He loves interacting with fans, so he can be found on numerous social media platforms, but posts most often to Twitter and YouTube.

Website - http://justusrstone.com
Twitter - https://twitter.com/JustusRStone
YouTube - https://youtube.com/user/JustusRStone
Facebook - https://facebook.com/JustusRStone

Get the latest news, exclusive content, and discounts by subscribing to Justus R. Stone's mailing list.
http://justusrstone.com/subscribe-mailing-list/

Printed in July 2019
by Rotomail Italia S.p.A., Vignate (MI) - Italy